The Fatal
Cape Cod Funeral

Also by Marie Lee

The Curious Cape Cod Skull

The Fatal Cape Cod Funeral

Marie Lee

AVALON BOOKS
THOMAS BOUREGY AND COMPANY, INC.
401 LAFAYETTE STREET
NEW YORK, NEW YORK 10003

FIRST EDITION

10   9   8   7   6   5   4   3   2   1

PRINTED IN THE UNITED STATES OF AMERICA
ON ACID-FREE PAPER
BY HADDON CRAFTSMEN, SCRANTON, PENNSYLVANIA

For Johnny,
son and agent nonpareil

Acknowledgments

Thank-you's are extended to the Maine Indian Tribal-State Commission for supplying me with material pertaining to the Passamaquoddy Tribe;

To Ellen Singing Bird Hendricks for her gracious tour of the Mashpee Wampanoag Indian Museum in Mashpee;

To Lieutenant Steve Burns, paramedic of the Eastham Fire Department, for enlightening me as to the priorities and procedures in an emergency response;

To all the personnel at the Eastham Library and, in particular, Sue Lederhouse, who has been so generous in her assistance.

We shall meet beyond the river
Where the surges cease to roll.

—Epitaph on the tombstone of
Captain Solomon Young,
Congregational and Soldiers Cemetery,
Eastham, Massachusetts

Chapter One

The robin refused to join in the mourning. Perched on the pinnacle of the roof, he warbled his insistent melody, so cheerful in contrast to the funeral procession emerging from the Indian meetinghouse below. Or perhaps the robin's joyful tune was appropriate accompaniment to the burial ceremony in light of the Native American belief that everything in creation is part of a circle, with birth and death but two parts of the circle. The song might have been celebrating the release of a spirit from the constraints of aging and imprisoning flesh which would be returned to the earth to complete the circle.

For the deceased was a very old man. He had been content to live in the Baptist way but had expressed a desire to die and be buried in the old way, with the service conducted by his own spiritual leader.

Led by the supreme sachem, or medicine man, dressed in regalia, the coffin was being carried about two hundred feet from the meetinghouse to the grave, followed by the mourners. The sepulchral mien of Blue Feather altered abruptly as he reached the grave site. He peered intently into the hole and between the straps on which the coffin would be lowered, then turned and signaled silently to the pallbearers, hands upraised in the familiar motion meaning, "Halt!" The startled pallbearers stopped suddenly at the unexpected command, taking by surprise the family members behind them who, walking with heads bowed, overtook the coffin before realizing the cortege was no longer in motion.

Obviously disturbed, the supreme sachem approached the pallbearers and directed them to put down the coffin. Confused but compliant, they carefully lowered the coffin onto the grass and followed Blue Feather to the edge of the grave site, looked into it, and became as agitated as he. Sensing some disaster, the mourners rushed forward to surround the hole, knocking into it a few of the pine boughs that had been provided for the attendees to place on the coffin.

First disbelief, then dread, then gasps of dismay. There was a body in the grave! Not a body in a coffin but a body dressed in dark blue pants and a white shirt, sprawled facedown. As their shock dissipated, the men first on the scene came to the joint realization that it might not be a dead body but someone sick, injured, drunk, or otherwise impaired. Blue Feather took command and ordered everyone back from the grave site lest it collapse and truly entomb the unfortunate person.

Three of the youngest and strongest men present were selected to climb down and retrieve the person—dead or alive. They looked around the cemetery first and noted a long, wide board, part of a small scaffold that had been in use during repairs to the roof of the meetinghouse. The board was carried to the grave and, after removal of the chrome frame supporting the straps for lowering the coffin, was placed from the top of one of the short sides of the grave to the bottom of the opposite side, forming a sturdy plank.

The three men then looked at one another, each hoping that one of the others would volunteer to go first. Impatient at the delay, Blue Feather barked to the oldest of the three, "Why are you waiting? Someone needs help."

Abashed at the criticism, Willie Edwards gingerly descended the plank, exclaiming, "It stinks down here." Ducking under the plank, he examined the fallen man, for a man it proved to be. Willie attempted to turn the head so he could see the face but the neck was stiff and the head would not turn. Clearly frightened, but in his humanity attempting to brush the insects off the prone man, he called up to the other two men.

"I can't move him. He's too stiff. I need help. One of you better come down here."

A second man, Isaac Howard, cautiously descended the plank, barely squeezing into the now overcrowded space. He assessed the situation.

"We'll have to remove the plank to get room to pick him up, and hold him to one side while the plank is put down again. Then we can put him on it and someone at the top can pull him up while we balance him from here."

The plan was quickly adopted and the plank removed by the third man, Fred Minton, who had awaited topside. With great difficulty, Willie and Isaac lifted the body, for it was indeed a corpse, cool to the touch and well into rigor mortis. As they turned him around, they gasped.

"It's Ethan! Ethan Quade! And he's dead!"

Spoken loudly enough for the people nearest the grave to hear, the word spread quickly through the small group and speedily reached a woman and a girl farthest removed from the grave. The woman had retreated there to shield the child from whatever horrors were about to be revealed, never suspecting the proximity to them of the tragedy unfolding.

The girl heard it first, her curiosity impelling her to pay rapt, though distant, attention to the drama at the grave site. Clapping both her hands to her face, she cried, "It's Daddy! It's Daddy, Aunt Esther!" and began to run to the grave.

Her aunt made a belated attempt to stop her, then ran, following the child.

"Neil, that's Rosebud, Rose Quade, running to the grave," exclaimed Marguerite Smith, who was visiting the Indian Cemetery with her son, Cornelius, his wife, Katie, and their two-and-a-half-year-old son, Thomas. Standing at a respectful distance from the funeral procession, they had been aware of some disturbance at the grave site but were not close enough to hear what had happened. "Something must be wrong. She's crying."

"Who is she?" asked Neil, puzzled.

"She was one of my students."

"Out here in Mashpee? And she's too young. You taught high school."

Impatient at the need to explain, Marguerite responded rapidly, "Don't you remember I told you I accepted a long-term substitution at our elementary school this year? The regular teacher went out on a maternity leave. Rose was one of my students."

"Oh, yes. I remember," hastily added Neil, who had indeed forgotten his restless mother's latest venture.

By now the hushed murmurs of the mourners had swelled into a crescendo of dissonant sounds as, ever so slowly, the body was pulled and pushed up the plank and placed on the ground beside the grave. It was a horrifying sight. The face and formerly clean white shirt were befouled by the dirt so recently loosened by grave diggers. That was fortunate. What could be seen of the face was a ghastly purplish-red color. A spider searched along the perimeter of the partially protruding tongue. But the eyes! They were the worst of all—wide open, staring, lusterless, partially obscured by particles of dirt and by insects scurrying across the eyeballs into the dark recesses at the corners to escape the sudden glare of sunlight to which they were unaccustomed, living in the womb of the earth. Mercifully, an old woman, who had attended many deaths, reached down to close the eyes—unsuccessfully. The muscles of the eyelids were tightly constricted in their last movement ever and would not relent. Unfazed, she removed a light scarf from around her neck and placed it over the eyes, tying it in the back of the unyielding head.

A woman wearing oversized sunglasses sank to the ground and cradled the head crying, "Ethan! Ethan! What happened to you?" Reaching into her pocket, she withdrew a tissue and wiped it over his face in an attempt to clean him. The grave had been damp and her efforts caused the dirt to smear across his face, further distorting his image. Undeterred, she wiped harder, frantically, until the tissue fell apart and the gentle hands of the old woman restrained her.

The little girl, identified by Marguerite as Rose Quade,

pushed through the crowd encircling the body and fell across the chest. Her Aunt Esther, only a few steps behind, knelt down beside Rose and embraced both the blindfolded corpse and the bereaved child.

"Neil, that was a body taken from the grave! It's Rosebud's father. Someone should call the police."

"I'm sure they will, Maman."

"I don't think there's a phone here. Why don't you go to your car and use the cellular phone in that fancy rental?"

"But this isn't any of our business," protested Neil.

"A dead body is everyone's business," scolded Marguerite.

Thirty-six years old, the CEO of a leading import/export business in Seattle, a husband and father, Neil was still the dutiful son he had always been and reluctantly walked off to heed his mother's wishes.

All but forgotten, the coffin sat off to the side surrounded by a few family members whose duty to the deceased held them firmly in place despite the frantic activity surrounding the grave site.

The first to recover his equanimity was Blue Feather who, as community religious leader, had to proffer the respect due both corpses and two grieving families. Reassembling the pallbearers, he directed them to return the coffin to the meetinghouse. He was certain there would be no burial today, and he needed to restore order and dignity to this funeral. Stepping in front of the pallbearers, he led the coffin back from whence it had so recently been removed. Wearily, the family of the deceased fell into position behind the coffin. They had acceded to the request of their aged relative and allowed him to die at home. Taking turns caring for him, juggling work schedules, child care, and nursing, had exhausted them. When would this end?

With the coffin once again in place, and under the stewardship of the funeral director who had discreetly remained behind during the procession from the meetinghouse, Blue Feather returned to the grave site, where the body was com-

pletely surrounded. A police officer approached from the other
direction. The crowd, swelled by additional visitors to the
cemetery, curious passersby, and a couple of thrill-seekers
who listened to police calls, hushed expectantly as two au-
thorities—one civil, one religious—headed toward each other.

The policeman spoke first. "Who's in charge here?"

"I am," answered Blue Feather.

Officer Haines recognized the supreme sachem but had
never met him, and decided to follow formal police procedure.

"What is your name, sir?"

"George Percy," he replied, responding to civil authority
with his civil name.

"We had a report of a dead body found here."

"Yes, that's correct." Briefly, George Percy recited the sequence of events up to the discovery of the body.

"I'd like to see the body," said Officer Haines.

"Over there, on the grass."

"You removed it from the grave?"

"Yes, we did."

"You probably destroyed all the evidence of what happened!" cried the officer.

"We were not concerned with evidence. We were helping
a brother in distress. It wasn't a body until we confirmed he
was dead."

"Okay. Let's rescue what we can of the situation. I'd appreciate your help. Were all these people at the funeral?"

"No, some have just arrived."

Haines elbowed his way through the crowd and ordered
everyone to move away from the grave and the body. The two
women and the girl were still bent over the body. He approached them and spoke solicitously.

"There is nothing you can do for him now. We would like
to find out how this happened. Please move away from the
body."

Blue Feather had followed the policeman and bent toward
the grieving women, encompassing them with his arms and
gently coaxing them upward. Slowly they arose and walked
with him to the meetinghouse.

Haines had his hands full. He had to secure the body and the site while retaining all the witnesses. He needed help.

The three young men who had removed the body from the grave were still standing there, sweaty, dirty, and uncertain of what to do next. Haines hastily decided to enlist them as temporary assistants.

"I need your help until I can get backup. Stay here and keep everyone away from the body and the grave," he directed. "Move back a little yourselves and don't touch anything. We'll preserve whatever is left to preserve."

Haines then walked to the expectant crowd and noted that they had arranged themselves into three groups: the largest apparently comprised the mourners; a smaller group—some in business clothes, some in brightly discordant summer wear—appeared to be passersby sharing information as to who saw what and when; and a still smaller group, somewhat apart, of two women, a man, and a small boy. There'd be time to sort them out later, he thought as he called out for their attention.

"This is now a police investigation. Everyone stay where you are until I go to my car and radio headquarters. As soon as I get backup we'll be able to take your statements. I know this might be inconvenient for you but please be patient and we'll be as quick as possible."

The only sounds of discontent came from a few people in business clothes who now regretted their impetuosity at stopping. It was a summer Saturday. Cape Cod was crowded. They needed to get to their establishments. An indignant man started to protest but the policeman turned a deaf ear and walked rapidly away, longing to jog to his car but restraining the impulse so as not to increase the anxiety level of an already messy situation.

Raising headquarters on his radio, he quickly explained the situation and heard the lieutenant whistle in disbelief.

"Hang on. I want to tell the chief about this."

Walter Pedersen, Mashpee Chief of Police, was officially off duty today, a day for which he had planned for many weeks. His daughter, Sally, had graduated from high school on Thursday and he had made a deal with her. If she did not attend the all-night parties, increasingly popular as a graduation perk, he would give a barbecue on Saturday for as many friends as she wanted. And no reproving relatives to censure their music or reproach their attire. He alone would be there, manning the grill and remaining as inconspicuous as his six feet, two inches permitted.

The deal accepted, Pedersen had made extensive preparations. But only a few hours before the party, as he was leaving the house to pick up ice, he discovered that his ID case was missing. He must have left it in his uniform pants yesterday when he had changed into his clamming clothes before he left the office. Grilled clams were on the party menu, and the tide was right. Embarrassed at the implications of driving without a license, he asked his wife to drive him to headquarters so that he might retrieve his ID case. As he entered, the call came from Haines.

Signaling the hurrying chief, Lieutenant White asked him to listen to Haines. Pedersen tried to wave him off, but Oscar White was insistent.

"I know you'll want to hear this, Chief."

Impatient and annoyed at his forgetfulness that made this trip necessary, Pedersen reluctantly listened to the officer's report. His annoyance vanished quickly, replaced by urgency as he heard about the chief sachem's having discovered a body in a grave site during a funeral.

"Haines, we'll send another car over immediately to assist you. I'll be over myself as soon as I get a few things started here. In the meantime, don't move the body!"

"Chief, it's already been removed from the grave by some guys who were at the funeral."

The chief swore. "Okay. Then at least secure the area and keep the site undisturbed."

"Chief, about thirty people were walking around the body and the grave when I arrived."

The chief swore again—this time in Norwegian.

"Well, do whatever you can. Get everyone into the meetinghouse to wait for us. Ask the sachem to help you keep everyone calm. Remember, you're dealing with possible witnesses, not suspects. Be polite, Haines. *Very* polite!''

Chapter Two

Thomas Tadayuki Smith, age two and one-half years, was fussing. Whisked abruptly from the grassy, airy surrounds of the cemetery, hustled into a hot meetinghouse filled almost to capacity with over forty people, and restrained by his mother holding him tightly on her lap, he protested. Tearless cries and complaining whines, punctuated with petulant cries of, "Down! Down!", expressed his frustration, along with wildly pumping arms and legs. His father, Cornelius, was delighted. Separated too long from his phone and a fax machine, he also wanted out. He knew his mother relished adventure or even misadventure and would never voluntarily leave. Katie, his wife, was distraught at her son's unacceptable behavior and tried valiantly to calm him. Cornelius sat back and smiled. The tantrum was building nicely. They would soon be asked to leave.

Walter Pedersen was the son and grandson of fishermen. His grandfather sailed on many voyages from Norway to the rich fishing banks of North America until he decided to stop commuting to the fish and move to where they lived. Cape Cod, with its proximity to Georges Bank and its established fishing industry, beckoned him. Settling in Provincetown, he bought the cheapest boat available and fished every good day and most bad days, sometimes spending as much time bailing and pumping as fishing.

As a conspicuous minority—a Norwegian in a Portuguese

fishing village—he lacked the cultural, religious, and family support of the tightly knit community and had no hesitancy about looking elsewhere to live. The narrow streets and closely built houses of Provincetown made him claustrophobic and he longed for more space.

Neighboring Truro, largely undeveloped, satisfied this need. With the carefully hoarded money from his frequent fishing trips, he made a small down payment on a rickety one-room cottage that leaked as much air as his boat did water. He married, and as his family expanded, so did the cottage, but only after the purchase of a better boat. His sons followed him into the fishing business, as did their sons, with the exception of Walter.

On his first fishing trip at the age of twelve, Walter became violently seasick, much to the embarrassment of his father, who attributed this weakness to his wife's Polish heritage. ''Landlocked people,'' he would explain scornfully to anyone who asked—or who did not ask.

Tall, slender verging on gaunt, his blond hair with infringing gray strands worn in a military cut, his eyebrows so pale as to be nearly invisible, Walter relished his career as a land-lubber policeman and now a chief. His mind whirling with things to be done instantly and simultaneously, he hurried toward his office, reached for one of the doughnuts next to the coffee urn, and called out instructions to everyone in earshot.

''Radio Sergeant Odoms and send him to the cemetery. Call Yarmouthport and get Dr. O'Neill. Find her wherever she is. Call Barnstable and tell the DA's office what happened. Let them decide whether to send out the crime team or wait to hear from the medical examiner. It might just be some guy who keeled over with a heart attack. At this point we don't know.''

While he yelled out directions, he changed into the uniform now so fortuitously left behind the day before. Downing the last of the jelly doughnut, he rushed out of his office, briefly stopping to select a coconut-covered doughnut as he headed for the parking lot and his official car. Walter's slenderness was not due to a lack of appetite.

As he hurried to his car, he was brought to a sudden stop by the sound of, "Walter, what are you doing in uniform?"

Hand slapped against forehead, he winced. "Irene, I forgot you were waiting. I have an emergency."

"Yes, you do. Sally has fifty friends coming to a party *you* organized and now *you* are running out on it."

"I am not running out on it," he protested. "Everything's ready. All I need is ice. If you would pick it up and get the boys to carry it from the car to the coolers, we'll be in great shape. Sally and her girlfriend are decorating and hanging the lanterns; the boys promised to carry out the chairs and tables; and the food is ready to go. All I have to do is start the grill and I'll be home in plenty of time for that."

Upset, but reconciled to the exigencies of life as a police officer's wife, Irene quickly calculated that he was right. Walter was a meticulous planner. Nevertheless, she fired off a parting shot.

"You had better be there for the cooking. I married you for better or worse but not to stand over a hot grill cooking for fifty ravenous teens. They'll starve before I do that."

With this she raised her window and accelerated rapidly, leaving Walter, amidst flying gravel, to marvel at her feistiness, which he adored.

A house break-in and the theft of expensive stereo equipment indicated as clearly as a calling card the probable involvement of a group of local young toughs. Cruising around their usual haunts, Detective Sergeant Lloyd Odoms heard the police calls concerning the body at the Indian Cemetery (still called that although officially a town cemetery for many years). He was not surprised when his radio crackled and the dispatcher directed him to the scene immediately. As a Mashpee Wampanoag, he was the logical choice for the assignment.

Driving up the cemetery road, Odoms noted yellow police tape around an open grave site, a body next to the yawning hole, and three young men whom he recognized standing outside the taped area.

"Are you guys deputies now?" he jokingly called to them.

"I guess we are because we're not smart enough to be a fancy policeman like you," retorted Fred Minton. "Now that you're here, you can stand here looking pretty and we'll leave."

They started to walk away.

"Only kidding, fellows," Odoms answered. "Stay here just a few more minutes until I get Haines down here. Where is he?"

"In the meetinghouse. Everyone's in the meetinghouse."

Continuing up the short road, Odoms saw Haines rush out of the door, heading toward the grave. With his medium height, medium build, medium brown hair, regular features neither handsome nor homely, and no distinguishing marks, Haines would have made the perfect thief—everything medium, difficult to describe, impossible to remember.

He was far from bland right now, however. Face red, heart beating in overdrive, uniform clinging to him from perspiration, he was racing down the path, desperate to guard the body and grave which he had reluctantly abandoned to civilian protection in order to escort everyone into the meetinghouse as directed. It was with unabashed relief that he greeted Sergeant Odoms and updated him with a brief, coherent, albeit breathless, narrative of events, including the name of the deceased, the latter information unnecessary since Odoms recognized Ethan even in the brief glance he directed at the corpse. They had been high school classmates and fierce rivals for the affection of Anna Pochet.

"What's the status of the people in there?" inquired Odoms.

"Most of them were at the funeral. But some of the people were just visiting the cemetery and others zeroed in on the cemetery after the body was discovered. They need to be sorted out but I haven't had time. The sachem is in there. He can tell you who's who."

"Okay. Stay with the body for now. The medical examiner should be here soon. And tell those three guys down there to come up here."

As Odoms stepped from his car he seemed to shrink in size.

Of average height, he appeared larger when seated because most of his height was in his torso, which was formerly well muscled, but slowly losing its definition. Entering the meetinghouse, he quickly scoped the scene. With a seating capacity of about fifty, it was nearly filled. Obstructing the narrow front aisle was a coffin that contained the body of old Joe Harmon, deprived temporarily of his rightful resting place. His few relatives sat near it to the left of the center aisle. The remainder of the seats on the left and the two front rows on the right were occupied by members of the Indian community, evidently the funeral attendees. The three remaining benches were loosely filled by tourists and local businesspeople.

Blue Feather was in the front engaged in conversation with a man Odoms knew to be a funeral director. Assuming they were making plans for the temporary disposition of the body in the coffin, Odoms went first to the two women and the girl who had been so distraught at the discovery of the body.

The women were calmer now, holding hands, tears running silently down their cheeks, as the one identified by the child as her Aunt Esther rhythmically, almost absentmindedly, alternately stroked and patted the hair of the little girl who had her head buried in her aunt's lap and whose whole body shook from her sobs.

Expressing his condolences to them while unconsciously smoothing his narrow mustache, Odoms looked studiedly at the woman in the sunglasses.

"Anna, you don't need those glasses in here. Take them off."

Anna ignored his suggestion. Odoms reached over and lifted the glasses from her eyes.

"Who punched you, Anna? Was it Ethan?"

Thomas could no longer be ignored. He was now crying steadily. Even the normally imperturbable Blue Feather was unnerved by this added stress in an already tense situation. Concluding his conversation with the funeral director and hastily informing the Harmon family that the coffin would be returned to the funeral home for burial at a later date, he walked over to the Smith family. He was still in ceremonial garb, and his sudden appearance immediately caught the attention of Thomas, who was particularly attracted to the bright, beribboned shirt and reached toward it curiously. Since his crying had reflected no distress other then boredom, he was easily diverted and smiling again, which caused his father much chagrin. His ticket out of there had been canceled.

As Chief Pedersen headed up the path to the meetinghouse, he saw several small groups of people exiting it. Three people, a woman in a green summer dress and two men in dress slacks and short-sleeved white shirts, whom Pedersen recognized as local businesspeople, were hurrying away, anxious to man their cash registers. Another group, casually dressed in shorts, halters, tank tops, sandals, and baseball caps, was reluctant to leave. Two of them had cameras and were taking pictures of everything—the meetinghouse, the sign indicating it had been established in 1684, the yellow-taped grave site with Officer Haines glumly guarding it, various gravestones, even the police cruiser. Vacation memories to cherish.

Appalled that people were leaving the scene of an as-yet-to-be-determined incident, Pedersen stormed into the meetinghouse and bellowed, "Odoms!"

The effect was instantaneous. All sound and motion stopped, frozen in time. The chief was a tall man but his presence defied mere mass. His persona took up more than its share of psychological space. He was the Sturm und Drang of the law. Even Thomas dared not protest.

Odoms was the first to react and walked hastily to the chief.

"Why are those people leaving?" demanded Pedersen.

"They're just add-ons. They got here after the body was found. Thrill-seekers. I took their names, addresses, and looked at IDs, mostly drivers' licenses. We can find them if we need them, but for the moment it seemed best to get some people out of here. The group over there with the little boy is different. They were watching the funeral and saw the body discovered. The man, Cornelius Smith, used a car phone to call the police. I thought you might want to talk to them."

"Indeed, I do. I'll talk to them in the entry. Get them out there while I speak to the sachem. Is that the family whose funeral was interrupted that he's talking to?"

"No. They were at the funeral but they're the relatives of the guy found in the grave. At least two of them are—his sister and his daughter. The woman with the sunglasses has no connection to the guy," Odoms quickly added, stretching the truth, queasily aware that he was temporarily concealing information that he would later be obligated to reveal. "I was just about to question them when the sachem came over to talk to them. I'm waiting for him to finish before I go over there."

"Question them? Are you crazy?" hissed Pedersen, succeeding in making an angry whisper seem like a shout in Odoms's ears. "They're the bereaved family. They're in shock. Show a little sensitivity! Get on your radio and send for Officer McGrath. She'll take proper care of them."

Odoms nodded his head with the barest of movement and walked to his car with deliberately slowed steps, restraining the rage engendered by this chastisement. Sensitivity to the bereaved? Or was the chief sensitive to the presence of the sachem?

Although ten years older than Odoms, Pedersen had been appointed to the Mashpee police force only a few years before him. A resident of Truro, Pedersen had moved to Mashpee the day after his appointment was confirmed and had become the town's principal cheerleader, joining one civic association after another and expertly tiptoeing through minefields of controversial issues.

His rise in the department had been meteoric and he had become chief while Odoms was still a patrolman. It was Pedersen who recognized Odoms's steady, solid abilities and pushed for his promotion. While grateful for the stripes and the money, the move fueled Odoms's cynicism about the chief as a politician, something Odoms was not temperamentally suited to be. Despite an undercurrent of hostility, they complemented each other and were destined to waltz together in disharmony—the flier and the plodder.

Safely out of sight of the chief, Odoms kicked a tire and roughly grabbed his radio.

"This is Detective Sergeant Lloyd Odoms," he announced, emphatically enunciating every syllable.

"Uh-oh!" moaned the Mashpee police dispatcher in an aside to a passing officer. "It sounds like Odoms is having a bad hair day."

Released at last from his confinement, Thomas scampered happily across the grass, all complaints forgotten. The three adults, having told and retold their story, replete with minute details supplied by Marguerite, and having produced enough identification for them to be located anywhere on the planet, happily stretched their legs and took deep breaths of the clear air.

Running well ahead of them, Thomas cut across the area most proximal to the cordoned-off site, evidently attracted to the bright yellow tape. Stooping over and reaching into the grass, he picked up something and ran back to his mother.

"Mommy, look!"

Proudly he showed his treasure—a hypodermic syringe.

Chapter Three

The meetinghouse was being vacated slowly. Phineas Wharton, in his professionally lugubrious manner, had supervised the removal of the coffin to the hearse and was about to accompany it back to his funeral home when he was startled to hear his name called loudly by the police chief. Phineas lived in a somber world of hushed tones and recoiled at this brusqueness of manner, particularly in his current state of hangover.

Black-suited, black-shoed, slick-haired, web-nosed, and peppermint-breathed, Phineas glided soundlessly to where the chief stood, the peppermint aroma arriving a full second before him.

"When was that grave dug?" the chief asked without preamble.

"I really could not say," replied Phineas in his accustomed whisper.

"Why can't you say? You were in charge of this funeral, weren't you?"

"Yes, but I do not supervise the digging of the grave. That duty is performed by a contracted service."

"When do they usually prepare a grave for a morning funeral?"

"Usually the day preceding the sorrowful event."

"Didn't you check to see if the grave was ready?" Pedersen gave no quarter.

"There was no need. My secretary handles the routine de-

18

tails and would have assured herself that the duty was performed. However, I am ever mindful of my obligations and, after the coffin was placed in the meetinghouse for viewing prior to the service, I walked over to the grave and found all in readiness.'' Phineas recited this last with head bowed and hands folded.

"Did you see a body in the grave?"

"No, indeed!"

"What time was this?"

"About nine-thirty."

"You are stating, then, that at nine-thirty this morning there was no body in that grave."

"No, I never said that. You asked me if I *saw* a body in the grave and I said I did not. There might have been one that I could not see."

"And why wouldn't you have seen it?"

"The grave is not adjacent to the path. It is about thirty feet removed from the walk, necessitating passage over grass and dirt. I must maintain my appearance for the service and you can see . . ." He paused, pointing to his glossy patent leather shoes.

"If I understand you correctly, you checked the grave from thirty feet away, decided it was okay, and didn't come any closer because your shoes might get dirty.'' Sarcasm edged Pedersen's voice.

Phineas Wharton was not too hungover to react to this reproach. Drawing himself to his full height of five feet, six inches, he countered, "Chief Pedersen, I have been in this business thirty years, as were my father and grandfather before me. It has never been suggested that I am anything less than thorough in my funeral preparations. For you to imply that—"

He got no further in his complaint, as the chief interrupted. "That's all for now, Mr. Wharton. Before you leave give the name of the grave-digging company to Detective Odoms."

Pedersen walked away dismissively, leaving Phineas sputtering with frustration. His indignance abated swiftly as he walked to the hearse and mentally calculated how much money he could squeeze out of the police department for this service. The meager insurance on Joe Harmon had already been pledged for the funeral and the family would not likely pay these additional costs. Two extra trips in the hearse and per diem cold storage costs might balance the books this week. Wharton Funeral Home was no longer the destination of choice in Mashpee. People were not dying to go there.

Detective Odoms had been interviewing, identifying, and releasing the funeral participants, starting with the family and working his way methodically down the rows. No one acknowledged looking into or even passing the grave site prior to the discovery of the body. They had parked in the area north of the meetinghouse and walked up the path leading to its door. The grave was south of the meetinghouse and not visible to anyone using the north entrance.

About a dozen people remained to be interviewed. They were slouched uncomfortably on wooden benches, fanning themselves with whatever came to hand, inhaling the sickly-sweet scent of a decaying floral wreath left behind by the funeral director, when Haines, his medium-brown hair now appearing black from perspiration, burst into the hall excitedly.

"Chief, the ME is here. And guess what that kid found. A syringe! And right near the grave, too!"

Immediately, the aura of lethargy encompassing the funeral participants dissipated. As one, they sat up and tuned in. But they were deprived of further titillation as the chief barked, "Haines!", effectively building a dam stopping the flow of gratuitous information.

Dr. Miranda O'Neill was dressed for the occasion, not the weather—jeans, long-sleeved shirt, canvas sneakers, socks, red hair severely pulled back in a rubber-banded ponytail, except for a few unruly tendrils that resisted restraint and broke free to frame her pale, freckled face. A plentiful supply of rubber gloves and face masks nestled in a capacious bag crammed with the tools of an on-the-scene medical examiner. Low rubber boots, as well as high fisherman's waders, were stored permanently in her car trunk for those occasional forays into the bogs and marshes with which the Cape was replete.

In her early thirties, Dr. O'Neill was temporarily on leave from her profession as a family practitioner to assume the role of wife and mother to her husband and two young children. Congratulating herself on this self-sacrificing decision, she had plunged into housekeeping and mothering with avidity—for about six months. Slowly, her normally ebullient personality became lackluster. At the end of the day she was enervated, not by overwork but by understimulation. Devoid of sufficient mental challenge, her brain was dozing.

The O'Neills' longtime family physician, about to retire, suggested she apply to replace him as local medical examiner. The pay was negligible, one hundred dollars per call, and the hours terrible, usually in the middle of the night, but it fit Miranda's needs perfectly. Her husband was home for the night calls and her mother nearby for the rare day calls. She eagerly responded to police summonses, about ten per month, and just as eagerly returned to her clean and peaceful home, relieved to leave behind the ugly sights and nauseating smells of violent or unexpected deaths, so unlike the orchestrated and antiseptic hospital deaths.

This call was easy. The body was accessible, obviously dead for some hours, and just as obviously an unexplained death that had to be referred to Dr. Mann of the state medical examiner's office for autopsy and determination of cause of death. All she had to do was certify his death, fill out the forms, and arrange for transportation of the body to the morgue.

But, of course, the police were never satisfied with this. Autopsies took time; chemical tests took more time. They wanted answers there and then.

"Andy, you can do better than that! What did he die of?" the chief implored.

Miranda O'Neill had long ago developed a response to anyone who called her Andy. She ignored him and continued writing.

"How about that needle we found? Could that have been his?"

She continued writing.

Bending over and shouting in her ear, he queried, "Are you deaf?"

"No, but I will be if you keep yelling in my ear. If you have any questions for Dr. O'Neill or for Miranda O'Neill, I shall be glad to answer them," she replied haughtily, chin jutting aggressively, all five-feet-two of her defying his imposing physical presence.

"Okay, *Dr. O'Neill,* how about that needle?"

Unable to resist a final jab, she replied, "You mean the one the little boy found?" as she arose from the rock on which she had been sitting, and motioned him over to the body, now covered by a plastic tarp. Pulling up his left sleeve which she had previously unbuttoned, she indicated a needle mark in that arm.

"This is recent. It could have been from that needle and it could be the cause of death. It's puzzling, though. There's only one needle mark on this arm and none on the other. People who OD are usually junkies with a full needle track. This needle mark could be from a blood test, or maybe he was a conscientious citizen and donated blood. I can't tell you anything further. You'll have to wait for the autopsy and the tox reports. We'll send that needle along with the body."

"How long has he been dead?"

Miranda sighed. "You know I can't tell that just by looking. The advanced state of rigor mortis indicates he has been dead a minimum of six hours and possibly as long as twelve hours. I doubt the latter, however, because the weather has been hot and he would probably be in complete rigor by now."

"Did he die in that grave or was he thrown in there afterward?"

"I don't know, but I understand he was discovered lying prone and I'm fairly certain that he either died in that position or was placed in that position shortly after death. You can see on the anterior portions of his face, neck, and arms the evidence of postmortem lividity. That's the purplish-red color of his skin. Note that the color occurs on the portion of his body that would be lowermost in the prone position. When he's examined during the autopsy, the torso and legs will also be inspected for this lividity. It occurs because the heart stops pumping blood and the blood pools in the lowermost part of the body.''

"How soon after death does this start?'' Pedersen asked with a tinge of respect in his voice.

"It usually begins in about twenty to thirty minutes and is complete within six to eight hours. That's consistent with his eyes, too. The corneas are cloudy.''

"So you have no idea if he died where he was found?''

"Not from the information I have. However, I can make a suggestion. The bladder relaxes after death and the urine is released. You can't notice the stain on the front of the pants much because the pants are dark colored and covered with dirt. You might want the crime team to take samples of the dirt on the pants and the dirt in the grave. I don't know whether urine traces can be detected in soil after this period of time. It might dissipate or break down too quickly but it's best to be on the safe side. Another problem is that the body has been moved and we don't know the exact location or orientation of it. The only hint I can give you is that I have been informed that the coffin-lowering device was in place and since there is a strap at each end, the body had to fall or be pushed through the center. Check that region. Of course, two men were also walking around in there and any dirt with urine might have stuck to their shoes or been moved around the bottom of the hole.''

Pedersen walked away talking to himself. He was in a delicate situation. Was this an accidental overdose, a suicide, a murder? Or was it a natural death having no connection with that needle or with the rubber tourniquet they had just found? Only the pathologist and lab tests could determine, but that took time and he did not have time. He had a grave and a body that was supposed to be buried in it. If he permitted the burial to proceed, the site would be destroyed for examination if it later proved necessary. But did he have enough reason

now for an extensive search of that grave or for a prolonged
delay of the funeral? He decided not to decide and walked to
his car to notify the DA of the situation. Let him decide.

Officer Lois McGrath searched the shelves in the large cupboard masquerading as a kitchen in Esther's condominium,
looking for tea bags, instant coffee, cocoa, anything she could
serve hot to Esther and Rosebud.

Arriving quickly after having been grudgingly summoned
by Odoms, Lois had smoothly separated the two Quades from
Anna, who, Odoms had warned the officer, was not a relative
and was about to be questioned by him. Lois efficiently propelled the Quades to a police cruiser parked directly in front
of the meetinghouse, Rosebud walking huddled against Esther,
whose arm encircled her narrow shoulders. The flowered cotton dress, hanging from neck to knees in a straight line, made
the child look even thinner than she was.

Settling both of them in the backseat, Lois backed expertly
down the narrow drive, avoiding the grave site and the curious
crowd lingering in the cemetery.

Lois was too smart a cop to misinterpret Pedersen's motive
in assigning her to this detail. She was the fabric softener of
the police department, guardian of the victims or families of
victims of violent occurrences whether they be criminal or
accidental. Comfort them, soothe them, calm them, do anything except question, harass, or importune them. No charges
were going to be made against his department while Pedersen
was chief.

Lois was also smart enough to know that this was not the
way to the top. She was a baby-sitter in uniform. But she had
plans. Oh, she would perform her duties meticulously. But no
one prohibited her from listening. People liked, even needed,
to talk after a tragedy. Tea and sympathy were as effective in
loosening tongues as were threats and coercion. Cautious
though he was, Pedersen would surely listen to and appreciate
any information she produced that had been offered gratui-
tously.

If she could only find some tea bags!

*   *   *

Marguerite studied her grandson, Thomas, sleeping peacefully in his car seat, for some resemblance, however small, to his namesake, her beloved father, Thomas Fallon. Even her predilection toward such could not unearth any similarity. But why should there be? The boy's mother, Kazuko, Katie, was Japanese-American and his father, her son Cornelius, seemed to have inherited his entire gene pool from Marguerite's French-Canadian mother, whom Marguerite herself resembled.

At five feet, eight inches, sturdily built, with dark hair, a beard which exhibited five-o'clock shadow by noon, and a fluent command of French including the patois spoken in Quebec, Neil was a Le Grande more than a Fallon or a Smith. As a child he loved to sit in his grandmaman's kitchen, inhaling the aromas of cassoulets or potages by which Genevieve Le Grande turned simple ingredients into chefs d'oeuvre. Thomas Fallon never ceased to wonder at the ease with which his grandson chatted in a "foreign" language, one whose pronunciations eluded Thomas's tongue, and whose nasalities eschewed his tenor range. His only attempt at the language was playful, as he called Genevieve "Le Grande maman"—a pun on her name and her role.

A stop at a red light interrupted the rhythm of motion and Thomas awakened. His first words, "I'm hungry," were not surprising since it was past his usual lunch hour.

"So am I," agreed Marguerite. "Neil, let's stop for lunch."

"Good idea. How about this seafood stand?" he asked as he was swinging into its driveway. No one objected.

Marguerite was thinking pleasurably of fried clams before the car even stopped. Not those puny strips some places pass off as fried clams, but the whole clams—known locally as belly clams—succulent, sweet, and satisfying.

Already worried about future clogged arteries in her toddler son, Katie was scanning the outdoor menu for something not fried.

"Good. They have broiled fish. I'll order that with a salad and share with Thomas." Katie was always happy to share meals as her small appetite precluded her finishing a normal restaurant portion.

Neil opted for fried shrimp and French-fried potatoes. His arteries would have to fend for themselves.

"Neil, I can't help thinking about little Rose Quade. Especially when I compare her with Thomas—so happy, so secure with two loving parents," said Marguerite as they ate their lunch.

"And don't forget a doting grandmother," Neil interjected, trying to lighten the conversation.

"Two of those," she corrected gently, "as well as two grandfathers, at least one of whom is doting."

This last remark reflected her residual bitterness at the husband who had left her more than ten years ago for another woman.

"Rose is an orphan now. Her mother died when she was just a baby. I believe there was something mysterious about that death, too. Rose seems to be star-crossed. Such a lovely, bright child," Marguerite said musingly.

"I was surprised when you said she was in your class in Eastham. Don't most of the Cape Indians live in Mashpee?" Neil inquired. Despite himself he was becoming interested in the story of Rose Quade.

"Yes. Most do, but not all. And Rose's mother was not Indian. She was Caucasian."

"Is there anyone to take care of her now?" asked Katie in a concerned voice.

"I believe her grandmother, or maybe it's her great-grandmother, lives with Rose and her father. Occasionally, I see her and Rose at arts and crafts fairs. The grandmother sells her handmade beadwork, mostly chokers and bracelets, but they're of finer quality than most of the ones I've seen. The designs are more intricate, the beads are smaller and the handwork exquisite—no big knots or ties that fall off. They make wonderful gifts."

Catching herself straying, Marguerite returned to the question. "However, I think she is too old to assume responsibility for a ten-year-old. Of course, there's Ethan's sister. I met her at a parents' open house which was during the day, and Ethan couldn't come. He normally made a point of attending every function. He was devoted to Rose.''

Katie's face was becoming progressively sadder. "Maybe her aunt will take her,'' she volunteered hopefully.

"Maybe, but Esther is single and works as a nurse's aide. That involves night and weekend work. That's why she was able to attend the open house in the daytime.''

"Poor child,'' murmured Katie. Her small portion of fish was nearly untouched, her appetite further diminished by empathy for an orphaned little girl.

The somber mood was broken by the emphatic voice of Thomas. "More! Want more!''

Smiling again, Katie happily placed more of her fish on Thomas's plate. The cares, perplexities, and griefs of existence were swept away by that simple entreaty, "More!''

Chapter Four

Robert Maleski, in coveralls and rubber gloves, was crouched in the open grave sieving dirt. Topside—perfectly aligned, evenly spaced, and meticulously labeled—were an assortment of specimen jars, some containing detritus from the sieve and others preserving dirt samples from the bottom and sides of the hole. He would continue his painstaking examination until every inch of the grave was inspected, and each specimen coded on a map of the grave drawn on graph paper. Maleski was a type A personality.

His more eclectic colleague, Arnold Roche, was posturing and posing and snapping pictures of the corpse rapidly in the manner of the fashion photographer he used to be. No matter that these on-site photographs were of dubious value since the body had been roughly handled and moved. Every Roche picture was a signature piece. His personality defied letter typing.

Maleski and Roche were members of the Crime Prevention and Control, or CPAC, unit, dispatched to the cemetery by Lawrence Hartung, district attorney of Barnstable County. Though the cause of death had not been determined, and the likelihood of foul play was negligible, Hartung wanted no charges of racial insensitivity to haunt his career.

The unburied body of Joe Harmon was cooling in Phineas Wharton's refrigerator and the body of Ethan Quade lay decomposing on the grass. The grave belonged to each of them: Joe Harmon by deed, Ethan Quade by mischance. How to mollify both families and fulfill his professional responsibilities?

A former college football running back, Hartung preferred offense to defense. Acting quickly, he ordered a trooper to obtain the signature of the closest Harmon relative on a consent-to-search form specifying the grave. In return, the family would receive permission for a Monday burial.

Confident of the successful outcome of the trooper's mission, he then ordered the CPAC unit to the cemetery for photographs and evidence collection. They were directed to conduct a diligent search of the site and, pending permission, of the grave itself. He wanted no more surprises from two-year-olds.

The CPAC unit worked with fluidity, never in one another's way. As Arnold Roche and his appendant camera moved away from the body to photograph the surrounds, Ralph Donato, another crime scene expert, moved smoothly in, rubber gloves on anxious hands, and began to collect and record the deceased's possessions. He removed a wristwatch from the right arm and a wedding band from the left hand. Deftly taking fingernail scrapings, he then secured a plastic bag around each hand for further examination by the pathologist. The pants' pockets contained only a handkerchief, a ring of keys, and a small penknife with multiple attachments. No wallet. Every item was placed in a separate plastic envelope and labeled with an evidence tag.

Dr. O'Neill, delayed from removing the body by the decision to send the CPAC unit, waited nearby, sitting on a rock and stamping her feet occasionally to discourage the encroaching ants whose territory she was occupying.

Pedersen watched the routine and tediously painstaking procedures somewhat distractedly, his mind on the impending barbecue. His wandering thoughts were abruptly returned to the present by an item discovered in the pocket of the white shirt now so encrusted with dirt that the pocket was nearly hidden. Holding his find carefully so as not to puncture it, Donato displayed a fragile glassine packet containing a coarse powder—not quite white, not quite tan. Irene Pedersen would have called it ecru.

"That should wrap it up!" exclaimed Pedersen, the relief

evident in his voice. "Just another shooting. Only not with bullets," he added as Dr. O'Neill looked at him quizzically, having missed his meaning.

The tea for Esther and cocoa for Rosebud were achieving the desired effects. Aunt and niece sat quietly, sipping the hot drinks and relishing their warmth in the chill of the air-conditioning Lois had turned on high when they entered the sweltering apartment. Her ministrations successful, the officer sat back, unconsciously smoothing the sides of her luxuriant, tawny hair that was drawn tightly back into a French braid that fit neatly under her uniform cap.

"I can't believe it," said Esther, shaking her head. "Ethan wasn't sick, he wasn't in trouble. He never got in trouble. Here's a picture from his college graduation," she indicated, picking up a photograph in a silver frame that was displayed on a folding table against the wall. It was an enlarged snapshot of Ethan and Esther, he in academic gown, she in a bright summer dress, standing on a grassy expanse, arms clasping each other's waist from behind.

There were only two other pictures in Esther's small living room: one of an older couple whom Lois guessed to be her parents, and a recent school photo of a shyly smiling Rosebud. Lois studied the picture Esther handed to her.

Esther bore a remarkable resemblance to her brother. Her low end of medium stature, sturdy physique, glossy dark hair, dark eyes, and taut skin that highlighted her facial bone structure, were the anatomical manifestations of this similarity. To those who knew them, and unrevealed by this posed portrayal, it was the puckering of the nose in conjunction with the raising of the eyebrows, the slightly asymmetrical smile, the direct and unblinking gaze of the eyes when answering a question, that proved the closeness of their consanguinity.

"If only I had gotten to see him last night. If he had come home for dinner like he always does, maybe he would have told me if he had a problem," Esther speculated.

"Don't think that way. It wasn't your fault," soothed Lois.

"I went to his house last night, you know," offered Esther,

confirming Lois's hypothesis on the need to talk. "I usually go every Friday because I'm off that night. Most of the time I cook dinner. It gives Grandma Sunny a break and I enjoy it because I don't always bother to cook for myself. When I walked in Rosebud was talking to her father on the phone. He said he had to work late and wouldn't be home for dinner. He didn't want us to wait or even save something for him because he would pick up something in Hyannis. I heard her say 'Okay, Dad' and then she said 'Good-bye.' That's the last we heard from him."

Lois held her tongue, anxious to know more but disciplining her inquisitive instincts. After a brief and heavy silence she was rewarded. Esther, desperate for answers, turned to Rosebud.

"Honey, did Daddy say why he would be late?"

"No, he just said he was working."

"Was he okay in the morning?"

"He was a little quiet. You know Daddy. He usually likes to kid around. I get up for breakfast even in the summer because he's such fun. Yesterday he didn't say much. I asked him why he was so quiet and he said he had some business to take care of and it was on his mind."

"Tell me exactly what he said to you on the phone," demanded Esther, normally so solicitous, now manic in her quest for answers.

Even Lois recoiled at the aunt's insistent questioning of the child. But Esther was relentless, simmering in a mental cauldron of engagement with the intolerable. She had to know what had happened to her twin brother.

Motherless before her first birthday, orphaned now at ten, Rose Quade replied with a composure belying her youth and circumstances, repeating her conversation with her father. As she came to the good-byes her voice trembled, and a little tear squeezed itself out of her left eye and meandered down her cheek. She had just realized that the four o'clock telephone call had been the last time she would ever speak to her father.

"I should have stayed there last night," Esther chastised herself, hugging Rosebud tightly as the child softly lamented for her lost father. "Maybe he called again. I always sleep over on Friday but I wanted to take Rosebud to Mr. Harmon's funeral in the morning because it was an old-style Indian funeral and she'd never seen one. I want her to know something about our customs. After dinner, me and Rosebud drove here so we wouldn't have far to go in the morning. I don't even know if Ethan went home at all. Grandma Sunny must have been worried."

Suddenly she halted her narrative and sat upright.

"Grandma Sunny! She doesn't know yet! I have to get to her before she hears it from someone else or on the radio. Take us back to the cemetery. I need my car. Hurry, please!"

Esther automatically picked up the cups and saucers to put in the dishwasher and called out to Rosebud to turn off the blasted air conditioner. It was freezing in there.

Katie was not satisfied with her portrait of Blue Feather. It was a good likeness—one would have recognized him from it—but the character was missing. She yearned to do a pen-and-ink drawing of him, but lacking his presence, she had to forgo this very precise method of portraiture and settle for the more forgiving medium of charcoal, which she could smudge into a semblance of wrinkles in a manner suggesting but not accurately portraying the strong lines etched in his face by joy, sorrow, and sun.

The physiognomy of Blue Feather was easily reproduced by Katie. His broad face was so reminiscent of her own family traits. Blue Feather, like Katie, was a descendant of Asian immigrants, albeit much earlier ones. Thousands of years ago and for many generations, his forebears had trekked slowly north through Asia, east over the land bridge closing the Bering Strait, then south to populate two continents.

The Kazukos' trip was shorter and more comfortable but also had its travails. In 1930, Asian immigration to the United States was severely restricted. Katie's great-grandfather had received permission to enter the country because of unusual circumstances. A major botanical garden in San Francisco had inherited from a supporter a premier collection of bonsai specimens. There was no one on the staff capable of tending and enhancing this valuable bequest so the trustees, all powerful men, turned to Japan for a bonsai master and obtained the requisite visas.

Even their privileged status did not prevent the family from being interned on Angel Island in San Francisco Bay, the Ellis Island of the West. Used primarily to stem the immigration of cheap Chinese labor, the complex detained and housed Asian immigrants in drafty wooden barracks with barred windows for two to six weeks while they were extensively interrogated. The Kazukos' stay was short but the memory burned vividly when, in 1942, they were placed in a World War II detention camp for three years. Katie's father was only two years old when interned, the same age as Thomas now.

With Katie occupied drawing on the patio and Thomas napping, Neil seized the opportunity to catch up on *The Wall Street Journal*. Rusty, Marguerite's generic red dog, lounged in the shade of a hydrangea bush.

It was a tranquil scene. Except for the kitchen. Frustrated and troubled by the events at the cemetery, Marguerite launched a frenzy of activity, her usual antidote to worry.

Rummaging noisily among the excess pots and pans stored in the cellar, she returned triumphantly with an old marmite, an earthenware lidded pot higher than it was wide, the very one in which her mother had always made pot-au-feu. Into the marmite went large quantities of beef rump chunks and beef shank, a marrowbone, chicken wings and giblets, and pieces of oxtail, all of which were frozen because this meal had been planned for later in the week when she had invited a few friends to meet her family. Right now she had other things on her mind.

Mainly the police. And their cavalier attitude about Ethan's death. She covered the meat with water and turned on the stove.

Of course, they had to wait for an autopsy to determine cause of death but she was certain they already considered it a typical drug case.

Marguerite took from the refrigerator carrots, small white

turnips, leeks, and celery. *Chop, chop, chop* went the knife against the cutting board as she recalled how pleased the police looked when Thomas found the hypodermic needle.

The vegetables were added to the pot along with a clove-studded onion, salt, and a bouquet of parsley, thyme, marjoram, and bay leaves.

The officers were annoyed that they hadn't found the needle themselves, but they'd had such smirks. She was positive that they connected the needle with Ethan and just as positive that he didn't take drugs.

With the pot now boiling, Marguerite skimmed the liquid, added a lid, and placed it in the oven to cook slowly for two to three hours.

She did not know Ethan well, but even in her short acquaintance with him, she concluded that his hatred of drugs of all kinds had been obsessive. At a parents' meeting called to discuss ways of preventing drug use among children, he'd commented that parents gave mixed messages when they lectured about street drugs but continued to use alcohol, tobacco, and excessive over-the-counter drugs. He urged them to limit all of these products—addictions, he called them.

"*Ça va, Maman?*" inquired Neil, startling Marguerite from her soliloquy as he came into the kitchen.

This homely phrase signaled the beginning of conversation in French between the two. Marguerite eagerly anticipated these exchanges and the opportunity to refresh her skills in that language. The only other occasions to speak French came during infrequent encounters with Frank Nadeau, Eastham chief of police. But he was not nearly as fluent as Neil and she usually assumed the role of instructor in these instances.

"*Bien,* Neil. *Regardez!*" she commanded, opening the oven to exhibit the bubbling, aromatic stew.

"Who's coming for dinner?" he asked, still in French. "You're cooking enough for eight people."

"No one. But I did make a little extra to take over to the Quades. My mother always brought food to neighbors who had a death or an illness in the family. It's just an old custom."

"Old custom, my foot. You're dying to find out what happened and get in the middle of it," Neil surmised.

"Nonsense! I'm just trying to practice the good habits I was taught by Le Grande maman," she answered self-righteously.

"Le Grande detective would be more like it," insisted Neil as Marguerite walked huffily out of the kitchen. The conversation was over.

Chapter Five

Lloyd Odoms looked appraisingly at Anna Pochet. Time had passed gently over her. The years had softened the arresting angularities of youth, resulting in a sleek yet slender body. She could still cause heads to turn. His forty-year-old self felt twenty every time he looked at her.

Ethan, Anna, and he had been classmates from kindergarten through high school, the two men rivals for Anna. Saucy at six, sexy at sixteen, she was the eye of the hurricane, calm while the storm swirled around her. Ethan won. He and Anna were an item throughout high school.

A guidance counselor changed their lives when she informed Ethan of the new Native American program at Dartmouth College in New Hampshire. Founded in 1769 by Eleazar Wheelock, a Congregationalist minister, "for the education of Youths of the Indian tribes . . . English Youths, and any others," the school had graduated only nineteen Native Americans in its first two hundred years. In 1970, a program was established to recruit, retain, and graduate Native Americans. The counselor considered Ethan an excellent candidate.

In September 1972, Ethan entered Dartmouth, leaving behind a discontented trio—Anna, who missed Ethan; Lloyd, who yearned for Anna; and Esther, Ethan's twin sister, who adored Lloyd. The latter avoided Esther, could not abide her presence. She looked too much like his hated rival.

Anna considered herself engaged to Ethan throughout his college years. She even announced that they were to be married the summer of his graduation. Evidently, she forgot to tell Ethan. After graduation, he headed directly for New York and Wall Street.

Anna's trips to New York were disastrous. She was not comfortable with Ethan's new friends—cool, educated, worldly, pale. They talked finance passionately, ate nouvelle cuisine at midnight, and dressed like preppy clones. Though they drank sparingly, they experimented with the drug of the moment, which changed frequently in the '70s. Conservative economically, but liberal socially, they embraced Ethan, a manifestation of the union of their philosophies.

Over the next few years, Anna restyled her hair and revamped her wardrobe, even made shopping trips to Boston for "New York" clothes which she could ill afford. She was nervously preparing for her next visit to Manhattan when she met Ethan's mother, who had news—a telegram from Ethan announcing his marriage.

Lloyd was not sure whether his insistence on pursuing the cause of Ethan's death was to exculpate him or to incriminate him. Alone with Anna now, he began to question her.

"When did you meet Ethan yesterday?"

"What makes you think I met him?"

"I know you were with him," he answered, focusing intently on the black eye hidden again by the sunglasses.

"Do you follow me around?"

"No, I passed your house and saw his car."

"Always the cop, aren't you, Lloyd? I suppose you called in the license plates to see who was at my house. Or did you already know by checking up on him?" she spat.

"I knew it was his car because I saw him and Rosebud get in it one time at the mall."

"And you memorized the license plate? Like he was a criminal or something. Don't you ever act like a real person instead of a cop?" she retorted, raising her voice so that it echoed in the room, now empty except for the two of them.

"I am a real person, Anna. A real person who happens to be a cop. Don't you think it's important for Esther and Rosebud to know the truth instead of spending the rest of their

lives wondering what happened? Don't you want to know how
Ethan ended up in someone else's grave?''

She did.

Resignedly, she answered. "I met him about eight o'clock
last night. I was shopping at the Hyannis mall and went into
Smugglers Cove afterward for something to eat and a few
drinks. Ethan was at the bar."

"Was he drinking?"

"Yes, he was."

"Had you arranged to meet there?"

"No, it was just by accident."

"Did Ethan regularly hang out at this bar?"

"You know darn well, Lloyd, that Ethan didn't hang out at
any bar. He didn't drink."

"He was drinking last night."

"Yes, he was," conceded Anna. "That was what was so
strange. I never knew Ethan to drink since he came back to
the Cape. Even when he was in New York with that fast crowd
he hardly drank. Just enough to be sociable."

"Did you speak to him?"

"Yes. I was so surprised to see him that I went up to him
and ordered something to eat at the bar. I tried to get him to
eat but he wasn't interested. He just drank."

"Tell me what you talked about."

"We didn't talk about anything. He was very depressed.
Just rambled occasionally that life is an illusion and people
aren't what they seem to be. I couldn't make any sense of it."

"What happened then?"

"Well, I wanted to leave. It was no fun sitting there with
him in that mood. When I said I was leaving he came to his
senses. He said he couldn't go home like that because Rosebud had never seen him drunk. He asked if he could come to
my house to sober up. I said okay, but didn't think he should
drive. He insisted he needed his car to go home that night. So
we left in two cars and somehow he made it to my house."

"Was anyone there?"

"No, Lloyd. I live alone as you well know. You drive by
often enough."

"Just asking, Anna. Continue."

"The house was hot from being closed up all day. Ethan was sweaty from the drink and the heat. He took off his jacket and his shirt and sat down on the sofa while I went in the kitchen to make coffee. By the time I came out with the coffee he was sprawled across the sofa sleeping."

"How late did he stay at your house?"

"He slept until about midnight, then he woke up when I turned the TV off. He was all mixed up at first, then he realized where he was and said he had to go home. I heated up the coffee and gave him some. Then I gave him some aspirin for his headache. When he finished he put on his shirt and left. He forgot his jacket. It's still at my house."

"What time was it when he left?"

"I guess about twelve-thirty."

"Odoms, come out here!" called Pedersen, his voice sounding particularly strident in the hushed atmosphere of the meetinghouse.

Returning to Anna after a brief conference with the chief, Odoms resumed the questioning in a more aggressive tone, kindled by the information he had just received.

"Tell me about the scratches on Ethan's chest, Anna. Is that when he punched you?"

The pot-au-feu was ready and Marguerite ladled into another pot some of the broth along with a sizable portion of meat and vegetables. Traditionally, the broth was served separately with noodles added, but she did not wish to complicate matters for the Quades. They could just heat it together and serve it as a stew. She decided to deliver it to their house before she served her own family. Rusty followed her to the door.

"You want a walk, don't you, girl? Okay, I'll take your long leash and tie you to a tree while I go inside."

Marguerite had no qualms about talking aloud to a dog. Rusty was her only live-in companion.

Delicately balancing a large pot in one hand and holding the dog's leash in the other, Marguerite fervently hoped no rabbit would cross their path to set Rusty off on a chase.

The Quade house was only a short distance, set back from the road, nestled between the trees and a kettle pond. It was one of the older houses, originally a summer cottage. Though now insulated and heated, it was not fully modernized and was one of the few houses in the neighborhood that still had exterior propane tanks for cooking.

A knock on the door was answered by Rosebud, dressed in shorts and a baggy T-shirt. She was barefooted and long-legged, tall for her age.

"Mrs. Smith!" she gasped, surprised at finding her teacher at the door.

"Rose, I came to tell you and your family how sorry I am about your father. I only met him a few times, but he seemed like a wonderful father."

Noting the sadness spreading on Rosebud's face, working its way downward from the eyes, Marguerite quickly changed the subject. "And I brought some dinner for you and your family. I didn't think anyone would be interested in cooking," she added almost apologetically.

"Rosebud, who's there?" called a voice from another room.

"It's Mrs. Smith, my teacher."

"Well, ask her in," ordered the voice, becoming closer and eventually appearing in the person of Esther Quade.

Despite her good intentions—or was it curiosity?—Marguerite began to question the propriety of her intrusion on a grieving family. She offered a hasty repetition of her condolences, proffered the dinner, and began to retreat.

"That was very nice of you, Mrs. Smith. Please come in. Rosebud talked a lot about you. She liked you as a teacher."

Excusing herself to herself as merely being polite, Marguerite entered and told Esther the food just needed to be heated when they were ready. The ice broken, Marguerite accepted Esther's offer to sit down, looking around her while Esther carried the pot into the kitchen.

What she saw was a gem of a living room, small but exquisitely furnished in a style atypical of Cape Cod cottages. The floor was carpeted in a magnificent old Persian rug. An antique Federal sofa was comfortably married to a pair of Queen Anne side chairs. One of the lamps on the side tables appeared to be a Tiffany original. A small carved console table held a few choice collectibles: a faience vase, an English tole box, and an old wooden mantel clock. Tucked beneath the table was a wallpapered trunk on which rested a few large, glossy art books.

A small dining area was sparely furnished with a nine-teenth-century painted French country table, four chairs, and a low French corner cupboard. On the cupboard were beautiful but tarnished silver pieces: candlesticks, a tea set, and a serving tray. Windows in both rooms were simply but elegantly dressed with Brunschwig & Fils fold-up window shades.

What little Marguerite could see of the kitchen was surprising. Sagging pine cupboards, old fixtures and appliances, faded wallpaper hanging loose at the one corner in her view.

"Would you like to sit outside with me, Mrs. Smith? It's stuffy in here."

Marguerite was suddenly aware that Esther was talking to her and answered hastily to cover her embarrassment at having been caught inspecting the house.

"Oh, no. I don't want to bother you. I was just leaving."

"You're not bothering us. I want Rosebud to lie down for a while and Grandma Sunny is very upset and wants to be alone in her room. I'm not able to rest and I can't sit still or do anything. I keep thinking of Ethan. It would be nice to talk to someone besides the police. They won't tell me anything, not even when we can bury him."

So saying, Esther waited for no further protest and led the way to a back door that opened to a sunny garden and a bench overlooking the pond. She stopped first to pick up a portable phone to take with her, hoping that the police would call to give her some answers.

Her distress at Ethan's death was compounded by the apparent suspicion on the part of the police that he had died from a drug overdose.

"It's not possible, Mrs. Smith. Anyone who knew Ethan would know that he hated drugs. After what he went through because of drugs, he thought drug dealers were as bad as murderers.''

"What do you mean by what he went through?"

"Don't you know? I thought everyone knew about Joy, Rosebud's mother. It was in the newspapers and there was so much gossip at the time."

"When was this?" Marguerite asked.

"About nine years ago."

"That explains it. I didn't live here full-time then, only summers.'' Marguerite had overheard a reference to Joy's death but did not know the details.

"Since you seem to be the only one on Cape Cod who doesn't know, I might as well tell you. When Ethan and Joy married they lived in New York. Joy was in Ethan's crowd there. She was from New Hampshire. Ethan fell head over heels for her. She was tall, slim, blond, beautiful, and so lively. Just like her name, Joy.

"But Ethan's crowd was fooling around with drugs. It was hip in those days. Ethan tried marijuana but didn't like it so stopped and never tried anything else. If you knew Ethan you would understand that. Ethan was special. He was different. He always had a goal and knew he was going someplace. Ethan was in control of his life. When the rest of us kids were loafing in the summer or working in restaurant kitchens or motels, Ethan became a golf caddy. Can you believe that? A golf caddy. Learned to play, too, and became very good. He even made the golf team at Dartmouth. There was a picture of him holding a golf club in the Dartmouth school paper. The title over it was 'Mashpee's Mashie','' she added, smiling at the memory.

Marguerite, anxious to hear more, gently urged her, "What happened to Joy?"

"Ethan wanted to have a family but Joy was occasionally abusing drugs. He thought if they moved away from New York, away from that crowd, she would stop. You have to understand, that was a big sacrifice for Ethan. He was very successful in New York and was moving up. But Joy meant everything to him. He convinced her to move to Cape Cod with him. He made it sound very romantic. That's why they picked a house on a pond. They even bought a canoe."

"But why in Eastham?" queried Marguerite. "Why not Mashpee where Ethan came from and where his family lived?"

"That was Joy's only condition in moving to the Cape. She didn't want to live in Mashpee. You see, her family didn't approve of her marriage and she was an only child. She thought if she moved to Cape Cod, her parents would be able to see her more and learn how happy she was. But if she moved to Mashpee her parents would think she was abandoning them and living in the Indian community. So they picked Eastham. She even decorated this house the way her parents' house looked. They were very rich and had a big house with all antiques. Her mother gave her some of this stuff."

Esther's strained look softened. The stress lines on the forehead were replaced by smile lines at the corners of her mouth.

"I told Ethan the Wilkinsons should be ashamed of themselves for giving him a used rug. He laughed and told me it was an antique Persian rug and very valuable. That's how much I know," she joked, confessing her own ignorance.

Serious again, she continued, "They were remodeling one room at a time. They never finished. Joy got sick and after she died Ethan had no interest in continuing. Everything is as she left it."

The memory prevented Esther from continuing. But Marguerite was too involved in this saga to stop now.

"What happened to Joy?" she repeated.

Taking up the thread, Esther continued. "They moved to the Cape and Ethan got a good job in Hyannis. Not like he had in New York, but good for the Cape. Joy worked, too, and got away from drugs. She was never a serious user.

"When she became pregnant they were thrilled. Ethan was so proud of his baby. But things went wrong. Joy became depressed—you know what I mean, childbirth blues. Ethan did everything he could and so did the doctor. But somehow Joy got hold of some LSD, probably asked her New York friends to send her some. She had a bad trip. Rosebud was only eleven months old, but Joy left her alone at home, drove to the ocean, walked in with her clothes on, and drowned. The doctors said she might have been having hallucinations and thought she could walk on water. But nobody knows.'' Esther paused a minute or two before she continued.

"Ethan nearly went crazy. Then, as if that wasn't bad enough, the Wilkinsons tried to take the baby away. They claimed Ethan was an addict who got their daughter hooked on drugs and he wasn't a fit parent. He had to get a lawyer and have drug tests. He tried to get some of his New York so-called friends to testify that it was Joy, not Ethan, who took drugs, but they didn't want to get involved. They probably sent Joy the LSD. Anyway, he finally won after he tested clean on drugs and my mother testified that she would take care of the baby. She and Dad were big shots in the community. He was even on the Tribal Council. The Wilkinsons had nothing on them. So you see, this is why I know Ethan didn't die from drugs.''

"Esther, I'm sure they'll find that out in the autopsy. Ethan probably died of natural causes.'' Marguerite patted her hand encouragingly as she said this.

"Or maybe unnatural causes. Anna told me something was bothering Ethan but she didn't know what. He was talking about people not being what they seem.''

"Which people? Did he mention any names?'' Marguerite's antennae were waving.

"No, she didn't say. She said she couldn't make any sense of what he was mumbling.''

"Maybe you'd better ask her again when she's had more time to think about it.''

Before Marguerite could pursue this point, Rosebud emerged from the back door, hair tousled, eyes swollen, face sweaty.

"Aunt Esther, I can't sleep,'' she whined. "Can't I stay here with you?''

As Esther extended both arms to her, a soft chanting was heard emanating from an open window.

"That's Grandma Sunny," explained Rosebud. "She's praying for Daddy."

"Yes, she prays in her room mostly. She's Passamaquoddy, not Wampanoag. They're Catholic," added Esther. "She uses the rosary beads but chants it Indian style."

"Maybe she's even scolding Great Rabbit," said Rosebud with innocent resilience, a smile lighting her face for the first time since that dreadful morning. "She believes he has *m'teoulin,* great powers, and maybe he did something bad to Daddy."

"Maybe, Rosebud. Maybe she is," murmured Esther, gently smoothing Rosebud's hair. "You know, Ethan gave Rosebud her nickname. They agreed to name the baby Rose after Joy's mother. But the first time Ethan held her he said to me that Rose wasn't a baby's name. It was too ripe, too mature for a little baby. She was more like a flower bud. Then he said, 'Rosebud—that's what I'll call her until she's old enough to be a Rose.' It was so beautiful the way he said it."

The poignant moment suspended time and reality. Marguerite knew she must leave and let the Quades confront their loss in private.

Arising, she kept her farewell brief. "Keep in touch with me. If there is anything I can do for you, I would be glad to help."

With a parting squeeze to Esther's hand and a hug for Rosebud, Marguerite hurried out the door, untied Rusty, and urged her toward the road faster than she was wont to travel. There were a few unexplored rabbit holes around this pond.

Chief Pedersen heard the blaring music as soon as he turned the corner. "What is Irene thinking of? Someone will call the police."

Unable to enter his driveway, which was crowded by the addition of two pickups and a Mustang, he parked on the road and hastened toward the smoke billowing from the unattended grill. Three spareribs, blackened on one side but with enough fat on the bottom side to be causing flare-ups, lay abandoned, a sacrifice to the coals.

Walking along the flagstone path to the patio on the other side of the house, he winced at the increasingly raucous music of Pearl Jam and came to a sudden halt at the edge of the patio. In the midst of the wriggling, writhing, short-skirted and baseball-hatted crowd of teenagers, was Irene—feet stomping, hips swaying, arms waving. Spotting him, she ceased the gyrations and squeezed her way over to him.

"Walter, where have you been? I've had a terrible time here alone trying to cope with feeding this crowd. I'm exhausted."

It was past quitting time but Odoms was still working, cruising around the seamier bars looking for Louis Perry, Anna Pochet's ex-husband. Odoms was not officially on a case. No charges had been brought against Perry. No overtime would be accrued. But he couldn't go home. Not like this.

Married twelve years, the father of three children, Lloyd Odoms was content ninety percent of the time. But, oh, the other ten percent! He was obsessed by Anna. He was besotted, bedeviled. The sight and sound of her kicked in all his old hurts, his regrets, his speculations of what if, but mostly his desires. Those were the times, like now, when he could not face his family. He must first dispel the devil within.

So at seven o'clock on a Saturday night he was looking for Louis Perry. Faced with the discovery of the scratches on Ethan's chest, and his accusation that Ethan struck her, Anna had gone beserk in the meetinghouse.

"You can't let go, can you, Lloyd? You still hate Ethan after all these years. He's dead and you won't let go. You're really cruel. Do you beat prisoners, too?"

Sitting patiently through her outburst, thankful no one was around to hear her partial truths, Lloyd said nothing until she had vented her anger and sank back on the bench. She was ready to answer him.

"Yes, I scratched Ethan. But it was accidental. When he said he was leaving I was afraid to let him drive home. He was still a little drunk, and it's a long trip. I begged him to stay overnight. But he wouldn't listen. When he reached for his shirt, I grabbed hold of his shoulders to stop him. He

shoved me away. That's when I scratched him. I was trying
to grab him so I wouldn't fall.''

''And he hit you.''

''No! Ethan wasn't like that. I was surprised that he even
shoved me. He just went into the bathroom to wash the blood
off his chest. There wasn't much. Then he put his shirt on and
left.''

''How did you get a black eye?''

''You're the detective. You figure it out.''

He thought a minute, then said, ''Louis.''

''Yes, Louis. He was on the Cape and decided to visit me.
It's just like Louis to think of visiting me after midnight. He
was drunk, too. And mean. He came in just after Ethan left.
He's always been jealous of Ethan. Claims that's why I left
him. Louis never blames himself for anything.''

''You should bring charges against him, Anna. Get a restraining order.''

''What good would that do? It's a piece of paper. How
many women do you hear of who get killed after getting a
restraining order? I'd rather let him go back to New Bedford.
He doesn't come to the Cape much anymore. I guess he has
enough drinking buddies in New Bedford. Besides, his diabetes will kill him soon, anyway, the way he abuses himself.''

Anna had wed Louis in a fit of pique after Ethan's marriage.
He started beating her on their two-day honeymoon to New-
port. A drifter, moving from job to job, he decided that New
Bedford offered more opportunity and moved there. Anna,
rebelling after almost six years of torment, refused to go and
used his move as an opportunity to divorce him. He still returned to harass her but the intervals were becoming longer
and gave her some hope of his eventual disinterest in her.

Incensed by Louis Perry's abuse of Anna, after Odoms
completed his interview with Anna, he searched for Louis. He
spotted him in the parking lot of the Happy Hour tavern. It
was misnamed. Happy people were not to be found there. It
was the haunt of rejects, misfits, and people without résumés
who lived in the shadows of life.

Pulling his car across the driveway so as to prevent Louis

from exiting, Odoms approached and began to question him about his visit to Anna last night. Amidst a string of profanities, Louis managed to convey the message that Odoms's interest in Anna extended beyond his police duties, that he, Louis, had outsmarted Odoms by capturing Anna, and that he could make several suggestions as to what Odoms could do. Colorful language aside, Odoms knew all too clearly that Louis Perry, maybe for the first time in his life, was right.

Time to go home to the family.

Chapter Six

Esther arose at dawn after a sleepless night. Unable to acknowledge the finality of Ethan's absence, she declined to use his room and occupied the other twin bed in Rosebud's tiny room. After crying herself to sleep, Rosebud slept peacefully and Esther did not wish to awaken the child prematurely with her own tossing and turning.

It had been a night of torment for Esther. Her thoughts were discordant, in disarray. Although her emotions at her brother's death were primarily those of great sorrow, there were secondary emotions, more self-serving, of which she was ashamed. Esther's feelings about Ethan were bittersweet. As his twin, she loved and admired him. But, as his female twin, she bore the burden of inequality, always in his shadow.

In high school her grades were equivalent to Ethan's; however, no guidance counselor urged Esther to go to college. After a series of no-account jobs, she became a nurse's aide and remained so. Diffident, lacking self-confidence in her ability, Esther could not have been more different from Ethan in personality. She never complained about their disparate paths and everyone assumed she was happy with her less ambitious choices. No one ever thought to ask her.

Now, at forty years of age, she had to pick up the pieces of Ethan's wrecked life—one piece in particular, Rosebud.

Sunny, Esther's grandmother and Rosebud's great-grandmother, was eighty years old. Although healthy and vigorous, she could not be left to manage a ten-year-old; indeed, she should not herself be left to live alone.

Where would they all live? The house in Eastham would belong to Rosebud free and clear—Ethan had mortgage insurance—but Esther did not want to live there. Her friends and social life were in Mashpee, where she lived in a one-bedroom condominium.

If Esther's parents, Israel and Amelia, were alive, the situation would be different. But they had been killed in an automobile accident four years ago, returning from a Rhode Island conference late one Sunday night. Israel apparently fell asleep at the wheel and hit a pole. Both died instantly.

As Esther reviewed her options and made coffee, she heard the newspaper deliveryman leave the Sunday paper. Dreading it, but unable to resist, she ran out and unfolded it quickly. Staring at her from the front page was the young, eager face of Ethan in his high school yearbook picture. The heading over it read: EASTHAM MAN DIES IN GRAVE FROM DRUG OVERDOSE.

Marguerite gently nudged the unlatched door, opening it just enough to poke her head through it, and addressed the occupant of the desk, Chief of Eastham Police, Francis Nadeau.

"Bonjour, François. J'ai un petit problème."

"Un autre?" inquired the seated figure, still cool and fresh looking at this early hour in his white uniform shirt.

"François," she replied reprovingly.

"Alors, qu'est-ce que c'est?" he said with a sigh.

Taking this as an invitation to enter, Marguerite opened the door wider, revealing a foil-covered dish in her right hand. Frank groaned. When Marguerite visited him at police headquarters speaking French, she wanted something. When she came in speaking French and offering food, she *really* wanted something.

Marguerite and Frank had started their habit of conversing in French about two years ago when they met at the circulation desk of the library. He was requesting books in French and Marguerite, standing behind him, offered to lend him some of hers. Frank was struggling to learn the language spoken by his forebears who left Nova Scotia over two hundred years ago to settle on Cape Cod. They were in the vanguard of the mass deportation of Acadians, most of whom traveled further and settled in Louisiana where they retained much of their language and culture. They had been forced by the British to leave Canada because of the imminence of war with France and the uncertainty of Acadian neutrality.

Unwrapping the package on the plate, Marguerite revealed one of her carrot-raisin-nut breads, a small tub of cottage cheese, and a knife. Frank noted that the bread had been cut on one end and there was some cottage cheese on the knife. She probably used that slice to bribe her way past Joanne, he concluded, referring to the dispatcher in the front office.

Wasting no time, Marguerite talked while he ate. Pulling from her purse that day's newspaper article about Ethan, she began.

"Frank, you really ought to look into this. He was not a drug user. He did not give himself an overdose."

"How do you know that?" he asked between bites.

Marguerite succinctly reviewed everything she knew of Ethan, including what she had gleaned from Esther.

"So you see, it's not possible," she concluded, sitting back satisfied with her powers of persuasion.

"I read that article, too. It says preliminary findings indicate a drug overdose and that toxicological test results are awaited. There is no conclusion yet."

"You know perfectly well, Frank, that those preliminary findings are pretty accurate."

"I thought you just told me that he couldn't have died from drugs," commented Frank, confused.

"No, I did not. I said he did not take drugs. If he died from them, it was foul play. Someone else is involved," she concluded smugly.

"Now wait a minute, Marguerite. Just because you got yourself mixed up in one murder last year doesn't mean that everyone who dies was murdered," he exclaimed, exasperated. "Besides, he wasn't found in Eastham. This is Mashpee's problem. Let Pedersen worry about it."

"I'm surprised at you! He was one of our residents whom

you are sworn to protect. His family, his orphaned daughter, are still here. Does your oath end when someone dies?''

Expecting him to respond angrily, Marguerite was surprised to see him smiling and shaking his head.

''Marguerite, how did I know you were going to be here this morning? What inspired me to call the State Police and find out what the CPAC team turned up?''

''You mean you already investigated this?'' she sputtered.

''Of course. My oath, remember?''

''Why didn't you tell me instead of letting me go on?'' she demanded.

''That carrot bread looked mighty good. I thought I'd let you bribe me a bit, as well as Joanne.'' Now he was the smug one. ''To get you off your tenterhooks, I'll tell you as much as I can that is not confidential police information. This will come out in the papers tomorrow anyway.

''I spoke to Al Medeiros at the State Police barracks. You remember him from the Dafoe case.* He's a lieutenant now. The packet they found on the body was a drug—a particularly lethal one called fentanyl. It's a synthetic form of heroin, only one hundred times more powerful, sometimes as much as four hundred times when sold illegally, depending on how they cut it. Medeiros told me a lethal dose could be about the size of three grains of salt. They believe it to be the cause of death but need more test results. Of course, even then they won't be one hundred percent certain. After heroin is injected into the body it is rapidly metabolized to morphine and the lab tests usually can't distinguish heroin from morphine. It was just lucky that they found some on the body.''

Marguerite sat back nonplussed, almost at a loss for words. But not quite.

''Frank, that just proves what I said. Ethan was a very intelligent person. He wouldn't take a drug like that.''

''Neither would any run-of-the-mill junkies if they knew what it was. But they don't know. The pushers don't tell them it's going to kill them.''

*The Curious Cape Cod Skull

"But where would he get something like that?"

"That's what has Medeiros worried and that's why he wants it in the papers. As a warning to drug users. The DEA people are involved, too. If someone here is making this stuff again, it could set off a rash of deaths."

"What do you mean, making it again? Was it made here before? On Cape Cod?"

"Yes, it was. Somewhere around 1990 or '91. A guy from a drug ring rented a house in an exclusive neighborhood of West Falmouth and had the stuff manufactured right there. It was a perfect cover, an expensive oceanfront home in a quiet neighborhood where no one would suspect drug activities. The ironic thing is that the neighborhood even had a guard in the summer to keep out trespassers."

"Were they caught?"

"Not at that time. The guy left the house without being discovered. But about two years later he was fatally shot gangland-style, just one day before the feds were going to arrest him. They got his buddies who were in Kansas by then. That's when they learned about the Cape operation."

"Frank, there's more to this than meets the eye."

"There sure is. And your friend, Ethan, might have been in it up to his eyeballs. I feel sorry for that kid of his."

"I'm not convinced you're right, but I'll have to give this some more thought." Gathering her knife and dish after first shaking the crumbs into Frank's wastebasket, Marguerite left the office more diffidently than she had entered.

Walter and Irene Pedersen were at breakfast later than usual. The barbecue had lasted until one A.M., the cleanup till three A.M. Pedersen had already been in touch with the State Police and received the shocking news about the possibility of a renewed outbreak of fentanyl deaths. Right now, at the beginning of the summer season with all those additional people, some of whom were bound to be drug pushers and others drug users, this could be disastrous.

As he read the newspaper account of the discovery of the body at the cemetery, a thought struck him.

"Water," he murmured. "That's the key to this case. Water."

"You're absolutely right, Walter," chimed in Irene. "It's a beautiful day. Let's go down to the water."

Leon Roberts sat down to Sunday breakfast and the newspaper feeling good. Sales were up, his third and last child had finally finished college and gotten a job, and it was the week before he would get away from the plant for a European vacation with his wife.

His first glance at the paper made him dyspeptic. Staring at him was a picture of his plant manager, Ethan Quade, and the revelation that he had died of a drug overdose.

Bacon and eggs were left to congeal on the plate as he dashed for the phone to call his brother and partner, James.

"Jim, have you read the news about Ethan?"

"No, what happened?"

"He's dead! From a drug overdose."

The silence on the line was palpable as James struggled to refrain from saying, "I told you so." They had fought over hiring Ethan. James had wanted to promote from within the plant, someone who knew the company and was known by the company. Leon had wanted to bring in new ideas, get ready for the twenty-first century, as he put it. He insisted on this hotshot Ivy Leaguer with financial experience on Wall Street. Leon claimed it would also be good for their image to diversify their employees. Some image they would have now!

Always the pragmatist, James quickly recovered and thought of the company.

"Leon, we have to call Henry. He's got to check those books right away. You know how addicts are. They steal you blind."

Anna was not a beauty on Sunday morning. The red of her good eye was sharply contrasted by the nasty purple bruise on the other, and by the black circles underlining both eyes. Her face was puffy, her hair limp and uncombed. She was wearing a drab brown and tan housecoat which made her skin look sallow and which belonged to her sister-in-law, Ellen, a woman thirty pounds heavier than Anna. Alone in the house while her brother's family were at church, she was close to despair.

Despite her bravado with Sergeant Odoms, Anna was frightened—too frightened to spend the night alone in her house, too frightened to return there yesterday for a change of clothes.

Louis had been mean and nasty from the day she married him, but Friday was different. Spotting Ethan leaving her house appeared to confirm his years of suspicions and galvanize his hatred. After one stunning blow to her eye and a shout of "Liar!" he ran from the house. His tirades usually lasted for hours. Temporarily relieved at the brevity of his visit, she became terrified when Ethan's body was found. Where had Louis gone in such a hurry?

Afraid he might come after her, she had taken refuge in her brother Nelson's home. Built like the bear from whom his Indian name was derived, Nelson was not only strong, but was fit, agile, sober, and despised Anna's erstwhile husband. Louis might get his kicks from hitting a woman, but never, even in his most dissipated state, would he attack Nelson.

Not unarmed he wouldn't. That was Anna's gnawing fear. Was Louis moving to the next level of violence? She had to leave her brother's house before she brought harm to his family. But where could she go? How could she hide?

As she glumly considered her plight, her nephew, Todd, back from church, reached past her, looking for the sports section of the Sunday paper that lay unopened on the table.

"Hey, look at this, Aunt Anna. Some guy OD'd at the Indian Cemetery yesterday. Do you know him?"

Thomas splashed the tidal pool with the peculiarly flat-handed splash of a child. The stranded minnows turned in one mysteriously coordinated move away from the assault. Again and again he splashed, entranced by their graceful motion, unaware of the havoc he was causing to these peaceful creatures. Each splash decreased the likelihood of their survival until the

next high tide rippled in, softly covering the sand and freeing
the minnows from their imprisoning pool.

The adults sat nearby on the dry sand, able to watch Thomas
and pursue their own interests at the same time. With the tide
low, nothing but the sand flats, eel grass, and shallow pools
remained at First Encounter Beach as evidence of the lunar
ebb and flow of the ocean. Off in the distance could be seen
the broken remains of the World War II target ship, gradually
taking form in Katie's pencil sketch and exhibiting a delicacy
in its demise that it lacked in its design.

Neil sprawled in the sun on his beach chair, absorbed in
The Wall Street Journal while munching a salami sandwich,
delicately balancing a can of soda between his knees to keep
it out of the sand.

Shaded by an umbrella, Marguerite was reflective behind
her sunglasses, contemplating the book she was reading, a
brief history of the Mashpee Indians. The book, purchased
months ago, had been unopened until today. As she sampled
her tomato and cucumber sandwich—the veggie lunch meant
to compensate for yesterday's pot-au-feu—she reviewed the
salient information.

The Mashpees, People of the First Light, were a tribe of
the Wampanoag Nation, long settled and still residing on Cape
Cod. In the 1630s, Richard Bourne, a missionary, assisted the
Indians in the Mashpee area in registering with the county
their ancient Indian land claims.

In 1790, Congress passed the Indian Trade and Intercourse
Acts, which prohibited the purchase of Indian land by individuals or states without the consent of the federal government. Despite this, in the mid-1800s the Commonwealth of
Massachusetts divided the land which had been held in common by the Mashpee tribe and apportioned most of it among
the tribe members, who were then permitted to sell their holdings. This land division made the property subject to local
taxes, as a result of which some land was lost to tax sales and
some sold privately.

The Mashpees complained about the land loss but were told
the Indians in the thirteen original states were subject solely

to state law and not covered by the federal act of 1790, which applied only to federally recognized tribes, most of whom were in the west and gained recognition as a result of a treaty of war.

As the years went by, more and more land was bought by non-Indians. By the 1960s, the Mashpees began to lose control of the Board of Selectmen and other town boards.

Marguerite's reflections were short-circuited by a loud cry from the direction of Thomas and the rapidly depleting tidal pool. He had succeeded in lowering the water level to a point where his last splash had hit bottom and thrown sand up into his face and eyes. Perhaps it was the minnows' revenge.

As Katie ran to him, Marguerite, long inured to the sine qua non of beach life, sand in one's eyes, joined Neil in rummaging through the Playmate cooler, evaluating its offerings. They both longingly eyed the remaining half of Katie's smoked turkey sandwich but refrained from claiming it.

Every move was watched by a gathering of seagulls, so habituated to the customs and generosity of beach-going picnickers that they searched through unsealed bags and pecked at the sides of picnic coolers lying on temporarily unoccupied blankets.

Sand washed from his eyes by the natural healer, tears, Thomas scurried back to the blanket, abandoning the surviving minnows. Katie delved into her capacious tote bag, came up with a small box of raisins, and offered them to her son. The blatantly begging seagulls moved closer. Katie shooed them away while Thomas enticed them with his raisin lures. Shrugging her shoulders, Katie returned to her drawing, having decided that it was more instructive for Thomas to feed birds than to kill fish.

Neil settled for a bunch of grapes and continued with his newspaper. Savoring a ripe nectarine, Marguerite cranked her mental recording of what she had read and refocused on tribal status.

In 1974 the federal court found that the 1790 acts did apply to the thirteen original states and that this protection covered both federally recognized and nonrecognized tribes. The

Mashpees filed a lawsuit seeking claim to their original land holdings. This suit created havoc in the town of Mashpee, as every property title was now clouded.

The central issue in the case became the question of whether the Mashpees were a tribe and if they had been so continuously since 1790. The jury decided that there were times when they had not been a tribe based on two indicators: one, that they were no longer all of the same or similar race since blacks and Caucasians had intermarried with the Mashpees, theoretically changing Indian society and culture; and, two, that they had long been subject to state and federal law rather than tribal law. Federal recognition was also denied in a separate decision.

The Mashpees were preparing to file a second request for recognition and were optimistic of success this time.

Water tickled Marguerite's toes and Neil snatched a couple of towels away from the encroaching water.

"I think it's time to go," suggested Katie.

"Yes, the tide does turn, doesn't it?" mused Marguerite, obviously thinking of events other than the physics of tides.

Chapter Seven

There were several messages on Henry Lawrence's answering machine when he returned home at three o'clock Sunday afternoon. They all made him tremble. But, then again, it did not take much to make Henry tremble.

His high school yearbook portrayed him as "Class Genius," but, perspicaciously, not as "Most Likely To Succeed." His obsequious manner failed to endear him to employers whose rule of thumb was that anyone so self-effacing must be deservedly so. They preferred confident men.

So did women. Lacking the ability to engage in the badinage requisite to flirting, he had settled into bachelorhood, not contentedly but resignedly. He could not believe his good luck at meeting Felicia. Attractive in a neat, not gaudy way; intelligent, but not boastful; ambitious, but not greedy; she attended the college reunion alone and unfettered, just like Henry. They had not known each other at college, but in a class of four thousand, that was not unusual.

Henry had approached her at the bar where he had noticed her forlornly nursing a drink for forty-five minutes, absorbed now in draining the ice. That was a good sign, he had thought; he wasn't a big drinker either. When he had introduced himself, her answer was slow in coming, her stammer painful to watch and hear. Sensing a kindred lonely spirit, he'd joined her and ordered two drinks. The transformation occurred slowly, as trust replaced fear. Felicia had relaxed, gained control of her wayward tongue, and spoke carefully and deliberately as years of training had taught her to do, and by the next drink they were chatting amicably. Her speech betrayed her only in circumstances where she felt insecure, such as in crowds or when faced with strangers or aggressive people.

No one was less aggressive than Henry. Timorous to a fault, he walked with shoulders stooped and head bowed so low that the bald spot on the back of his crown could be seen from the front. His carriage made him seem shorter than his five feet, ten inches and his softness around the waistline contributed to his amorphous appearance. Sandy-haired, gray-eyed, pale-complected, bearing a small nose paired with a hint of a chin, he was the invisible man, perfect for Felicia, who had finally met someone she could dominate. Her speech was flawless around Henry.

But she was still single. They dated steadily for almost three years; the friendless Henry relished her company but hesitated to marry her. She tried to control him, just as his parents had before they retired and moved to South Carolina. Living alone had been a revelation to Henry. Free to run his own life, he faltered. Cupboards were sometimes bare, oranges moldy, and laundry unwashed.

Henry loved it, mold and all, and was reluctant to cede his liberty to Felicia. Independence had enlightened him. He was an underachiever and that knowledge nagged at his soul. His job in the business office at Roberts Instruments was adequate but routine. Any reasonably competent accountant would suffice. It did not require the class genius.

Discomfitted by his mediocrity, Henry had decided to break out of this gelatinous mold and take charge of his life. He, and he alone, would decide when to marry Felicia.

Despite his commitment to audacity, the phone calls unnerved him. One was from Felicia, petulantly asking why he had not called her that morning. Two calls were from James Roberts, his boss, demanding that Henry call him immediately. Sensing trouble from both directions, he decided to have a Twinkie first.

* * *

Just as Marguerite was stepping from the outdoor shower, she heard Rusty barking. Not wanting her to awaken Thomas, who was napping, she ran around to the front of the house still in her terry-cloth robe, and saw Rosebud approaching the front door with Marguerite's pot in hand.

Marguerite simultaneously ushered Rosebud into the house and patted Rusty to quiet her.

"Mrs. Smith, I want to thank you for the delicious dinner last night. You were right about no one wanting to cook. Aunt Esther and Grandma Sunny thank you, too."

Marguerite accepted this gracious little speech with a triumphant eye on Neil, who was puzzling over the crossword. Her expressive look said, *I told you so.*

"Neil, this is Rose Quade. Why don't you get her a cold drink while I finish dressing? Sit down a minute, Rose. I'll walk back home with you. Rusty needs a little exercise."

Noting the distaste on Rose's face when he mentioned iced tea, Neil brought her a Coke, along with one for himself. In the awkward silence that ensued after he expressed his condolences, Neil searched for a neutral topic of conversation. He commented on the purple and white necklace she was wearing and asked what it was.

"Oh, this is wampum," Rosebud replied.

"Wampum? Wasn't that used as money at one time?"

"It was used for trade, in the same way that money was used later," she answered, correcting him slightly.

"I didn't know it was made into necklaces," Neil continued, impressed by the mature demeanor of this child.

"Oh, it was. It was made into fancy necklaces and collars. I guess it showed how rich or important you were," she surmised.

"Is that an old necklace?"

"Oh, no," she responded, relaxing now in her role as instructor. "Grandma Sunny made this for me out of some of her rejects. This isn't even a fancy necklace. You should see some of the real ones. Daddy took me to the Museum of the American Indian once when we were in New York. They even had hair ornaments and strings of wampum that were sent when someone dies. And there were beautiful wampum belts that were used as records—like for treaties and other important events.''

"What do you mean by your 'grandmother's rejects'? Does she make wampum necklaces?'' asked a curious Neil.

"She makes a few of them. That's why she goes clamming so much. Most of the clamshells don't suit her so she has to have a lot to pick from. She wants the ones with a lot of purple. Of course, she won't throw the clams away and waste them, so we have to eat them. I think she knows a hundred ways to cook clams. Me and Daddy get sick to death of them,'' she replied jokingly, but her upward-turning mouth quickly reversed itself as the corners turned downward to reflect her sudden awareness of what she had said.

With the living room in torpid silence, Marguerite swept in, vibrant and scrubbed looking, dressed in Black Watch plaid shorts, yellow shirt, and white sneakers. Her dark, curly hair was still wet and she wore a touch of lipstick. Nearing sixty, she looked ten years younger. She liked to think her youthful looks were due to disciplined habits of diet and exercise. In truth, her exercise was sporadic and her eating guidelines had more exceptions than rules. Her appearance owed more to nature than nurture, particularly to her mother, whom she resembled in every way except for Marguerite's blue eyes.

Gloom not permitted in her presence, she chucked Rosebud under the chin and asked, "Has Neil been pestering you with a million questions? He wants to know everything. I wonder where he got that habit?''

Taking Rosebud by the hand, she left with Rusty in tow. Rosebud walked in shrouded silence. Marguerite respected her privacy, content to offer the child the comfort of a caring, adult presence.

The quiet mood was shattered as they neared the Quade house and heard a woman shouting at someone to leave. Suspecting that reporters were camped around the house, Marguerite ran quickly ahead, letting go of Rusty's leash as she did. Nothing like a barking dog to scatter trespassers.

As the path broke through the cover of trees and brush, Marguerite spotted a gray-haired man leaning against a Mercedes and ignoring both the dog, who barked while wagging her tail, and an old Indian woman screeching at him from the doorway.

His granitic expression softened as he noticed Rosebud trailing Marguerite.

"Rose, get your things. I'm taking you home," he greeted her.

"But, Grandpa, I *am* home," she protested.

"You call this shack a home? And with no one but that crazy old woman to mind you? I'm taking you to your real home where you'll be properly cared for and go to good schools. You'll have all the opportunities your mother had until she threw it all away. Too bad you don't look more like Joy, though. But when we get you properly dressed, you'll look better," he added, disdainfully eyeing her long, baggy T-shirt, knee-length shorts, and chunky shoes. Matthias Wilkinson was ill informed about ten-year-olds. Rosebud was actually dressed in the height of current fashion.

Without a word to Marguerite or Sunny, he took Rosebud by the hand and led her into the house, brushing Sunny aside, impervious to her escalating shouts. She was now almost frantic in her attempts to thwart him.

It would take more than an old woman to stop Matthias. Sixty-four years of age and the multimillionaire owner of a chain of pharmacies, he did not resemble the cartoon or movie version of the neighborhood pharmacist. Born and raised on his father's struggling New Hampshire dairy farm, he had the physique of a farmhand used to manual labor. He maintained his muscle tone in later years not by mucking out barns, but by working out in his fully equipped home gym, never having cultivated the rich man's exercises of golf, tennis, or squash. He just missed being handsome. A hardness in the ice-blue eyes and a touch of parsimony in the mouth sabotaged nature's efforts.

Matthias had become a pharmacist by sheer grit. He worked two years after completing high school, in addition to helping at the farm, and saved every dime. With enough money to enter pharmacy school, he managed to remain there by working nights as a waiter and summers in the post office while continuing to help his father when at home.

After graduation, he returned to his hometown and filled prescriptions in the local drugstore owned by an aging pharmacist. That was part of his plan. In a few years he bought the business, modernized and expanded it, and paid off the loan. His credit now established, he obtained a bigger loan for a second store and the beginning of a New England chain of stores.

Married to a hometown girl, Rose Potter, he longed for a family on which to lavish his wealth. Rose had three miscarriages, then a baby girl. Ecstatic, they named her Joy, for that was what she represented to them.

At the age of twenty-eight she died, the victim of LSD. Two years later, Rose died of pancreatic cancer. Scientists may have grappled with the cause of cancer, but not Matthias. To him, Ethan Quade had killed his wife by destroying their daughter. Now he had come to rescue the only vestige of them remaining to him.

Marguerite stood frozen at the spectacle. This man was evidently Rosebud's grandfather and she was a stranger with no standing. Her pensive hesitation exploded into action when she heard Rosebud crying, "No, Grandpa, please, I don't want to go. I want to stay here."

Bursting into the house, albeit wearing an apologetic expression she thought appropriate for her uncertain status, Marguerite inquired formally, "Sir, may I ask who you are?"

"Yes, you may ask. I'm Matthias Wilkinson, Rose's grandfather. Who the heck are you?"

"I'm Marguerite Smith, Rose's teacher. I walked home with her and found you ready to take her away, apparently against her will," she replied feistily, reacting in kind to his arrogant tone. "Do you have guardianship papers that would give you the right to take her?"

"I'm her grandfather, the only relative she has left. That gives me the right to take her. Rose, get in there and pack anything you need for a couple of days. After that you'll have new clothes, decent ones." He pointedly turned away from Marguerite, dismissing her objections.

"That's not true," Marguerite insisted. "That woman is her great-grandmother and she also has an aunt, her father's sister. And if Ethan had a will, he probably appointed a guardian for her. You'll just have to wait to see about a will."

"Any guardian appointed by a drug addict will be disregarded and overturned. I'll make sure of that."

"But—" Marguerite began, but she got no further. A whirlwind—tanned to a mahogany hue, pony-tailed, six feet tall, muscular but not bulky—invaded the room, grabbed Rosebud, and stood defensively in front of her as she hugged his waist and cried, "Uncle Cat, I'm so glad you're here!"

Chief Pedersen did not have the peaceful beach day he and Irene envisioned. His belated sleep last night had been troubled by his harsh reproof to Officer McGrath yesterday when she had reported to him the conversation between Esther and Rosebud. He knew his criticism of her was hypocritical and he despised himself for having yielded to it.

Yes, he did want to know what they had said about Ethan's actions and whereabouts but he should have waited a respectful time and then questioned them openly. He dared not risk being suspected of sending officers as spies in the guise of protectors. Not sure of Lois McGrath's discretion, he elected to cover his back and denounce her tactics. And it bothered him all night. He had to find a way to assuage her injured feelings. She had been trying to please him.

With an opportunity to catch up on his lost sleep, he lay facedown on a beach towel that accommodated only half his length. He barely had time to get sand on the sunscreen lotion when his beeper sounded. Ignoring Irene's sigh of martyrdom, he walked promptly to the outdoor phone near the dressing rooms. Since no one beeped him to wish him good day, he knew he would soon be heading for those showers.

He was right. It was a DEA agent. In light of the fentanyl discovery, they had decided to move promptly on several drug connections they had been watching. This premature operation would risk losing some of the big guys but they had to confiscate as much powder as possible to see if fentanyl was circulat-

ing. Since one of the selected sites was in Mashpee, they were
notifying him and would work jointly with his department.

Turning from the phone, he was rehearsing his explanation
to Irene when she nudged him in the side with an elbow, both
her hands already laden with beach chairs and towels.

"Let's go, Lone Ranger," she jested, not regretful at leaving the beach. The sun was too hot, the water too cold, and
she had gone to bed too late last night. A nice nap at home
would be just fine.

Marguerite walked dejectedly up the driveway, her normal
exuberance subdued by events. When she saw Neil gazing at
her from the deck she commented, "*Quelle tristesse,* Neil.
Malheureuse jeune fille. Poor little girl," she translated
quickly as she noticed the uncomprehending Katie looking
quizzically at her.

"I guess the loss of her father is just beginning to register
with her," commented Neil.

"Oh, it's even worse than that," she offered, and described
the latest chapter in the Quade saga.

"Who is this Uncle Cat who came to her rescue?" asked
Katie.

"His name is Herbert Catlaw and he has a store in Hyannis
that sells Indian jewelry, among other things. Evidently he
buys some of Sunny's handwork. He'd heard of Ethan's death
and came to offer condolences and to see if they needed anything. He seems to be very fond of Rosebud and she of him.
After he forced Wilkinson to leave, he decided to stay, at least
until Esther came home. She took off from work today but
went to Mashpee to make funeral arrangements for when
Ethan's body is released. He'll be buried in the Indian Cemetery next to his parents. Joy isn't buried on Cape Cod. Her
parents insisted on returning her to New Hampshire to the
family plot and Ethan was too broken up to object at the time.
How very strange their story is. It's like a Greek tragedy."

Marguerite, emotionally weary, sank into a lounge chair
absentmindedly patting Rusty, a comforting presence in a vex-
ing world. Thomas, jealous of the attention given to the dog,

climbed into her lap and sat on the petting arm, much to the dog's consternation. Foxy as to the ways of these miniature humans, Rusty began to lick Thomas's leg and was rewarded by the irregular patting motion of the child. It was less satisfactory than Marguerite, but it would do.

"Maman, do you know the name of Mr. Catlaw's store or its address? I would like to meet him. You know my business tends to be more import than export and I'm searching for unique export goods. Indian jewelry might be just the thing. Especially with so many newly rich entrepreneurs who like to have something different." Neil evaluated every new encounter through the eyes of a businessman.

"I don't know, but I can ask," replied Marguerite.

"Good," said Neil. "Now let's get down to immediate concerns. We're supposed to go out to dinner. Where are we going?"

"Neil, why don't you and Katie go? Just the two of you. There are enough leftovers for Thomas and me. Go out and enjoy yourself. It's your vacation."

"Are you sure?" inquired a concerned Katie. "Are you all right?"

"I'm fine, just a little sad about Rosebud. It looks as if there will be another custody battle. I hope someone takes her preference into consideration."

"Okay, but if we're not taking Thomas we'll go out a little later. That will be a treat in itself," said Neil.

"It certainly will," agreed Katie. "But we'll miss the early-bird specials we're usually in time for," she said with a laugh. "I'll feed Thomas before we go so you won't have to bother. Can I get you anything?"

"Nothing to eat, but perhaps Neil could fix me a gin and tonic. I'll relax here on the deck a while."

As Neil moved around the kitchen preparing the requested libation, a voice called to him from the deck.

"Neil, while you're doing that, why don't you put a few of those smoked scallops on a plate for me? And perhaps a few crackers. Just to tide me over." Marguerite's mood was improving already.

*   *   *

Lloyd Odoms was engaging in the summertime male ritual—
standing over an outdoor grill attempting to cook to individual
specifications. Rare, medium, just a little pink, a lot of pink,
no pink, were the requests. The resultant products never
seemed just right, and complaints followed. Each week he
vowed never to cook again. Next Sunday he would be right
back at the barbecue taking orders.

The ring of the telephone set off a race among his three
children. A disappointed call of, "Daddy, it's for you,"
emerged from the house.

"Odoms, Pedersen here. The DEA is going to close in on
a few of their targets. One is in Mashpee. I thought you might
want to be in on it since you've been eyeing it. It's the Happy
Hour tavern."

"Sign me on. What time?"

"Be at headquarters at nine o'clock. They want to move in
about ten when it's in full swing."

"Okay, Chief. I'll be there." *With bells on,* he added to
himself, and hurried back to his grill with more anticipation
than he usually felt for hamburgers.

Marguerite finally bestirred herself, refreshed from her drink
and snack, and began to think of dinner. Noticing that the pot
returned by Rosebud was still sitting on the stove, Marguerite
removed its lid preparatory to storing it. Inside was a small
envelope. Opening it she read a short thank-you note in the
backhanded writing common to left-handers. In place of a signature was a delicate colored-pencil drawing of a rosebud.

Chapter Eight

At three o'clock Monday morning, Detective Sergeant Odoms was heavy lidded and steel hearted. Louis Perry sat before him in the interrogation room, staring at Odoms with eyes black as hate. He was thinner than Odoms had remembered and his skin was yellow, with none of the ruddiness expected in a man who worked outdoors—when he worked at all. A fatal race was in progress. Could his alcohol-damaged liver succeed in killing him before his diabetic pancreas did so?

"Perry, you're really in trouble this time. With mandatory drug sentencing, you're going away for ten years. Especially since it's not your first offense." Odoms had been playing this theme for three hours. Louis never budged.

"It's a frame, man. You're setting me up to get rid of me. Who are you doing the favor for—Anna or yourself?"

"The stuff was found in your car, which you were driving."

"I don't know nothing about no stuff in my car. Especially no Marlboro cigarettes. That ain't my brand." The cigarettes he was disclaiming were found on the dashboard of the car in which he and another barfly were trying to escape the drug raid. Three vials of crack were concealed in the space behind the four cigarettes showing at the opening. "Why don't you ask the other guy in my car? Maybe it was his. Or maybe you put it there?"

Pretending to be shocked, Odoms replied, "Me, an officer of the law? Why would I frame you?"

"Because maybe you want something from me."

"There are certain questions that need answering by you and perhaps if you were more cooperative, we might be inclined to investigate your friend a little harder. It might just happen that the rocks are his," agreed Odoms with mock pedantry.

"You *know* it ain't mine. But even though I'd like to get out of this dump, I can't help you about Friday. I told you a hundred times I don't remember anything."

"Do you remember going to Anna's house Friday night?"

"I only remember telling myself to go visit Anna. I don't remember going there."

"What time was it when you told yourself to go visit Anna?"

"I already told you. When I was driving here from New Bedford—about seven o'clock."

"Where did you go?"

"Man, are you stupid or something? I told you."

"Tell me again. I like the sound of your voice." Odoms was searching for the slightest discrepancy. He resisted the impulse to pity Louis Perry. A talented carpenter, he was wasting his life on liquor and laziness. Obviously unwell, he sat hunched over his sunken chest, sweating and nervously cracking his knuckles.

"I went to Rose and Joe's and ate."

"Then what?"

"I went to the Happy Hour. Had a few drinks."

"When did you get there?"

"About nine o'clock. I'm not sure."

"When did you leave?"

"I don't know."

"When did you go to Anna's?"

"Don't know. I don't even remember going."

"Did you follow Ethan?"

"I never seen Ethan."

"Yes, you did."

"If you know all the answers, how come you're bothering me?"

"What's the last thing you do remember about Friday night?"

"Waking up in my car about five o'clock Saturday morning. Some crows was making a racket in the woods. I must have pulled over to the side of the road and fell asleep. It was on the road to the beach. I was hungover and couldn't remember how I got there. Didn't even know where I was right away."

His story never varied. He was either telling the truth about being too drunk to remember or he was a remarkable liar.

"You'll have plenty of time to remember. If your head clears up, call me."

Odoms left the room. So did Louis. He was taken to a cell.

The DEA agents had already gone home in disgust, leaving the local detectives to deal with the disappointing crop of miscreants. For the drug busts had been failures. Worse than failures. They had blown away months of surveillance at five sites. The cases were not ripe. This gangbuster deal had netted a few vials of crack, two packets of cocaine, and four marijuana joints, all in the possession of pathetic users, not the sought-after pushers. No fentanyl or heroin surfaced. That was the good news. The bad news was that the dealers were warned and would establish new bases of operation. If any of them were selling poison, it would be harder to find.

Thomas awoke at five A.M., conversing with himself. Was it the continuance of a pleasant dream, or did he pick up the thread of his last thought before going to sleep?

Marguerite did not wait to discover the answer. She was out of bed, into his room, and had him in her arms before he put a period to his thoughts.

Neil and Katie had come home late. They had driven to Provincetown and walked the length of the pier to observe the boats, all kinds of boats: commercial fishing vessels, recreational fishing boats, whale-watch cruisers, sun-shaded harbor tour boats, dinghies, rowboats, sailboats, and inflatable craft, some moored at the pier, others in the tranquil harbor, secure behind its stone breakwater.

After lingering over dinner, they had gone to The Moors and were entertained by Lenny Grandchamp as he played piano, sang, and cajoled both regulars and tourists into a comedic dialogue. This was Katie's first trip to Cape Cod and Neil wanted her to experience a variety of locales from the canal to the tip.

Marguerite hoped to let them sleep late. Why was it, she wondered, children inevitably woke up early when their parents went to bed late? Slit-eyed and yawning, she hastily dressed Thomas and herself, took the keys for Neil's rental car, which had the child safety seat, and drove away.

Now what? The beach had no appeal in gray light. It was still too early to find a restaurant where they might have breakfast. Aha! That gave her an idea—Stop and Shop supermarket. They were open twenty-four hours a day, had a counter for doughnuts and other goodies, including coffee if it was brewed this early. Thomas and she could eat, then she would shop before other people were aware they needed anything. Katie might raise her eyebrows at a doughnut breakfast but, after all, Thomas was on vacation. He was entitled to a treat.

As she came to this decision, she stopped for a red light at the corner of Samoset and glanced over at the octagonal windmill, an Eastham landmark. As the only Cape Cod windmill still on a working site, the others all having been moved in order to preserve them, it was a favorite stop for tour buses. This venerable town centerpiece was believed to have been built in the 1680s by one Thomas Paine. Constructed in Plymouth, it was moved first to Truro, then to Eastham in 1793. Still a popular local gathering site, it was feted at Windmill Weekend, held every year in the week after Labor Day.

Since it was not yet full light, Marguerite thought the shadows were playing tricks with her eyes. Nevertheless, she was concerned enough to turn right and pull up beside the windmill green. She gasped, not able to comprehend the macabre sight. Lashed to one of the four sails was a man. Hoping it was merely a dummy placed by a prankster, she ran from the car to the sail, which rested about two feet above the ground. The man was real; the blood on the walk was real; the broken nose and blackened eyes and smashed cheekbones and crooked jaw were real.

Her soundless screams echoed only in her brain. First a body in a grave, now a man—or a dead body?—on the windmill.

She could not take him down. The ropes were tied out of her reach.

Her stomach rebelled, her body quivered, her legs wobbled, her brain protested. *Do something!* As the paralysis of mind and body subsided, she turned and noted the fire headquarters across the highway; in her shock, she was surprised that it should be there. Testing her legs, putting one slowly in front of the other, she headed for the road but was brought to a halt by a call of, "Gramma, Gramma!" Thomas! What was she doing abandoning him? Legs now in full throttle, she hastened to the car, reversed direction, and sped across the road, stopping directly in front of the door of the fire department and emergency medical services.

It was that quiet time of day for emergency personnel. By dawn, the violence of the night abated while the crises of the day incubated. It was the time to stretch, yawn, daydream a little, and head for a cup of coffee.

But it was not to be so this morning. Marguerite burst through the door, babe in arms, shouting, "Help him! Cut him down!" pointing vaguely toward the windmill.

The desk officer had seen his share of hallucinating and deranged persons and, in her present state of agitation, Marguerite seemed of that fellowship. She gave no information as to an accident or health crisis, nor even a clue as to who needed help or why or where. Only the repeated demand, "Cut him down!"

Of most concern to Jerry Barbato was that the woman was holding a child, obviously not her own. Calmly and slowly, he talked to Marguerite, encouraged her to put down the child, and endeavored to soothe her. All of which succeeded in making Marguerite angry, frustrated, and louder. She was screaming now, trying to penetrate the mask of placidity worn by Barbato as a trained reaction to hysteria. As the drama escalated, the sound penetrated into the back of the station and a firefighter who was her neighbor came through the door.

"Thank heaven, you're here. He needs help. I don't know if he's alive or dead. Bring something to cut him down. And tell him"—a scathing glance was directed at the occupant of the front desk—"to send over an ambulance immediately. And the police, too. Why are you standing there? Let's go!"

Confident of being followed, she hastened through the door, her back to the two bewildered men who were shrugging their shoulders and rolling their eyes. Nevertheless, they did as she directed, so commanding was her voice and attitude.

Thomas was goggle-eyed, never having heard his grand-maman shout. This was great fun.

And so the week had begun.

Joe Harmon's relatives were awake now, preparing to attend his second funeral. It would be earlier, nine o'clock, to minimize the time needed to be absent from jobs. It would be smaller, because friends and acquaintances were not notified of the new arrangements and might not have come if they had been notified. How many days can one allot for the same funeral? And, most of all, it would be quieter—they hoped.

Anna Pochet was at her own home hurriedly dressing for work. Detective Odoms had guessed she might be hiding at her brother Nelson's house when she did not answer a six A.M. phone call to her home. He contacted her at Nelson's to assure her that Louis was tucked away for the present and she could resurface. Only when she put down the phone with unsteady hands did she come to the full realization of the trauma Louis had inflicted on her life. If only he could disappear—permanently.

Esther and Rosebud slept late, their emotional skein unraveled and in need of rewinding.

Grandma Sunny was up at her usual time, six-thirty A.M. Her movable joints were less so after prolonged inactivity and, by early morn, lying in bed was more penance than pleasure. With no breakfast to prepare yet, Sunny took a walk around the pond to loosen and lubricate her protesting bones.

Finding the house still dark when she returned, she went to her room, hung a magnifier around her neck, turned on a bright lamp, and began running minute beads through a string of artificial sinew. The pattern was unrecorded on paper or disk, etched only in the mental software of its creator who stored dozens of such patterns and changed them at will.

What might be tedious work to some was relaxation to Sunny. Seventy years ago she had been tutored in this skill by an old woman who had not only taught her the ancient art but had given Sunny her own simple tools, including a stone drill for piercing the shell and stone beads that had been part of Indian culture long before the introduction of European glass beads.

Sunny's full name was Lily "Sun Child" Barnes, which soon became Sunny to everyone. Born amidst the poverty of the Passamaquoddy tribe in Maine, she went to work and live, at the age of sixteen, in the household of a wealthy family. They frequently traveled and brought her along to care for their two children. When she was eighteen years old, the family summered in Mashpee on Cape Cod. On her first half-day per week off duty, she met George Sims, a Mashpee Indian, and continued meeting him secretly for the remainder of the summer. Averse to returning to Maine and lifelong servitude, she ran off with George and married him on the day before the family was to leave Mashpee.

She never regretted her marriage. She did sometimes regret her self-imposed isolation. A Passamaquoddy among Wampanoags, a Catholic among Baptists, a young woman among strangers with no kith or kin nearby, she was reserved and never quite at home in Mashpee. Beading became her outlet. She retreated to the company of shells, stones, and beads. The rudiments she had learned in Maine were perfected over the years and her work became a source of supplementary income, small but welcome during those terrible years of economic depression in the 1930s and '40s.

She continued her work to fulfill an emotional need. Her work defined her. It made her who she was—Sun Child. In each of her beaded pieces, no matter what the design, she incorporated the letter S, sometimes so stylized as to be hidden to all but her. Today her signature would change. This choker would bear an E, her memorial to Ethan.

The respective police chiefs, Pedersen and Nadeau, had divergent prospects for today. Pedersen's problems at the Indian Cemetery were resolved. The interrupted Harmon funeral had been rescheduled for this morning. As a precaution, he had sent a policeman to keep at bay incidental sightseers or expectant reporters who had two columns to fill on a slow Monday morning.

The Quade death appeared to be a straightforward case of drug overdose. True, there were a couple of unresolved questions rumbling in the back of Pedersen's head, but the state police were in charge and they were leaning toward accidental overdose. Best to let them decide.

Frank Nadeau was less sanguine this Monday morning. In fact, he was humiliated. A spine-chilling, cultlike crime had been committed diagonally across the road from police headquarters. An as yet unidentified man was found tied to Eastham's historic windmill, beaten to a pulp, his hold on life as fragile as the spiderweb being woven above his head when he was taken down.

The paramedics, almost as stunned as Marguerite by the bizarre scene, had worked feverishly to save him. Their first obstacle was his location. The ropes were too high to reach and they had the additional problem of needing to grasp and lower him gently as they freed him to avoid injuring him further. A race across the road to headquarters brought two team members running back with stepladders, which they mounted while donning rubber gloves to avoid contact with the victim's blood. As one of them cut the ropes, the other supported the victim, reaching between the old boards, some broken and splintery as a result of this outrage. Luckily the object of their rescue was a small man, because balancing a deadweight on a shaky ladder was treacherous for both savior and saved.

Lying him carefully on a spine board, trying to minimize

the movement of any broken ribs lest they puncture his lungs, heart, or other vital organs, they checked him for signs of breathing. Respiration was barely, even questionably, perceptible. No pulse could be felt in the wrist; none in the upper arm. Finally a faint but fast throbbing was located in the carotid artery. Life, however frail, persisted.

After checking the airways for clear passage, oxygen was administered and a transfusion begun of lactated Ringer's solution. Judging by the sidewalk beneath the windmill sail and by his blood-soaked clothes, the victim had lost a lot of blood and needed fluid replacement. A quick body check revealed that the bleeding had stopped, at least externally. Finally, they covered him with a blanket on this warm morning and elevated his feet, the low blood pressure and rapid heartbeat indicating shock.

This well-choreographed operation had taken only minutes. The presence of police on the scene, as per Marguerite's instructions, had saved them valuable time. When paramedics were the first respondents to a crime scene, they had to defensively assess the site to determine if there was lingering danger to themselves or the victim, and take care to preserve evidence. Relieved of these responsibilities, they rushed the scarcely alive man into an ambulance and arrived at the hospital in record-breaking time. Somehow he survived—both the beating and the ambulance ride.

Cornelius Smith enjoyed his drive to Hyannis. The solitude enabled him to focus on his goal. He had not become a CEO by default.

With Asia now the fastest-developing market in the world, the competition for position among the trading companies was fierce. The business was not static. Every day brought another challenge, another competitor, another trade regulation enacted or repealed, another tariff increased or reduced. He kept one eye on the competition, one eye on the federal regulators, and the proverbial eyes in the back of his head on new opportunities for export.

The possibility of establishing a market for Native American articles excited him. Not just jewelry either. He was interested in articles believed to promote good fortune or ward off bad fortune. Asian cultures were replete with customs and artifacts to ensure health, wealth, fertility, or whatever else one desired. He planned to widen accessibility to their dreams.

Thus, he was on his way to visit Mr. Catlaw. Finding his business address was easy. It was listed under his name. But Neil needed to know Catlaw's suppliers. Learning this information would be tricky. If Catlaw was a shrewd businessman he would not give away his sources. On the other hand, Neil had succeeded in outfoxing many self-styled shrewd businessmen. He was eager to engage the competition.

The most intriguing activity that Monday was at Roberts Instruments. Henry Lawrence had reluctantly returned his phone calls Sunday and had been advised by his boss that Ethan Quade was dead of a drug overdose and the books should be checked immediately, particularly any requisitions emanating from Ethan.

Consequently, Henry arrived early at his office and started pulling all requisitions signed by Ethan. By the time Ethan's secretary arrived, Henry had piles of pink and blue purchase orders on his desk. Requesting Mrs. Lopes to open Ethan's file cabinet, he rummaged through it and extracted two folders containing similar forms, one folder labeled "Completed" and the other "Pending."

This rainbow of papers was the company's way of originating, processing, tracking, and paying orders. A four-part purchase order was typed and signed by the originator of the order—in this case, Ethan. The originator retained the back, or green copy, then sent the remaining three pages to the accounting office—Henry and a clerk. The top copy, white, was sent to the vendor; the pink copy to the receiving department; and the blue copy remained in the business office. When the items were delivered, the receiving department released a signed pink copy and returned it to the business department, which paid the bill, retained the pink copy, and sent the blue one back to the originator of the purchase order after stamping it "Received."

Ethan had kept the green copies on orders which had not yet been filled in the file labeled "Pending," and sets of stapled-together blue and green copies of completed orders in the file labeled "Completed." Henry took all of them back to his office and separated them, matching the sets in his possession with those from Ethan's files. All sets correlated.

Next to come under scrutiny were the vendors. With the purchase orders divided between them, Henry and his clerk, Doris Grimes, began to phone suppliers to verify the accuracy of the orders. It was time-consuming. Vendors had moved or gone out of business. Some did not keep records that long, or kept them in a basement or storeroom where they were difficult to locate.

Patiently and methodically, Henry and Doris continued calling. Everything appeared to be in order until they reached the orders placed from about four years ago to the present time. Independently, they came upon vendors who could not be located. There were no telephone numbers on those purchase orders. Neither new nor old telephone books listed them. Calls to the town clerks of the respective towns in which the businesses were located proved inconclusive. Single proprietorships or partnerships were supposed to register with the town clerk but often failed to do so. None of the four firms in question were registered. The chambers of commerce had no listings for them.

But what about the addresses? Those orders had been mailed from the business office and not returned as undeliverable. A trace of those addresses resolved the conundrum. The addresses were those of mail services that rented letter boxes to people who wished to have a mailing address other than a post office box number.

So it was discovered that certain firms to whom Ethan had given orders did not exist. He had used phantom vendors to embezzle the company out of about fifty thousand dollars per year for the last four years.

Chapter Nine

Matthias Wilkinson paced the small motel room. From the window, blocked by a tiny, round, plastic-topped table and two orange upholstered chairs soiled by sweaty backs and dirty hands, to the opposite end of the room, with the door flanked by a bathroom and a makeshift closet, it was ten steps. Back and forth he went, hundreds of times.

Matthias had stopped waiting almost forty years ago when he bought his first drugstore. This was intolerable.

He was anxious for the telephone to ring, and when it finally did, he jumped, startled at the intrusion on his irritation.

"Wilkinson here," he growled.

"Matthias, I'm glad to hear you're finally taking a vacation. What can I do for you?"

"This is no vacation. Where have you been? I've been trying to get you since nine o'clock this morning."

"In court, Matthias. Duty calls."

"Your duty is to me. Or have you forgotten that, Simon?"

"Not at all, old friend. I'm yours to command. But we do have stockholders to consider now. One little coalition of them is suing to have more of a say in decision making. They want to halt the building of mega-stores. It seems they are concerned about the local pharmacists."

"I *am* the local pharmacist and I'll decide where and when we build mega-stores. Those kooks own about ten shares each and they bought them just so they could attend meetings and make nuisances of themselves. Who do these stockholders think they are?"

"I guess they think they are partners in the company, Matthias," replied Simon Wagner trenchantly.

Matthias rejected that concept. He did not attribute any importance to stockholders. Three years ago, on advice from his lawyers and financial advisers, he had taken his chain, Hampshire Drugs, public, reaping a second fortune from it. Loath to relinquish power, he became chairman of the board and remained majority stockholder, but no longer managed the day-to-day operations. A new group of whiz kids did that.

But he never let go and still controlled the important decisions. In his home was a complete office with fax machine and a direct telephone line to the new president. His disdain for the stockholders was so evident, the company management tried innovative ways to keep him from the stockholders' meetings. They failed. He chaired every meeting and, when questioned about his expansionary, anti–small business attitude, he called his questioners Luddites, a reference to the nineteenth-century British workers who destroyed laborsaving devices.

Today, however, he had no interest in business matters. Without preamble, he ordered the lawyer, "Get me the papers I need to obtain guardianship of my granddaughter, Rose. Her father's dead of a drug overdose. I want to take her home with me tomorrow."

Unprepared for this sudden shift of conversation, Simon Wagner, in his best lawyerly fashion, stalled to collect his thoughts.

"My condolences, Matthias. That's a terrible tragedy for a young girl."

"It's the best thing that could have happened to her. Just get me whatever I legally need to be her guardian. They stopped me once, but they won't succeed this time." He paused to emit a whinnying laugh. "I've won by outliving most of them."

The autopsy results were as expected. Ethan Quade died of a drug overdose, probably from the same batch of fentanyl found in his shirt pocket. Further toxicological tests were pending, but they would not likely make a positive determination of fentanyl because it converted quickly into its metabolite, morphine.

Lieutenant Detective Albert Medeiros of the state police had received the results and was now sharing them with Chief Pedersen of Mashpee.

The blood alcohol level was .12 percent, above the legal limit for driving in Massachusetts.

"Too bad he wasn't stopped for drunk driving," mused Pedersen. "He might be alive now."

"He might be," agreed Medeiros, nodding.

"What about the time of death?" asked Pedersen.

"Well, they have some indicators on that," answered Medeiros, perusing the report to refresh his memory. "Dr. O'Neill made some of the observations, and the pathologist in Dr. Mann's office who performed the autopsy made the others. Dr. O'Neill noted at eleven-thirty A.M. fixed lividity and extensive rigor mortis. Fixed lividity usually takes six to eight hours and we have to stop the clock on that at the time the body was taken from the grave because they turned him on his back and the blood remained on the upper side where it had already clotted when he was lying facedown. Of course, no one knows yet if he died in the grave or was put there later."

"What time does that give us roughly?" inquired Pedersen. "Since the body was removed at about ten o'clock and lividity takes six to eight hours, that makes it any time before four in the morning," he calculated.

"Right, and that six to eight hours minimum is confirmed by the eyes, because the corneas were cloudy. But the rigor mortis seems to make it a little earlier. Dr. O'Neill claims it was nearly complete at eleven-thirty A.M., only a little flexibility in the extremities. That usually takes about eleven or twelve hours but the pathologist claims this state could have been reached in nine or ten hours because the weather was warm. If we go with the full twelve hours, though, it takes us back to eleven-thirty P.M."

"But according to Anna Pochet, Ethan didn't leave her house until about twelve-thirty A.M.," remarked Pedersen.

"Yes, if she's telling the truth. Remember no one else has admitted seeing him after he left the bar with her," reminded Medeiros. "Her claim that Louis Perry saw Ethan leave hasn't been confirmed by Perry. And so far he's her only alibi."

"Alibi for what? I thought we were talking about an accidental overdose."

"Just keeping my options open," said Medeiros. "Women who have been given a black eye by a boyfriend have been known to kill them while they sleep."

"Do we have anything else to go by in that report?"

"Yes and no. It seems Dr. O'Neill also took the body temperature of the corpse at eleven-thirty-five A.M."

"Andy didn't tell me she did that," interrupted Pedersen, vexed at this omission.

"Maybe you didn't ask. Or maybe you called her Andy."

"I guess I did, at that," agreed Pedersen, smiling. "She sure is touchy. Sounds like a perfectly good name to me. But getting back to the point, what did she find?"

"The body temperature was eighty-four degrees Fahrenheit and the air temperature was eighty degrees. A corpse cools at an average of 1.5 degrees per hour, so that works out to about nine hours before she took the temperature, or about one-thirty A.M. However, the doc maintains that in warm temperature a body can cool slower, so he could have died later than that. Or even earlier, because some bodies cool at two degrees an hour."

"That one-thirty A.M. time sounds a little better though," mused Pedersen. "Anything else?"

"Yes, it seems that Dr. Mann has a new young pathologist on staff who is hep on insects. According to him, flies lay eggs on a corpse right after death and the eggs hatch into maggots in about twelve hours. Dr. O'Neill didn't notice any maggots. She did notice a few other insects but that is to be expected in hot weather when a body is lying in dirt. However, when this bug doctor examined the body at three P.M. there were some maggots and lots of unhatched eggs. That means he was dead at least twelve hours, which brings the latest time of death to three A.M."

"That narrows it down an hour from the four o'clock time. How about stomach contents?"

"I was leaving that for last," said Medeiros. "It's interesting. There was no food but there was coffee, which was consumed one to two hours before death. That agrees with what Anna Pochet said about him having coffee at her house. If we take her statement as fact, Ethan drank the coffee about twelve-fifteen, making the time of death between one-fifteen and two-fifteen. The problem with that estimate is that we have only Anna's word about the timing and she's not free and clear in this case. It sounds like a logical time of death, but we should keep our options open and expand the parameters if we decide to check alibis in case she's covering for herself or someone else."

"That *is* interesting," confirmed Pedersen.

"I didn't get to the interesting part yet, Walt. The stomach also had some alcohol ingested shortly before death. According to Miss Pochet, he had nothing to drink after leaving Smugglers Cove except for coffee. If she's telling the truth, he drank after leaving her house."

"But where? No one has come forward to admit seeing him."

"That leaves two options. Either he was with someone who doesn't want to come forward, or he had liquor in his car and was drinking alone. Anna said he was depressed."

"But we found his car parked at the cemetery and there were no bottles in it, empty or full," said Pedersen.

"Perhaps he drank somewhere else and threw the bottle away, then drove to the cemetery. The question is, what did he have to be so depressed about?" Medeiros wondered aloud.

Pedersen's desk phone rang. It was for Medeiros. A call was being forwarded from the Barnstable police. Medeiros would soon learn the answer to his last question.

The man on the windmill was a John Doe. No identification on him. No wallet, no keys, no business cards. He was not wearing a jacket, so no label gave a hint of his shopping haunts. He was dressed in lightweight, pale blue, elastic-waist pants and a short-sleeved plaid shirt, both with brands sold nationwide, and sandals on sockless feet; his clothes offered no clues.

By mid-afternoon, Chief Nadeau of Eastham had exhausted the possibilities of identifying him promptly. A police car had searched the road around the windmill green looking for an abandoned vehicle. Store and private home owners in the area were questioned as to whether an unfamiliar car or truck had parked on or near their premises overnight. Negative. The missing persons reports were scanned fruitlessly. The incident had happened too recently for anyone to have been reported missing. Publishing the victim's picture in Tuesday's paper would have been an option, but this victim was so heavily bandaged it would have been like identifying a mummy.

A search of the green itself yielded some information as to the locale of the attack on John Doe. One of the benches on the perimeter of the green had stains that appeared to be blood, as did the grass in front of the bench. Samples from both areas were taken for testing.

JD, as the police now called him, might have been seated on the bench when attacked. Were he and his attacker chatting chummily? Did one suddenly go berserk? Were they business rivals? Were they vying for the same woman? Or did the missing wallet indicate robbery?

Frank dismissed robbery as a motive. One blow would have incapacitated JD enough for a wallet snatching. The viciousness of the beating and the symbolism of tying him to the windmill at the risk of being discovered signified something much deeper. This was a message crime. But what was the message?

Whatever the motive, the violence seemed to have been one-sided. The victim had no defensive wounds. There were no skin fragments from the attacker under his fingernails, or cuts on his hands, or bruises on his knuckles. The grass around the bench, though apparently soaked with blood, showed no signs of a scuffle. JD was either a compliant victim or a defenseless one. Frank suspected the latter; consequently, he ordered that toxicological tests be done on the victim and the results forwarded to him.

This would take time and, for now, JD was out of the loop, recovering from the emergency surgery required to halt internal bleeding.

With nothing more that could be done on this case right now, Frank turned to the mass of papers on his desk and sighed. There must be a genie assigned to piling papers on the desks of police chiefs.

The Smiths were at the beach again. Today it was Coast Guard Beach as a continuation of Neil's program to show Katie all of Cape Cod. It was Marguerite's favorite beach, considered by many to be the most beautiful beach on the Cape. Adjacent to the expansive Nauset marsh, the beach nestled precariously between the ocean and low sand dunes. On the highest dune perched the old Coast Guard station, sheathed in the familiar white clapboard and capped by a red roof. Storms frequently changed the contours of the beach as the water steadily advanced landward and the white froth of the waves erased man's footsteps, claiming the territory for Neptune.

It was at this site that Henry Beston lived in a cabin for one year and wrote his memorable account, *The Outermost House*. The cabin had yielded to the sea. A couple of hundred yards north, Henry David Thoreau began one of his three beach treks which he later combined into the classic *Cape Cod*.

The water was still very cold this early in the summer and only Neil and Thomas had braved it. Neil was now sunning to warm himself without admitting how chilled he was, and Thomas was snuggled in a capacious, fleecy sweatshirt, digging a hole that never got deeper as sand from the sides collapsed into the bottom with every shovelful he removed.

"How did your meeting with Mr. Catlaw go, Neil? You haven't had time to tell me," said Marguerite.

"Whose fault is that? If you would stop finding bodies, perhaps we could talk about the things normal families discuss."

"We *are* a normal family," she insisted. "Now, tell me about Mr. Catlaw."

"Cat, you mean. That's what he told me to call him. He's a rather picaresque character who has had an unusual life. It seems he was born in upstate New York near an Oneida reservation. He became interested in Indian art and culture and managed to become a licensed Indian trader. He hated the weather in upstate New York though, so he obtained a license in the Southwest. According to him, he was honest and gave fair prices for the articles he bought and sold in his store. He was content there but his wife hated it and divorced him.

"On one of his trips to Santa Fe he met a woman who he fell head over heels for. The trouble was that she was only visiting there from Massachusetts. When she returned home they kept in touch and visited back and forth. They wanted to marry but she wouldn't even consider living out in the desert where he did. Eventually, she convinced him to give up his post and move east. They settled in Cape Cod because it has a lot of tourists and he wanted to continue selling Indian jewelry he could obtain from his contacts in the Southwest."

Neil paused for a cold drink. The sun had finally countered the chill of the ocean.

"That sounds like a good solution," commented Marguerite.

"That's what he thought. But it didn't work out. After a couple of years they broke up. It seems they got along better when they had a couple of thousand miles between them."

"I guess you could say that about a lot of marriages," agreed Marguerite. "But what about the business you wanted to discuss with him?"

"He was more open about his personal life than he was about his business. Cat is well named. Friendly up to a point, but doesn't let you crowd him. He's very circumspect. His jewelry pieces are tagged with the name of the artisan and the tribe, but those tribes cover a lot of territory and he wouldn't give me any specifics as to how to locate the artisans or who I might contact to expedite their location. In fact, he keeps the tags turned under so that anyone just perusing the items in the cases, as I was, can't obtain much information. After all his years in the business he can smell out the serious buyers and ignore the browsers.

"He offered to broker any deals I might want to make, but that would mean a commission for him. That's not the way I do business."

"It looks like you came up against a brick wall," sympathized Marguerite.

"Only temporarily." Neil grinned. "I took a good look around and found out what was available. That will save me a lot of time when I travel to the Southwest looking for direct suppliers. Besides the jewelry, I was particularly interested in an item called a dream catcher. It's basically a circle filled in with webbing and there's a small hole in the center of the webbing. It's placed above a baby's cradleboard or bed so that the web will filter all dreams and let the good dreams pass through the center hole while the bad dreams are trapped in the web where they perish in the light of dawn. The design is also used now for beautiful silver and turquoise earrings or pendants, but the original hanging dream catcher should be a hot item in China, with its one child policy. Parents are very protective of an only child."

"At least your trip wasn't a waste of time," said Marguerite.

"No, indeed, it was not. Cat was very helpful even though he didn't intend to be."

"Did he say anything about Rosebud?"

"Yes, he did. He's very fond of her. Cat has no children and regrets that. He's become a surrogate uncle to her and would hate to see her grandfather take her away. He also seems very fond of Esther."

"That would be nice for Esther. She seems very lonely. It would also make it easier for her to take care of Rosebud."

"Maman, you're matchmaking," chided Katie, speaking for the first time.

"Not really," responded Marguerite thoughtfully. "Because one has to consider the other side of the story. He's already had two failed marriages. Maybe he's better at being a surrogate uncle than being a real husband.''

''It's certainly a lot easier,'' cried Neil as he jumped up to capture Thomas, who was dashing toward the water. Returning with the wriggling child, he said, ''Katie, Thomas has had enough beach for today. I think we ought to go home.''

''Good idea,'' seconded Marguerite. ''Some of us are tired from getting up so early.''

''Al, this new information makes the case look more and more like a suicide. But something has been bothering me right from the beginning.''

''What's that?'' asked Medeiros. He and Pedersen were on their way to Roberts Instruments to clarify the revelation of Ethan's embezzlement. Though it was out of Pedersen's territory, Medeiros had invited him to come along and listen. It might be connected with Ethan's death.

''Water, that's what. If Ethan used the fentanyl he had in his pocket and injected it with that hypodermic syringe, how did he dissolve it? Where did he get water? Sometimes the powder even needs to be heated and we didn't find any cooker.'' Pedersen's forehead was screwed up into questioning wrinkles.

''I've been thinking about the same thing and there are answers if we don't limit ourselves to the practices of conventional junkies. And Ethan wasn't a junkie. I didn't get time to tell you before the phone call but the autopsy discovered no other needle marks on his body and the preliminary lab tests show no other drugs in his system except alcohol. His nose was okay, too. No signs of snorting.

''But back to the problem of water,'' Medeiros continued. ''Remember, Anna Pochet said he went into the bathroom right before he left her house. It was supposedly to clean the scratches, but he might have already decided to kill himself and taken water in some sort of container. We'll have to ask her to check her medicine cabinet to see if anything is missing. As for mixing it, he could have used the same container to mix the stuff. He might have thrown the container somewhere in the cemetery or he might have filled the syringe and discarded it somewhere along the road so as not to implicate Anna.

"Another possibility is that he used one of the cups or little boxes I noticed on some of the Indian tombstones. I doubt if he was a religious guy or concerned about tradition."

"I guess he could have done any of those things but it's a mighty cumbersome way to commit suicide," responded a skeptical Pedersen.

"Perhaps he didn't want it to look like suicide but wanted it to appear an accidental overdose. We'll have to check his insurance policies to see if he had any recent ones that had a waiting period before paying off in a suicide," suggested Medeiros.

Pedersen chuckled at this. "You know, Al, it's ironic. We investigate, question, analyze, lose sleep, and rack our brains. But the final decision as to accident or suicide is liable to be made by some clerk in an insurance office who's never seen a dead body but will be considered expert enough to challenge our decision if it's unfavorable to his company."

The relaxed camaraderie between the officers abruptly halted as Medeiros pulled his car into the No Parking area in front of the office at Roberts Instruments and an obviously choleric James Roberts came hurtling through the door, hair disarranged, tie askew, glasses on top of his head, shouting, "That lying snake! I never wanted to hire that Indian in the first place. I told my brother he would be trouble."

James Roberts could not resist. He had finally said, "I told you so."

Chapter Ten

James Roberts was peripatetic; Leon Roberts, subdued. James babbled without punctuation; Leon sat tongue-tied, rubbing his forehead as if to wipe his brother's sounds from his brain.

Medeiros and Pedersen tolerated the spectacle for several minutes, expecting James's incomprehensible monologue to cease, before Medeiros shouted, "Quiet!"

James looked startled; Leon, relieved.

"If we're going to find out what happened, we need to start at the beginning, quietly and logically. Now, you called and said Ethan Quade was defrauding the company. How was he doing it?"

"With fake companies!" shouted James, florid now.

"By phony purchase orders," declared Leon simultaneously, imparting cacophony to their answers.

Medeiros, sensing an impasse in his quest for calm, changed course. "Who discovered this fraud?"

"Henry did."

"Our accountant did." Once again they answered in unison.

The brothers' agitation escalated as a third police officer stepped into the crowded office. Detective Glenda Watson was a member of the Barnstable police force, to which Leon Roberts had reported the alleged crime, and which encompassed the village of Hyannis in the town of Barnstable.

She was tall, slender, tawny-complected, her facial features in sharp relief due to her severe haircut. Less than one inch of curly hair crowned her head. It was a power hairstyle, an aggressive statement of confidence. The effect was calculated. In the dangerous world of police work, any edge was vital.

The detective was on plainclothes detail, dressed to simulate a well-off tourist. She wore tailored brown cotton slacks with a salmon-colored silk shirt and shiny brown loafers. Her soft, glove-leather brown shoulder bag concealed the appurtenances of her work—gun, handcuffs, police radio, miscellany. The heft of it caused an indentation in her shoulder.

Watson had been delayed questioning a holdup suspect, so the other officers had reached the scene first. She had the jurisdiction Pedersen lacked, and a competitive tension filled the room, seeming to suck the air out of it.

Medeiros stepped into that vacuum. "I think we would like to talk to the accountant. Where is his office?"

"I'll send for him," answered James as Leon was already picking up the phone to dial Henry's extension.

"No! Don't send for him," ordered Medeiros, anxious to shed the brothers. "Just direct us to his office."

That command was easily complied with since the business office was only two doors away. The Roberts brothers were frugal in allocating office space. Money was made from the factory floor, not from fancy offices.

In a rarely applied officious tone, Medeiros informed Roberts and Roberts that he did not wish accompaniment. He stepped out of their office and, as Pedersen positioned himself to follow, Detective Watson moved smartly in front of him, staking out her ground in the pecking order. The chief cursed himself for having accompanied Medeiros and thought unkind thoughts about Detective Watson.

Henry was waiting for them, anxiously sorting and resorting his incriminating piles of multicolored papers. Before they even introduced themselves he began to talk, his voice shrill with nervousness.

"I suspected something was wrong. I just didn't know what. Sales have been up but profits weren't up as much as sales," he announced. "On several occasions I mentioned it to Ethan and said the brothers ought to examine their pricing structure.

He just dismissed the problem and said costs were up and they were afraid to lose business if prices rose. Said they were discussing ways to alleviate the rising costs and not to bother them about it. Now I know why.''

Hoping to avoid another time-wasting discourse, Medeiros raised his hands and gestured for silence. ''Suppose you start at the beginning and just tell us what you claim Mr. Quade was doing. And not too fast. We want to take notes.''

Timidly, Henry began the odyssey of the four colors of purchase orders, where they embarked, where they traveled, and where they finally landed.

The officers made notes on the disposition of each color and, after spending a few minutes absorbing the sequence, Watson asked, ''How was Mr. Quade able to defraud you? This seems like a pretty foolproof system.''

''Yes, but with a weak link,'' Henry said teasingly, not elucidating his answer directly but launching into an explanation of the phantom vendors with rented mailing addresses.

Another few minutes of silent fact-digestion passed before Medeiros summarized his observations.

''As I see it, Mr. Quade kept the green copy, the phony vendor received the white one from you, and you held the blue, only paying the bill when you received the pink copy that verified delivery. But you claim that you sent every pink copy to the receiving department. If there was no company and no delivery, how did you get that copy back with delivery affirmed?''

Henry smiled patronizingly, as if congratulating the progress of a slow student. ''That's exactly it, Lieutenant. That's the weak spot.''

''Please explain yourself.''

''Well, you have to understand. The receiving department is run differently from the professional offices. The procedures are a little . . . well, sloppy. Red, he's the boss, just keeps the purchase orders in a file folder on his desk. It would have been a simple matter for Ethan to go down there and remove the fake ones. No one would have noticed him because he was plant manager and was all over the place. Red goes home at four o'clock—he comes in at seven—and Ethan was always here until five or six, sometimes later. He just took them, forged Red's signature—it's only a scrawl really," he added disparagingly, "and forwarded them to the business office."

"Where you paid them," added Watson.

"Of course I paid them," said Henry defensively. "Everything appeared to be in order. After all, Ethan was in a higher position than I was."

Ignoring Henry's petulance, Medeiros informed him, "We're going to need all the fraudulent purchase orders, the three forms for each—you can make copies for your records—and the canceled checks that were used in payment of these orders. Thank you very much for your cooperation," he said dismissively. "We'll be in touch with you if we need more information."

The three police officers walked out, cutting off all questions and leaving a distinct air of disappointment behind them. Henry had expected at least a smidgen of congratulations on his detective work. *Probably jealous of my superior intellect,* he thought, deriving enough comfort from that observation to cease pouting.

The Smiths were dining "early and easy" tonight. Marguerite's five-o'clock-in-the-morning wake-up call by Thomas, the horrific discovery on the windmill, and a long afternoon at the beach had enervated her. She would like to put up her feet and get lost in a mystery story, someone else's problems.

Neil readily agreed. An early dinner and no family excursions afterwards would leave him lots of time for working. He planned to price out an order he had just received, relayed by fax along with the pertinent wholesale prices. His secretary was a gem. After completing this routine business, he wanted to plan a strategy for contacting suppliers and buyers for his proposed trade in Indian jewelry. Anxious to dispose of dinner quickly and effortlessly, he offered to pick up Chinese food, an offer accepted willingly by Marguerite, grudgingly by Katie.

A postprandial Marguerite took Rusty for an evening walk,

then settled comfortably and picked up her latest whodunit.
For a bookmark, she had used Rosebud's thank-you note. Absentmindedly perusing it, she again noted the trademark left-
handed slant to the writing.

Which reminded her of Ethan. Which reminded her of his
body being dragged unceremoniously from the grave and
pulled up a plank. Closing her eyes for clearer recall, she
remembered something flashing as he was lifted. It was only
momentary, but then it had flashed again and once more,
enough to enable Marguerite to locate the source of the glitter.
It was Ethan's wristwatch catching the sun's rays.

Marguerite concentrated hard to recollect the body's orientation vis-à-vis her location. To reenact the drama she stood,
pretended the rectangular coffee table was the grave, and mentally reconstructed the scene. Ethan had been removed while
lying with his back on the plank, the top of his head toward
her. With the picture clearly in her mind, she saw the watch
flash on the right. He was then lifted and placed on the ground,
still on his back, but facing the opposite direction, feet toward
her. Closing her eyes, focusing internally, she saw the sun's
rays strike the watch again—on the left. Ethan's wristwatch
was on his right hand. Only left-handed people wore it there.
Rosebud took after her father.

But why was that important? Marguerite knew it was but
not why. She was too tired. Perhaps if she slept on it, she
would remember.

"Chief, I want to talk to you." Detective Odoms stood in the
door to Pedersen's office early Tuesday morning, hesitant and
diffident, an unusual posture for him.

"What is it, Odoms?"

"It's about this Quade death. I remembered something that
might be important."

"Well, come on in and spit it out. You look like a school-
boy about to be whipped."

"They don't whip schoolkids anymore, Chief," Odoms retorted, refusing to be charmed. "It's something Anna Pochet
said when I questioned her. She mentioned that Louis Perry

was a diabetic. I didn't think anything of it at the time, but when I questioned him yesterday he sure looked bad, and it reminded me later of what she said.''

"You're too late. We found that out when he collapsed last night. He never told anyone he needed insulin. He's in the hospital.''

"Exactly. That's my point,'' affirmed Odoms. "He needs insulin. That means he has hypodermic needles. He also had access to fentanyl because he moves in those circles. I don't think he's much of a user—prefers liquor—but he occasionally handles small amounts. It pays the rent when he isn't working. He might have learned that stuff was no good and didn't sell it but held onto it anyway and stashed it away for a couple of years. It could have been how Ethan was killed.''

"I thought you were convinced Ethan was a junkie and OD'd.''

"I was at first. But the autopsy overruled that. If he was murdered it was probably Perry. He hated Ethan and saw him leave Anna's house.''

"According to Anna,'' added Pedersen.

"Yes, according to Anna,'' snapped Odoms defensively. "That's how she got the black eye.''

"Let's turn this around a little and look at it the way the DA might or even a defense attorney for Perry. We only have Anna's word that Perry was there and that he hit her. No corroboration. Now if I were a smart lawyer, I would remind everyone that Anna had been married to him and still lives in the same place they used to live. I don't imagine that Perry is a careful packer. When he split and went to New Bedford he probably left some stuff behind—maybe a few needles and some drugs he didn't have any use for because he couldn't sell them. This puts the stuff squarely in Anna's lap.''

"Anna! You're crazy! She would never kill anyone, especially Ethan. She was in love with him. Has been ever since we were kids.'' Odoms was sputtering.

"Yes, and he didn't marry her, did he? Dumped her for some fancy chick in New York. Didn't even marry her after his wife died and Anna divorced her husband.''

Pedersen was well informed about his officers and knew all about the love triangle involving Odoms. Though publicly disclaiming gossip, privately he stored it away in his memory bank.

"But he was at her house. They were probably getting together again."

"Maybe. And maybe he was just drunk and looking for a place to sober up. She might have suggested resuming their romance and he rejected the idea," proposed Pedersen.

"But what about the black eye? And how could she give him an injection?"

"Ethan was drunk. Men have been known to hit women when they are drunk. And women have been known to kill when abusive men fall asleep," suggested Pedersen, testing Medeiros's theory. "In fact, it makes a lot more sense than your theory about Perry. He and Ethan were enemies. Can you imagine Ethan letting Perry walk up to him and jab him with a needle? Remember, there were no bruises on Ethan. No signs of violence. Except, of course, for the scratches your friend, Anna, admits inflicting."

"Right. And then she carried him into her car, drove to the cemetery, and dragged him all the way to that open grave to dump him in. Nothing to it for a woman who weighs about a hundred and fifteen pounds."

"He could have died in the cemetery. Maybe she tricked him into going there. Then she took his jacket after killing him and put it in her house as proof that he had been there and not at the cemetery. It's unlikely that a man would leave to go home and forget his jacket with his wallet."

"No way, Chief! No way! It wasn't Anna," objected a distraught Odoms.

"Relax. I was just punching holes in your theory. It probably wasn't either of them, much as you would like to pin it on Perry. We have new information. Quade was stealing from his company. Something must have happened that made him think he was going to be discovered. It looks like suicide."

Odoms sighed in evident relief. "That's it, Chief. He committed suicide. That's what I thought all along."

*   *   *

Mary Healey hummed softly as she trundled her cart of cleaning supplies along the walk from room to room. This job had turned out better than she thought. In the United States for summer work while on vacation from her college in Ireland, she had not been enthusiastic about cleaning rooms. But the work was light, and the people generous. They responded to her bright smile and lilting speech. The tips reflected their pleasure. She would finish early today. Tuesdays were slow.

The next room on her work schedule, room 112, had a DO NOT DISTURB sign on the door. The same sign had been there yesterday morning, and she had moved on, completing her other assignments before returning to room 112. Noting that a car was parked outside the room, she had verified at the desk that it was the room occupant's car. Since renting a motel room did not nullify one's right to privacy, she decided to skip the room and notified the manager as to the reason. The harried manager was on the telephone sorting out some confusion as to a reservation for the coming Fourth of July weekend, one of the busiest times of the season. He waved her off.

Faced with the same situation today, and the car still parked, Mary was troubled. She dared not skip the room again. Perhaps the tenant was ill. Knocking and calling produced no results. She turned her key in the lock and tested the door. If the dead bolt had been engaged, the door would not open.

But it did. She pushed cautiously. The room was dark. Softly calling the occupant's name, she entered slowly and, as her eyes adjusted to the darkness, she observed a scene of havoc. The room had been ransacked. Beds were stripped, mattresses dragged onto the floor, pictures taken down, drawers pulled out and overturned, furniture moved away from the walls.

She saw no one. Fearfully, Mary looked in the closet and in the bathroom. No one there. She ran straight to the manager, who was again on the telephone and annoyed at her importunate interruption.

The police officer came upon it quickly. On the floor, under some clothes fallen from the overturned drawers, was a wallet with picture identification indicating the room occupant was a private investigator from New Hampshire. Other papers on the floor revealed that the car parked outside with Massachusetts license plates was a rental.

That was unusual in itself. New Hampshire bordered Massachusetts and people usually drove from there to the Cape in their own cars. Additionally, the male occupant of the room had not been seen for two days. Coming on the heels of the windmill episode, the coincidence shrieked. The only paramedic on duty that day who had also been on duty early Monday confirmed it.

John Doe had a name—Ralph Horton.

Marguerite was indulging herself in a third cup of coffee. It was her first leisurely breakfast since Neil had arrived *en famille*. Katie and Thomas were in the school playground where Thomas had discovered the thrill of gravity, scooting down the slide. Neil was in nearby Orleans, feeding a fax machine in which he would soon have a proprietary interest, judging by the volume of his patronage.

Ethan Quade remained front-page news. Marguerite read and reread today's coverage. The case had changed from accidental overdose to suspected suicide. Ethan was a thief!

Could she have been so wrong about his character? No. Besides, what was his motive? He had a good job, lived in a modest house, drove a moderate-priced car, had only Rosebud to support. Sunny required very little and probably supplied her simple needs by jewelry sales. He was not a drug addict— the police confirmed that. Gambling or a demanding girlfriend could explain a financial drain, but Ethan gave indications of neither. Something was wrong.

Recalling her observation after studying Rosebud's note, Marguerite remembered what had been nagging at her subconscious. Running down to the basement, she began rummaging through Sunday's newspapers, stored temporarily while awaiting transport to the recycling shed at the town waste-disposal site.

Here it was! The initial story on the discovery of Ethan's

body. The reporter had been on the scene shortly after the police call was intercepted and, though kept at a distance from the body, had sharp eyes and keen ears.

Through most of Dr. O'Neill's discourse with Chief Pedersen, she had kept her head averted for privacy; but, when she showed him the arm with the needle mark, she had been forced to turn, facing the reporter. He caught every word and was able to record the presence of a needle mark in the left arm.

"That's it!" cried a triumphant Marguerite to a basement devoid of listeners unless one considered the resident spiders. "I knew something was bothering me about that note. I've got to see Frank."

Changing rapidly out of chino shorts and into a chino skirt—she thought it made her look more credible—Marguerite ran a comb through her hair, gathered the newspaper and Rosebud's note, and hurriedly left the house. No need for food bribes today. She had evidence!

"Good morning, Frank. I have something important to tell you," she announced as she bustled into Chief Nadeau's office.

"In English! What a surprise," he countered, though fully aware that Marguerite spoke in French at his request and for his benefit.

"I have to tell you this in English because I want you to understand every word and your French isn't really that good." She took no prisoners.

"Marguerite, you hurt my feelings. And no cake?"

"No. No cake. No French. Just honest-to-goodness facts. Ethan did not administer himself with a drug overdose, either accidentally or to commit suicide. He was murdered! Which means he wasn't a thief either."

"Whoa, Marguerite! Let's back up. First of all, the Quade death is not my case. If you have some evidence, as you claim you have, I suggest you take it to the state police."

Marguerite waited for him to continue and when he did not speak further she asked, "And what's second?"

"What do you mean, what's second?"

"You said first of all it was not your case. If you have a first you must have a second."

"*Vous êtes bien trop exigeante.* You are too demanding."

"Stick to English, Frank. This is too important to mess up. Because if you don't have a second reason, I do. Look at this thank-you from Rosebud. She's left-handed."

"Congratulations! Did you figure that out for yourself?"

"Yes, I did. Then I recalled that left-handedness runs in families. Which made me think back to Saturday when Ethan's body was removed from the grave. The sun caused a flickering as the body was moved. He was wearing a wrist-watch."

"Most men do," commented Frank, restless at this waste of his time.

"Yes, but his was on his right arm. So I went back to the Sunday paper and the article claims he had a needle mark on his left arm. Frank, only a left-handed person wears a watch on his right arm. And a left-handed person would inject himself in his right arm, not his left."

Frank was suddenly attentive. Marguerite might sometimes try his patience, but she was bright and intuitive. Her conclusion made sense if the facts were correct. He hated to admit it.

With an air of feigned nonchalance he told her, "Since you seem so intent on this, I'll pass it along to the people handling this case. They can verify the watch and the needle mark. Even if they do it would be inconclusive. Didn't you ever hear the word ambidextrous? Now, if you don't mind, I have a million things to do. We've just identified your man on the windmill."

"Who is he? Does he live here? Is he a tourist?"

Frank had said the wrong thing in trying to get her to leave. He had piqued her interest.

"He doesn't live here and we're not sure yet if he was a tourist. It's more likely that he was working. He's a private eye. From New Hampshire," he added as an afterthought.

"New Hampshire!" Eyes and mouth agape, expression unguarded, she was clearly startled.

"Why are you so surprised? Do you know a PI from New Hampshire?"

"No, but I know a grandfather from New Hampshire. Rosebud's. He was at her house Sunday waiting to take her away, back to New Hampshire with him. He was trying to do it forcibly and would have succeeded if Cat had not come along. I wasn't able to stop him. And, of course, Sunny couldn't."

Frank's head was spinning, trying to absorb this complicated monologue. Nevertheless, he was interested.

"Marguerite, tell me the whole story, exactly as it happened, one step at a time."

And she did. With concise and accurate reportage, Marguerite recited the pertinent events so that even a reluctant Frank Nadeau was cognizant of their relevance.

"So you see," she concluded, "the cases are definitely related. The man on the windmill has some connection to Rosebud's grandfather and her father. Now you have the grounds to be involved in both cases. Isn't that good?"

"Wonderful, just wonderful. You've made my day."

State Trooper Stephen Fleming removed his sweaty cap to wipe the perspiration from his brow and to permit any stray breeze to flutter his damp, drooping hair. He wished he could remove his stiff new shoes to perform the same service for his feet.

It had been a frustrating day. To Braintree then Quincy then Boston, he had traveled with Ethan Quade's picture in his pocket in an effort to locate someone to identify him as the man who rented the mailboxes for the sham companies or who cashed the checks payable to those vendors.

The fraud had been planned for maximum efficiency and required only a few hours on a Saturday morning once per month to execute. Two mailing addresses each were housed in Braintree and Quincy, towns on the route between Cape Cod and Boston. Furthermore, a study of the now-infamous pink slips revealed that, in any given month, the two slips released for payment were in the same town.

On a Saturday morning, Ethan could drive to either Braintree or Quincy, pick up checks totaling between four and five thousand dollars, and return to the Cape in time for lunch.

Trooper Fleming visited each mail drop, interviewed every employee on duty, showed Ethan's picture, and obtained the names, addresses, and phone numbers of employees not at work that day but who worked Saturdays, as well as the last known addresses of employees who had left within the previous four years. Fortunately, the staffs were small, and he was able to locate all but two of the present or past employees.

No luck. The phony addresses had been arranged four years ago. Two establishments had changed ownership. No one remembered who opened the accounts or recognized Ethan's picture. This was not surprising since the employees rarely saw clients picking up their mail. The uniformly small offices were intentionally separated from the boxes. People with addresses of convenience cherished anonymity.

Continuing to Boston and the banks, Fleming experienced the same head-shaking, shoulder-shrugging reaction to Ethan's picture. Four years and thousands of accounts later, no memory existed of the originator of those accounts.

Armed with an order to check the activity of the accounts, information quickly available on the computer, Fleming was impressed at the methods devised to limit personal exposure. Once the accounts were opened, Ethan never visited the bank. Deposits were made by mail; withdrawals by ATM cards; some of those withdrawals were right in Braintree or Quincy on Saturday mornings, others in Hyannis and several other Cape towns. Fleming was willing to bet his next pay raise that those ATMs had no cameras.

The accounts themselves were carefully selected business checking accounts that paid no interest, thereby eliminating the risk of the banks reporting such interest to the IRS and exposing the false Social Security numbers. Only the minimum required balance remained in each account.

Police departments stressed that most cases are solved not by dramatic denouements but by good old-fashioned legwork. They were proud of this.

I guess it depends on whose legs they are, thought Trooper Fleming, resting his.

Chapter Eleven

Ronald "Red" Aumack had been dubbed with the nick-name in his youth. Too bad he had not been called Ron or Ronnie. Red had proven inauspicious for a man who began to lose his hair in his twenties and, by forty, sported only a fringe of graying hair. Hirsute everywhere but his head, he wore his shirts short-sleeved and open-necked, defiant of even the worst weather, as if to corroborate his name.

Red had worked for Roberts Instruments for twenty years, starting in maintenance and working his way through a pro-gression of jobs until attaining his present position in charge of receiving. The title was misleading, as he was in charge of only himself.

But his duties involved more than the title implied. He did not merely stand on a platform accepting cartons of goods, although he did that, too. Red opened every carton, counted and inspected each item, and, with a working knowledge of the company's requirements, informally assessed the quality of the shipment.

Every item in the factory was catalogued, from machine tools to paper towels: where it was stored, where it was needed, and where it was purchased. Working closely with Ethan on inventory control, he assisted in maintaining that dynamic balance—an inventory not so low as to delay pro-duction, not so high as to tie up cash. Despite Henry's egre-giously condescending attitude toward him, Red was highly valued by management.

The door to Leon Roberts's office was open. That was a policy at Roberts Instruments. No closed doors. Employees were unsure whether this reflected a spirit of collegiality or an atmosphere of distrust, but never asked, fearing that the question would inspire the latter.

Red strode into Leon's office and slapped a file folder and notebook on the desk, scattering papers and startling his boss.

"He's got some nerve! That namby-pamby nerd doesn't have the slightest idea of what goes on outside of his precious ledgers."

Red was inclined toward colorful language. He was restraining himself in deference to his boss—a distinct honor, because Red usually deferred to no one.

"I'm fine, thank you, and how are you this morning?" replied Leon, pursuing his effort to convince Red that a conversation proceeded more amiably if begun less confrontationally.

"Pretty lousy, since you asked," snarled Red. "I just heard that Henny Penny learned Ethan was stealin' and he's pointin' a finger at me."

"No, no! No one is accusing you of involvement. You heard that wrong," said Leon in a soothing voice.

"I don't mean he accused me of stealin'. He accused me of bein' stupid. That's even worse!" Red's priorities were interesting.

"He simply claimed that some receiving orders had your signature forged. I believe the police showed you the ones in question and you agreed they were forged."

"Yeah. But they didn't tell me the whole story. Now I find out that Ethan was supposedly coverin' up by stealin' order slips out of this folder and sendin' them to Henny Penny for payment."

"Yes, that's what we believe. And let's call Henry by his right name. It doesn't help anything for you to be displaying such anger toward him. He isn't the guilty party. Ethan is."

"Maybe Ethan did what you claim, but he didn't do it in the way you claim he did. Look at this," demanded Red, indicating a black-and-white, hardcover notebook, known to generations of schoolchildren as a composition book. "This is the proof. Sure, I keep the pink slips on my desk in this folder just like Henny Penny says." Leon grimaced.

Red pushed forward a grimy file folder with its tab bent, the whole much fingered. "But what he didn't say, and didn't know even if he is so smart, is that I also keep this notebook. And that's kept locked in my file." Red paused, triumphant.

Leon looked expectantly at Red. It seemed as if some momentous revelation was about to unfold. From his chair, he leaned far over and knocked three times on the wall to the adjoining office. This was the low-tech signal the brothers used to summon each other.

James responded to the rapping and walked in rapidly, reflecting his style, and chewing an antacid, reflecting his stomach. Requested by his brother to sit down and listen to Red, he complied wordlessly, reflecting his distress.

"Continue, please, Red. Tell us about the notebook."

"Every time a pink slip comes to my office, I log it in here before I put it in the folder. I divide the pages into columns. Look!" he directed, opening the notebook and pointing to columns headed *Date, P.O. Number, Vendor, Date Rec'd.* "Every order is put in here personally by me. If Ethan stole pink slips from this here folder, they would still be listed in the notebook because I don't put nothin' in this folder until I write it down in the book first. I might not notice it right away, but when I look at the notebook and see that an order didn't come in after a couple of months, I check it out and take the pink slip out of my folder and call the vendor. There's no way an order could sit in this book for four years without being received and me do nothin' about it."

"Did you check the purchase orders that the police were questioning you about to see if they were listed in that notebook?" asked James.

"Nope. I didn't know what was goin' on then and when I finally found out today, I didn't have the numbers on the orders. How could I check them?"

"Well, that's easily corrected. Henry made copies. I'll go get them," volunteered James.

"But there's somethin' else, too," offered Red, stopping James from leaving.

"What?" the Robertses asked in unison.

"I smelled a rat so I went through all the pink slips in this here folder and marked them with a check in my notebook to make sure they match. Look!" He held up the book again for them to see.

"So? What's the point?" asked Leon.

"The point is that all the orders in this book still outstandin' have a check mark, which means the pink slips are still in my folder. There's none missin'. No slips were ever stolen after they reached me."

"I still need to get the POs from Henry," stated James, starting to leave again.

"Wait! I'm not finished. After I checked the orders that were in the book and took out the slips that matched them, there were three leftover pink ones in the folder slipped in with the others. I never seen these slips. I'm positive, because they're not in my notebook and I never even heard of them vendors. Someone planted them."

James slowly reached into his shirt pocket and withdrew his roll of antacid tablets.

Marguerite was a celebrity, pursued by the media. The man on the windmill was attracting national attention. War, famine, and politics were everyday events. Bored with reporting these and run-of-the-mill, unimaginative assaults and murders, jaundiced reporters felt a renewal of their journalistic blood in the pursuit of this scoop and a possible byline. The symbolism of a man lashed to a windmill was magnetic. Allusions were made to Captain Ahab and, yes, even to Christ.

The first reporter to knock on Marguerite's door was young, inexperienced, and respectful. Marguerite's natural affinity toward young people came to the fore. She invited him in, bade him be seated, answered his questions fully but without hyperbole, and even gave him a glass of iced tea.

He had scarcely closed his notebook, thanking her profusely as he did so, when the phone rang and a woman reporter apologized for taking her time but wondered if she could ask a few questions. Marguerite graciously complied.

While she was talking with this reporter, Rusty began barking as a car pulled into the driveway and a man and a woman emerged and walked toward the house, the man carrying a camera. The barking awakened Thomas, who was napping. Unable to attend to the phone, the door, and her grandchild, Marguerite excused herself and called out the window to Katie who was drawing, her easel set up on the patio. Neil was at his now-familiar fax machine in Orleans, transmitting the results of last night's labors.

Katie soothed Thomas, whose nap was prematurely interrupted, while Marguerite ran to the door, asked the two people on her doorstep to wait, then completed an abbreviated telephone interview. Hurrying back to the door, she opened it again and was greeted by the flash of a camera. Appalled at the rudeness of startling her this way without first asking permission to photograph her, she pulled herself up to her full height and reprimanded the photographer.

"Young man, that was impolite. You should have asked me first and not flashed that in my face unexpectedly."

"I beg your pardon," began the accompanying reporter, but she had to stop because Rusty's barking reached a new crescendo as a television van pulled into the last space in the driveway and two men began to assemble equipment.

Katie had Thomas in arm and telephone in hand, politely but firmly fending off another caller. Chaos loomed.

Her innate sense of order surfacing, Marguerite took Rusty by the collar, led her to the basement door, and firmly ushered her through it, then went back to the front door. The television camera was moving and, without notice, a microphone was roughly stuck before her face. Chagrined as much by her lack of cosmetic preparation for a television appearance as she was by the perceived discourtesy, she opted out of it and made an announcement.

"There is nothing I can add to what you already know. This is a police matter and I suggest that you direct your questions to them. I *never* interfere in police investigations. Good day."

Inquiries as to the mysterious John Doe, aka Ralph Horton, were proceeding without his input. He had not regained consciousness.

A call to the car rental agency in Chatham, from which he had obtained the vehicle parked in front of his motel room, revealed the surprising information that Mr. Horton had driven to the agency in a car with New Hampshire license plates, and left that car parked in their lot.

The only reason Chief Nadeau could suggest for this switch was that Horton was on a case and did not want to be conspicuous with New Hampshire plates. The possibility of his being a tourist who was mugged was now an improbability. It never had much credence anyway.

Horton had been working, watching someone who would be alerted by New Hampshire license plates. A little alarm was ringing in Frank's head. Marguerite might be right after all. The Quade connection was seductive.

The suspicion that Horton's attacker was connected to his investigative work was supported by a complete search of the room, by what was found and what was missing. His wallet, containing money and credit cards, was in the room as were his car keys. Why would a man leave all his money and ID in a motel room? Possibly because he was meeting someone and did not want to be identified even if physically accosted by this person. Ditto the car keys. He had walked to the rendezvous.

Unless the wallet, car keys, and car had all been returned by the attacker. But why would he bother?

The room key was on the floor near the door. Horton must have taken that with him, of necessity, and it had the motel name printed on it. The attacker gained access, searched the room, and departed, leaving the key and placing the DO NOT DISTURB sign on the door. A nice touch.

The attacker evidently had found the object of his search, for the room was clean. Aside from clothes, keys, wallet, and car rental papers, there was nothing—no indication of Horton's assignment or client. No records, no files, no tapes, not even an itemized expense account, the constant companion of a private investigator. Although Horton had a permit, no gun was found. If he had taken it with him to the fateful meeting, he must have been assaulted skillfully and suddenly. Presumably, his foe now had the gun.

Identifying the attacker by dusting for fingerprints would have been a Sisyphean labor. The room turned over several times a week, sometimes five or six times. Hundreds of prints had impressed themselves on the furniture, which was rarely polished. Nevertheless, the police bagged a few items for the lab—the wallet, door key, and the DO NOT DISTURB sign—items assumed to have been handled by the searcher. The room was sealed off and, if necessary, could be checked for fingerprints when they had a suspect with whom to compare them.

The motel manager was apoplectic at losing a room for the Fourth of July weekend. To mollify him, they agreed to remove the yellow crime scene tape so as not to frighten the anticipated guests.

Telephone records were more informative. Horton had made two brief long-distance calls on Saturday. Both calls were made to the same number—the New Hampshire home of Matthias Wilkinson.

Chief Nadeau was uneasy. Seated across from him was Matthias Wilkinson. Frank had directed Sergeant Patterson to locate him. *Although,* he thought wryly, *I could probably ask Marguerite where he was.*

An old hand at detection, Patterson had started by calling the motels in Eastham. It only took two calls to find Wilkinson, registered and in his room at that moment. The sergeant calculated that a telephone request would suffice to bring Wilkinson to headquarters. He was not likely to flee, not with his access to an army of lawyers. Patterson was right.

Surprisingly, he came alone and greeted Frank cordially. That was why Frank was uneasy. Wilkinson's solo appearance and air of bonhomie were unexpected. He had assumed that a tycoon of this magnitude would not react kindly to a peremptory summons by a small-town police chief, or any police chief. His irascibility was legendary. Newspapers regularly quoted his latest tirade, be it toward supposedly ruthless competitors, uninformed stockholders, thieving pharmaceutical companies, or socialistic government regulations.

Prepared for an adversarial encounter, Frank was unsettled by this genial gentleman seated across from him dressed in off-the-rack clothes: navy blue shorts, white crestless polo shirt, white sneakers and socks. Such an uncharacteristic reaction had to imply guilt of something.

If he had no connection with recent mushrooming events, he would be screaming about police incompetence. This man was surely guilty. But of what?

"For what reason did you employ Ralph Horton?" asked Frank suddenly, attempting to catch Wilkinson unprepared.

"Frankly, Chief, that is none of your business." Congeniality faded. Matthias wasted no time in denials.

Frank had been expecting to waltz around this issue, with Matthias refusing to acknowledge the relationship between himself and the battered investigator. His direct and implacable answer indicated the quickness of his mind. In an instant he had concluded that the police knew of his connection with Horton and he would not demean himself by pointless lies.

"Maybe it isn't, but maybe it is," continued Frank coolly. "You see, I'm sitting here with a mess of coincidences in my hand, and I've been a policeman too long to put much stock in coincidence. Things that appear connected usually are." He paused, but no comment or question emerged from Matthias. Frank resumed his remarks. "Nine years ago a young woman in this town died leaving a baby. Despite the fact that the baby had a father living with her, the child's grandparents from New Hampshire started a custody suit to obtain the child."

Frank stared at Matthias as he related this history, utilizing shock treatment to obtain a reaction. There was none. He continued.

"On this past Saturday, the little girl's father was discov-

ered in someone else's grave, dead under mysterious circumstances. On Sunday, the girl's grandfather, the one from New
Hampshire, suddenly appeared and tried to take her away forcibly. He was prevented from doing so.

"Before dawn on Monday, a man was found near death
tied to our poor old windmill. When his identity is discovered,
he's a private investigator from New Hampshire driving a car
with Massachusetts plates, evidently because he's working on
something and doesn't want to be spotted. The only two phone
calls he seems to have made were to New Hampshire, to one
Matthias Wilkinson, the little girl's grandfather.

"Now do you see my problem? Too many coincidences."
Frank waited again for Matthias to speak. He remained silent
and seemingly unperturbed.

Changing tack abruptly, Frank asked, "Mr. Wilkinson,
when did you arrive on Cape Cod?"

"I checked into the Sand Palace Motel on Sunday at one
P.M., as I am sure you have already verified," answered Matthias, with an edge of sarcasm.

"Where were you on Sunday night?"

"Chief, are you charging me with anything?"

"Not at this time."

"In that case, I have nothing more to say. I suggest that
you devote a little more of your time to the criminal element
that seems to be running rampant on Cape Cod, instead of
harassing a respectable businessman. This is not a safe place
for my granddaughter to live. That's one of the reasons I am
taking her away from here."

With arrogance now burying any remnant of congeniality,
Matthias walked out of the office and the police station, his
aplomb unshaken. Savoring the pleasure of having shown his
mettle to that hick cop, Matthias was inattentive to his sur-
roundings as he strutted to his car. A lone reporter with a small
camera had been staking out police headquarters all day hoping for a break in the windmill case. The Mercedes with New
Hampshire license plates intrigued him and tickled his memory of an old case. As the car's driver walked toward it, the

reporter unobtrusively reached over the roof of his own car and rapidly snapped the shutter twice.

Before interviewing Matthias, Frank had estimated that there was a fifty-fifty chance of a logical and legal reason for the phone calls from Horton. Explanation given, they would shake hands and part amicably.

The odds had just changed. Time to call Medeiros.

Chapter Twelve

E sther glanced at the crowd during the funeral service and was satisfied that she had made the right decision. Initially torn between what she perceived as Ethan's right to an appropriate funeral and her desire to avoid a media feeding frenzy, she had toyed with the idea of a secret burial. Just as quickly as she had conceived it, she banished the idea. To slip Ethan into a grave unannounced and unmourned would be an admission of embarrassment at the circumstances of his death and a betrayal of his life. He was a victim, not a victimizer.

Her solution was Solomonic. Ethan would have a simple Baptist funeral service to which family and friends would be selectively invited by her via telephone. There would be no public notice.

Her strategy succeeded. Only one reporter was present, and she had the good grace to remain inconspicuous and refrain from taking notes during the service. About twenty-five people were present as Ethan was buried beside his parents.

Marguerite, in attendance at the specific invitation of Rosebud, studied the four women closest to the graveside.

Esther, her former submissiveness now imbued with defiance, stood erectly and proudly beside her brother's coffin, seemingly transfused with her dead twin's confidence. Rejecting the gloom of black mourning clothes, she was radiant in a simple white linen dress, belted by a multicolor woven Indian belt.

Rosebud's delicate, seamless face registered no emotion but

exhibited a preternatural stillness. She appeared somnambu-
lant, with reality suspended in favor of a dreamworld. She
wore the same flowered dress she had worn to Joe Harmon's
funeral the day her father's body was discovered. It was an
unhappy dress and she vowed never to wear it again.

Sunny, holding Esther's arm, was garbed as she always was
in a long, shapeless dress, this one in navy blue. Choosing to
adorn herself today out of respect for Ethan, she had added
an elaborate beaded collar in white, yellow, red, and blue, as
well as a beaded hair ornament. The unaccustomed finery
drew one's attention to her face, which contrasted markedly
with the jubilance of the jewelry. Her countenance could accurately be described as tired: tired eyes and tired facial muscles unable to maintain their tone so that everything turned
down, including the corners of her mouth.

To Marguerite's surprise, Sunny looked small and frail,
bearing little resemblance to the formidable woman who had
planted herself firmly on the steps to the house vainly trying
to thwart Matthias Wilkinson. It must have been the perspec-
tive of looking up at her from the walk that had made Sunny
look tall and strong. Or perhaps, thought Marguerite, her impending loss of Rosebud, coupled with the tragic death of
Ethan, had eroded her spirit and diminished her fortitude, leaving only the core of her former self.

The fourth woman was unknown by name to Marguerite,
but she recognized her as the one who had sunk to the ground,
cradling Ethan's head and calling his name the morning of his
disinterment. Still wearing oversized sunglasses, her face was
partially obscured, revealing a refined and beautifully struc-
tured composition of nose, mouth, and chin, a tantalizing but
incomplete picture. Marguerite was reminded of the classical
Greek statues, perfect as to form and face but with blank eyes,
the whole representing the facade of a human but not the
essence. She yearned to peek behind the mask but contented
herself with studying this slender figure who stood beside
Rosebud, with head drooped and shoulders sagged in marked
contrast to the sturdy Esther. Alone of the four women, she
wore black.

So rapt in her observations as to lose track of the funeral service, Marguerite was surprised when it concluded and people began walking away. Esther, detaching her arm from Sunny's and gently substituting Rosebud for herself, strode over to Marguerite who was hovering at the back of the group of mourners along with the discreet reporter.

"Mrs. Smith, thank you for coming. Rosebud is pleased that you were able to attend."

"I am glad to do whatever I can for her. Is there anything I can do to help you?"

"As a matter of fact there is. Ethan's lawyer, Mr. Shoemaker, asked me to come by his office as soon as possible. He wants to discuss Ethan's will, particularly about Rosebud. I arranged to go there today but didn't want to take Grandma Sunny and Rosebud, so Anna offered to take them home with her until I was finished. But Grandma seems so tired I think it would be better for her to go straight home. It would also save me the trouble of driving from the lawyer's office in Hyannis back to Anna's house in Mashpee."

To Marguerite's delight, Esther was indicating with her head the lady with dark glasses. So this was the woman who claimed Ethan was depressed on the night before he died and was mumbling about people not being what they seemed. She wished she could speak with her.

Esther continued. "If you're driving back to Eastham, would you take them with you?"

"Certainly, Esther. I'd be happy to. Can your grandmother walk to the car or should I drive up here?"

"Oh, we better let her walk. She hates to be babied. I'll go down with her."

Once in the car and away from the cemetery, Sunny revived and began to talk of the long-ago past in the way of old people. She spoke of growing up in Maine, the poverty of her youth which forced her into service, and the daring romance with George Sims. Underneath it all, one thread ran continuously: she wanted to return to her people—someday. But not until Rosebud was grown and no longer needed her. Sunny was eighty; Rosebud, ten. Marguerite marveled at the optimism of this charismatic woman.

They were home before the story ended. Marguerite drew up in front of the house, gave her arm to Sunny, and was rejected. As she headed toward the front door, intending to see that Sunny was settled comfortably despite the old woman's independence, Rosebud spoke for the first time.

"No, this way," she indicated, pointing to the walk around the house. "The front door is locked."

"And the back door is open?" inquired Marguerite.

"Yes, isn't that silly?" giggled Rosebud, the little girl in her irrepressible.

Approaching the back door, Marguerite noted a quantity of clamshells—properly called quahog shells—heaped in several piles. Pointing to them, Rosebud commented, "Just remember, Mrs. Smith, we ate every one of those clams."

Frank Nadeau felt like crowing. He knew it; he had known it all along. Ralph Horton had offered no resistance to his attacker because he was incapacitated, not by alcohol but by a drug. And the drug was not one of the usual "recreational" drugs—Frank thought that a strange connotation—but a drug not likely to have been consumed voluntarily or knowingly.

Horton had been given triazolam, the modern, sophisticated version of a knockout drug, replacing the more widely known chloral hydrate or Mickey Finn. Ground up and diluted in alcohol, the usual method of administration, it had no smell, no taste, and put the victim out in five minutes for a period of up to ten hours.

Ralph Horton was still unable to assist the police. Brain swelling rendered him unconscious and in critical condition. This might yet be a murder case.

Pondering the significance of the toxicology report, Frank made two notations on his crime sheet, an oversized pad of unlined paper set on an easel and designed for audiovisual presentations. Frank was an expansive man who required space for his jottings. He detested those little notebooks into which policemen squeeze notes in cramped handwriting.

The first notation, concerning the presence of triazolam, included a presumption on Frank's part. The victim must have known his attacker and was comfortable enough to have a drink with him. This was at odds with Frank's previous supposition that Horton had left his wallet behind to remain anonymous, but present facts often contradicted past conclusions. He had to keep his mind open.

His second notation was a reminder that the Quade and Horton cases, possibly related, both involved drugs and someone with familiarity and access to them. There were only two names thus far connected with the Horton case: Marguerite Smith, who had discovered the battered victim, and Matthias Wilkinson, who had employed him.

Frank's eyes lingered on the name of Matthias Wilkinson, drugstore czar.

Henry's nervousness was markedly decreased as he began his second interview with the police, but not his gratuitous insults toward the mental capacity and reliability of Red Aumack. The police presence emboldened Henry. Normally terrified of Red and his aggressive self-assertiveness—the bulging muscles, hairy chest, coarse language, merciless teasing—Henry avoided him assiduously, even scurrying into the men's room only when Red was clearly occupied elsewhere. It had not occurred to him yet that he might be required to testify in open court and repeat all his allegations with Red glaring at him. Faced with the white composition book, he theorized.

"That's what I thought might have happened. Red was in on it. Of course, he didn't record those pink slips because he would have had to account for the material, which was never delivered. He kept them for a reasonable period of time to allow for a fake delivery and then signed them and sent them to me."

Henry sat back, satisfied with this explanation. Medeiros was not satisfied.

"But Red claims his signatures on them were forged."

"He's lying."

Medeiros pressed on. "Why would he alert us to those three

additional purchase orders or even to the notebook? It complicates his role in this and points a finger at him. Why not be quiet and let Ethan take the blame?''

Henry merely pointed a finger at the side of his head, tapping it several times while making a face, the whole designed to denigrate Red's thought processes.

Detective Watson, more relaxed today without the perceived threat of competition from Chief Pedersen, joined in the questioning in an attempt to clarify her own understanding of the pink slips.

"Let me see if I have this straight. You claim Ethan submitted the orders through you, and you then sent the pink slips on to Red."

"My office did, yes," corrected Henry, distancing himself from the process and realigning the already perfectly aligned pencils on his desk.

"Your office consists of you and a clerk. Am I right?"

"Yes, that's correct."

"And you okay all the orders. Right?"

"Partially right. I have total confidence in Doris and rely on her to check them." Classic buck-passing.

Watson cleared her throat in a manner indicating disdain and continued.

"In any case, the pink slips went to Red, who put them in a folder, and then Ethan stole them back." She looked questioningly at Henry, who moved some ledgers an inch closer to the front edge of the desk to achieve symmetry.

"That appears to be what happened. Unless Red was in on it, in which case he signed and returned them to the business office himself."

Medeiros picked up the questioning.

"Let's assume for the moment that Red wasn't in on it. That means Ethan had to steal them back before Red listed them in his book. Red claims he enters them immediately."

"Immediately? What's immediately to Red? Tomorrow? Next week? Paperwork is not his forte."

"Leon Roberts confirms his inventory records are meticulous."

"There you go then. His record-keeping incriminates him. He didn't enter the orders because he's involved."

"And he planted three of the phony pink slips in his file and showed them to us to indicate that someone was setting him up."

"Evidently," Henry added, shrugging his shoulders. The only sound was the *tap-tap* of papers as he gathered a stack from his desk and made a neat pile neater.

"Maybe so," said Medeiros doubtfully. "But if he was involved, it brought down the stakes substantially. The whole operation netted only about fifty thousand a year. With two people splitting it, that makes only twenty-five thousand each."

"Ethan probably bought Red off for ten percent," offered Henry disparagingly.

"For five thousand a year? That's peanuts to risk jail for."

"People get mugged for ten dollars."

"But not by someone with a good job, a family, and no record."

"There's no accounting for people like Red," Henry said with a sigh. "Maybe he wanted a new pickup truck."

"There are a couple of other things we wanted to ask you. When did you last talk to Ethan?" casually inquired Medeiros.

"Let's see. It must have been Thursday. I wasn't at work Friday because I had to attend a funeral in Connecticut. My aunt died—my mother's sister."

"Did you talk to Ethan on Friday?"

"No, I didn't."

"Did he call your house and leave any messages?"

"No." The telephone was moved two inches to sit squarely in the upper left corner of the desk.

"That's funny," said Medeiros, scratching his head. "We had a different impression from his calendar."

"Calendar? What calendar?" Henry lost his air of casual unconcern and sat up stiffly.

"Ethan's," replied Medeiros, taking same from an expanding folder. "Mrs. Lopes gave it to us. Seems it was on her desk instead of Ethan's, and her calendar was on Ethan's desk.

The cleaning service came in Saturday and must have mixed them up. Has some interesting notations. For Tuesday of last week, he wrote, 'See about H.' For Friday, he wrote, 'Call H.' That must have been because you weren't here Friday and he wanted to talk with you,'' suggested Medeiros.

"Not me. That must have been someone else. I'm not the only person whose name begins with H.''

"No, you're not. There must be fifty names that begin with H,'' agreed Medeiros.

Henry took a deep breath, but slowly, trying to disguise his relief.

"However, you're the only one he called several times on Friday from his office.''

"I told you I was at a funeral Friday. If Ethan did call me on some business, I wasn't there.'' Henry was fidgeting in the chair. His synthetic, no-iron shirt had damp patches and was sticking to his flabby torso.

"Guess I'm not explaining myself clearly,'' said Medeiros mildly. "These were completed calls, not hang-ups like they would be if no one answered.''

"But I didn't answer! I wasn't there,'' protested Henry.

"Probably not,'' stated Medeiros, still low-keyed. "The calls were very brief. Just the right amount of time for an answering machine to pick up. Don't you play back your messages, Mr. Lawrence?'' he snapped.

No answer.

"Answer my question, Mr. Lawrence.''

"Of course, I do.''

"You just told us that you received no messages from Ethan on Friday. How do you account for these phone calls?''

"That's simple,'' replied Henry, focusing his eyes at a point above the lieutenant's gaze. "You asked me if I received any messages. Ethan didn't leave a message. He simply asked me to call him.'' The accompanying smile was ingratiating.

"And did you call him?''

"No. I got home late, after working hours. Since he didn't say it was urgent, I thought it could wait until Monday.''

"Were you home alone on Friday night?" pressed Medeiros, with something in mind other than fraud.

"No. When I came home from Connecticut it was about seven o'clock, so I called Felicia—that's my girlfriend. She had left a message for me asking if I wanted to have dinner with her at her place. I told her I would like to and went straight over to her condo in Centerville."

"What time did you leave there?"

"Late. I'm not sure when."

"Think hard."

Henry continued fidgeting and sweating. The guaranteed no-wrinkle trousers were being severely tested.

"About twelve or one o'clock, I guess. I'm not really sure."

"It's hard to believe that a person as precise about numbers as you are doesn't even know when he left a place. Try harder," Medeiros insisted, staring at him uncompromisingly. Henry blinked first.

"Midnight. I left about midnight."

"That's better," cooed Medeiros. "Did you go straight home?"

"Yes, I did." Handkerchief in hand, he swept his brow.

"Did anyone see you arrive home?"

"No."

"Did you receive or make any phone calls?"

"No."

"Can anyone verify you were at home?"

In his agitation, Henry had not realized the import of the questions about his whereabouts on Friday night. He suddenly recognized the implications of being asked for an alibi the night Ethan died.

"I refuse to answer any more questions. You have no right to question me without my having an attorney present. I know my rights," he concluded, more belligerently than he had ever spoken in his life.

"Do you think your lawyer would have any objection to your giving us your girlfriend's name and address?"

"I'll give it to you but it won't do you any good. She doesn't have to answer you either and I shall certainly tell her not to." Despite his challenging stance, he complied with the request.

The two police officers started for the door. Just as he was walking through it, Medeiros turned and theatrically clapped his hand to his forehead as if just reminded of something.

"I knew I forgot something. I want you to know everything, Mr. Lawrence, so when you speak with your lawyer you can give him a complete picture. It's about Ethan's calendar. There was a notation for Monday, the Monday after he was killed. It was written in the space for nine o'clock and the words were, 'See police about H.' Have a nice day, Mr. Lawrence."

Chapter Thirteen

Matthias assuaged his hovering paranoia by using a pay
phone to call his lawyer, convinced that the motel employees were as one with the police and were monitoring his
conversations.

Simon Wagner took the call at once with grave foreboding.
He remembered too well the rancor and failure of the last
custody battle for Rose and wished he could forestall this one,
which would be even less likely to succeed. Now how could
he convince Matthias of that?

" 'Morning, Matthias. How's everything on Old Cape
Cod?"

"Rotten. I want to get out of this motel room and off the
Cape as soon as possible. Do you have those custody papers?"

"Slow down, my friend. It's not that easy. First of all, the
papers have to be filed in Massachusetts and you should have
a local attorney for that. Goes a long way in smoothing things
with the court clerks and judges."

"It took you two days to decide that?"

"No, I've been doing a few other things, too. I contacted
an investigator down there whom I have used before and asked
him to check into some details about the child's situation. He
just contacted me."

"That was a waste of money and don't bill me for it,"
complained Matthias. "I can tell you all about her life. She
lives in a shack with a crazy old Indian woman and no one
else now that her junkie father is dead."

"Maybe you're not looking at this from the viewpoint of a

124

judge who would hear the case," suggested Simon. "Let me tell you what was reported to me."

"Make it fast. I'm on a pay phone."

"I think you can afford the call. Just listen for once. My guy managed to get information about Rose's school progress—I didn't ask him how—and she's doing quite well, near the top of her class. Her attendance is almost perfect and his source indicates she is well adjusted and doesn't seem to have any social problems. Her health is considered excellent, too."

"That's a lot of garbage. How about where she lives?"

"Compared with your mansion, Matthias, I guess a typical Cape Cod–style house might be considered a shack, but it's the most popular type of architecture on the Cape, and in many other places, I might add. Very likely your case will be heard by a judge who lives in one." That ought to do it, thought Simon. He should have known better.

"Forget the house then. How about who lives in it? Who's going to take care of her? Not that old woman."

The lawyer sighed. It was never easy with Matthias. "That's a two-edged sword, Matthias," he answered. "The issue of child care could also work against us. Rose has an aunt, her father's twin sister, Esther."

"I know that," interrupted Matthias impatiently. "Get to the point."

"I will if you let me continue. My investigator discovered that Esther has assumed much responsibility for Rose since her mother died. Takes her shopping, gets her hair styled, spends one night a week at the house, even visits the school to see the teachers. Esther is forty years old, unmarried, and has no children. It isn't likely that she will have any at her age. Ethan's will has not been admitted for probate yet, but chances are that he named her guardian. That would be hard to overturn. You have nothing on this woman. My man is still digging but if nothing comes up, I would advise you to drop this matter."

"Never! Not after the trouble I've gone to! And I hire you to tell me how I can do things, not how I can't. Compare this idyllic life you've described with what I can offer her. Go ahead! Just compare it.''

"I was hoping you wouldn't ask that, Matthias. But here goes. You are a sixty-four-year-old widower who lives in a huge house, alone except for a staff of hired help. It would ultimately be the hired help who would care for Rose—no doubt the best you could buy—but still not family, not even stability or certainty. Employees come and go. You personally have a public image, unjustified, of course''—Simon looked skyward and crossed his fingers as he added this last—''as an irascible, cantankerous, ruthless tycoon. And that little escapade of yours in trying to forcibly take the child won't help either.''

"How did you know about that?''

"My investigator is good, Matthias, very good.''

"How else have you been spying on me?''

"Not spying, just investigating. He informed me that you made a little visit to police headquarters yesterday. Not social, either. About the, er, accident to Ralph Horton. That isn't going to bode well for you. You'll be lucky to escape a criminal charge.'' Simon held his breath waiting for the eruption. It came.

"You sneaking, shyster worm! Paying good money to get something on me instead of those lousy Quades. You're probably in cahoots with the crazy shareholders who are trying to discredit me. Let me remind you, Simon, that I gave you a substantial block of shares. If I go down, their value goes down, too.''

Matthias was shouting. A leather-jacketed couple, trying to use an adjacent phone while astride their motorcycle, turned to glare at him. His return look was incendiary. Fools who rode those belching monstrosities were high on his contempt list.

"Matthias, my investigation and our conversations are private, they are privileged information. If you file for custody, the opposition will go public. They don't even need an investigator; they already know all this. Attempted abduction of a child, even by a grandfather, is a serious matter. They haven't filed any charges against you yet, but you can be sure they will be advised to do so if you become troublesome. Not to mention your involvement with Ralph Horton. The national media are hot on that one—a bizarre crime in a bucolic New England village. If they connect you with him, they'll have a picnic. That wouldn't do the company stock any good, including the shares I hold, which, if I remember correctly, I accepted as payment for legal services.''

Matthias was stubborn but not suicidal. He stood benumbed as the lawyer's warning penetrated his unreceptive mind-set. After all his planning, he could not lose now. In a chastened tone, he inquired, ''What do you suggest I do?''

''Mostly nothing. Lie low. Be a tourist. Go to the beach, catch some fish. I would suggest that you come home but it might look as if you were running away. Wait a couple of days and, if the police don't question you again, then come home. And a few warnings. Don't go near Rose or her house. Don't hire any more stumblebums like Horton. I wish you had asked me about him. His reputation is as bad as his breath. In fact, don't hire anyone for anything. If the police question you, insist on your right to an attorney and call me immediately. I can contact a fellow down there who does criminal work.'' Matthias blanched.

''Forget about custody for now,'' Simon advised. ''Let's wait until the will is admitted and the Horton mess dies down. Maybe we'll have some grounds when the dust settles. Your strong point is that you can provide for Rose's future. Her aunt is a nurse's aide and will likely be short of cash taking on two more people to support. Rose may end up in poverty and you can come to the rescue. Time, my friend, you need time.''

Simon Wagner was wrong on one point. Rosebud was not impoverished.

The small mortgage remaining on the house was covered by mortgage insurance and she owned the house unencumbered.

Ethan had a life insurance policy for two hundred thousand

dollars, written nine years ago and well past the two-year de-
nial of suicide benefits, if that should be the official cause of
death. He also had an annuity policy that guaranteed Rosebud
a monthly stipend.

Roberts Instruments participated in the federal 401(k) program, a tax-sheltered investment plan, in lieu of a traditional
pension, and Ethan had a large investment in that. Mr. Shoemaker, Ethan's attorney, did not have the latest figures but
would soon obtain them from the company.

Additionally, the child was eligible for monthly Social Security benefits until she was eighteen years old or graduated
from high school if older than eighteen. The attorney would
assist Esther in filing for those benefits.

Ethan's will named Esther as guardian for Rosebud. Esther
had anticipated this and had worried incessantly about her
ability to support Rosebud and Sunny. She should have known
better. Ethan never left loose ends.

Unlike the investigation into Ethan's death, which had a lot
of loose ends. Al Medeiros contemplated this tangled skein of
events as Detective Watson and he left a thoroughly agitated
Henry Lawrence to once again rearrange his desk.

There were three crimes, disparate yet interwoven, involving four police units. The dead body was found in Mashpee,
the assaulted private investigator in Eastham, the business
fraud in Hyannis. Add the state police, principals in suspected
murder cases, and one concocted a potpourri of police units,
each listening to a different drummer. Medeiros had to coor-
dinate these efforts and, to do so, needed to organize his own
thoughts.

The Ethan Quade case, whether suicide or murder, was
stalled. If it was murder, it was a remarkably clean one. No
physical evidence was discovered to indicate that anyone but
Ethan had been at the scene.

Fingerprint evidence was contradictory: Ethan's on the barrel of the syringe, none at all on the plunger or glassine envelope of fentanyl. These were mistakes, either on the part of
a killer or on the part of a suicidal Ethan intent on covering

his tracks. He might have held the envelope and the syringe with a fold of his shirt to avoid prints but forgot to wipe them first from the barrel. A killer might have put the syringe in Ethan's hands after killing him but forgot about the plunger and the drug packet. Arguments could be made for either point of view. The narrow rubber tubing, probably used as a tourniquet, had fragments of smudged prints that were useless.

The source of water was still a mystery but could be explained in several ways that Medeiros had already theorized when Chief Pedersen raised the question.

This case was as dead as the victim unless someone new came forward, or someone changed his story. Someone like Louis Perry who held the key to Anna Pochet's alibi as well as his own and, possibly, to the source of the needle and the fentanyl. That angle must be aggressively pursued as it was the only angle they had right now.

The notorious windmill case was also on hold, awaiting the anticipated recovery of Ralph Horton. This was an Eastham police matter but was of interest to the state police because of the peripheral connection to the Quade case through Matthias Wilkinson. It was another nearly perfect crime. No witnesses, no physical evidence. The items taken from the motel room for fingerprint analysis were clean.

Medeiros used the qualifier "nearly" to detract from the crime's perfection because the victim was alive and potentially able to identify his attacker. Or was he meant to remain alive and terrified, too terrified to admit remembering anything, a testimony to the shrewdness of the criminal? Assault was easier to defend than murder if the unthinkable happened and one was charged.

"Lieutenant, isn't that your car?" intruded a voice, interrupting Medeiros's mental gymnastics.

Medeiros halted his forward progress, which was leading him right out of the parking lot, and looked at Watson as if wondering why she was there.

"Oh yes, of course. I was just thinking."

"I noticed. Very hard thinking, too. What do you make of our conversation with Mr. Lawrence?"

"That's the part I was just coming to in my mind. Since I hadn't gotten there yet, and since you heard everything I heard, let's have lunch and talk about it."

Never one to work on an empty stomach—his expanding waistline aside—Medeiros firmly believed, contrary to physiological evidence, that his brain functioned better by the rush of blood to that organ when he indulged his favorite hobby, gastronomy.

"Good idea," answered Watson. "Where can we go?"

"Just follow my car. We'll go someplace quick because I have a lot to do."

Watson groaned as she followed him into a pizza palace, with its tantalizing aroma wafting from the oven, and heard him order a large pizza with linguica, a Portuguese sausage.

When their number was called and their pizza retrieved from the service counter, Medeiros hungrily reached for a wedge. Glenda Watson hung back. Pizza was an enemy. She had not attained her slender physique as a hereditary gift. Chubby as a little girl, from a family in which overweight was endemic, along with hypertension, diabetes, and a shortened life expectancy, she had exerted a tour de force of will to change the odds. Her strict regime had no niche for pizza.

But it was that or no lunch. This was not a salad bar and she never discussed weight or diet with colleagues. Avoiding personal colloquy entirely, she had effectively separated her professional and private lives.

Gingerly wielding a plastic fork, she removed the linguica from a slice, to the initial dismay and subsequent delight of Medeiros, who accepted her offer to add it to his.

Past the noon lunch rush, the pizza parlor was uncrowded and they had selected the booth farthest from the counter to ensure privacy. Skillfully turning her question back on her, he inquired, "What do you make of Mr. Lawrence?"

"I've been giving a lot of thought to that and I have some half-formulated ideas I'd like to explore. Will I disturb your lunch if I talk business?"

"Nothing will disturb my lunch. Fire away. I'd like to hear some fresh ideas."

"I'll start with our original assumption that Ethan was the initiator of these purchase orders and the only one involved. He would have typed them on his secretary's machine either before she arrived in the morning or after she left in the afternoon. The use of that typewriter has already been verified by your lab and Mrs. Lopes said she never heard of those vendors or typed any purchase orders involving them."

Watson paused to take a minuscule bite of linguica-less pizza while Medeiros affirmed the use of that particular typewriter. She went on.

"Now comes the complicated part. Ethan had to send them to the business office for the orders to be processed. They, in turn, sent the pink slips to Red Aumack. Henry Lawrence claimed Ethan must have stolen them back from Red's file, which was left on the desk. But Red claimed he entered every pink slip in a notebook before he put it in the folder and did so on the same day it was brought to him, usually waiting until late in the day to do his paperwork.

"That revelation means Ethan knew about the notebook and managed to steal the slips from Red's desk the same day they reached there. How else can we explain that for four years no phony pink slip ever got into Red's notebook? It would be difficult to believe that was just coincidence."

"It does stretch the imagination, doesn't it?" remarked Medeiros, who was quietly delighting in hearing his own doubts echoed by this keen detective.

"It certainly does," she agreed. "Unless Red was in on it. He couldn't have done it alone because he did not have access to the typewriter. If Ethan was alone in this, he had to know the business office routine to a T so as to know exactly how many days after he submitted POs, Doris would forward them to Red, and Ethan had to be on the scene to steal them."

"Exactly," affirmed Medeiros. "But we have pretty well discounted the idea of Red's being involved. Why would he complicate matters for himself and show the notebook and those extra purchase orders? No one else knew about them except Ethan, who was dead. Red just had to get rid of them and confirm Henry's statement that the pink slips were kept in a folder on his desk and that they could have been taken by Ethan. He would be in the clear.''

"Yes, we've discounted Red. Which brings us back to the theory that Ethan knew the business office routine and always managed to steal the pink slips the day they were sent to Red.''

"I sense a but at the end of that sentence."

"Very perceptive. You must have the very same question," surmised Watson.

"Are we both worrying about those three unexplained additions to Red's folder? Purchase orders to two of the fake companies?"

"I am; are you?" she asked animatedly.

"Yes, but you go first."

"Okay, but I'm not all clear in my mind on this yet. If we stay with the notion that Ethan alone planned this, then we have to assume he slipped up and forgot to steal those three slips.''

"Good," agreed Medeiros, who had been nodding his head to punctuate her words. "What next?"

"We have to wonder why they were not recorded in Red's notebook, and he showed us that they weren't. That gives us two options. One, that Red made a mistake and filed those POs without recording them. That's not too likely because his records are in otherwise perfect order and those three POs were processed on two different dates, so that he would have had to make two mistakes.''

"And the other option?" queried Medeiros expectantly.

"That we accept Red's word when he said someone planted them.'' Watson exhaled in a relieved manner, having given voice to a troubling thought that opened a whole new arena of suspicion.

"And that's what I'm inclined to do—accept Red's word," exclaimed Medeiros. "That creates an even more interesting scenario. Ethan would not have planted those pink slips. He would have been removing them, not adding them.''

"So someone else is involved." She finished his thought. "But who? And why plant those POs?"

"I'll answer your second question first. They were probably planted because the guilty party suspected there might be an inquiry when Ethan died of drugs and wanted to point the investigation in Ethan's direction. After all, it was his name on the POs and that was a perfect time to finger him even though it would end the scam."

"Good point."

"The who is a little more complicated, but we can draw some conclusions. It had to be someone who could use Mrs. Lopes's typewriter and not be noticed. That would include Mrs. Lopes herself during office hours, or anyone who had reason to be in the building early or to stay late. That limits us to the people with keys and the code to the security system."

"Who are they?" Watson asked excitedly.

"The Roberts brothers, of course, Ethan, and Henry Lawrence."

"Narrows it down a bit, doesn't it?"

"Yes. Now we have to narrow it a little further and prove it."

"What is the likelihood of Mrs. Lopes? She had access to both the typewriter and Ethan's files. She could have put those phony blue and green forms in his file after his death in order to make it look as if he did issue them."

"I considered the possibility of her working either alone or in partnership with Ethan. It seemed perfect. She typed the orders, Ethan stole back the pink ones, and they both destroyed or hid the green and blue forms that would link Ethan with those orders if the scam was discovered. He could deny ever receiving the blue ones from the business office. She might even have signed the original orders in an imitation of Ethan's handwriting so he could disclaim the signature.

"But those three extra purchase orders in Red's file made me rethink this. Someone planted them. We already dismissed the notion of Ethan doing so because he would have wanted them out of there. They had to be slipped in sometime between Ethan's death and Tuesday morning when Red checked his file. Mrs. Lopes doesn't have keys to the plant, so she couldn't have done it over the weekend, and it would have been nearly impossible for her to have done so during the workday on Monday. It's widely known in the plant that she never went near Red's office because she disliked him. Found his sense of humor offensive. She could not have gone to his office without being noticed.

"The same problem exists for those green and blue slips in Ethan's files. He wouldn't have kept them if he was guilty, but they were there on Monday morning when Henry obtained the key from Mrs. Lopes and they both looked in the file."

"Did you figure that all out while we sat here?" She laughed at her own question. "Of course not. You've been thinking this all along, haven't you?"

"Not all along. I suspected Ethan at first—until Red threw a monkey wrench into that theory. Then I began to look around."

"I don't know why we're so pleased with ourselves. We only had one suspect before and now we have three."

"Piece of cake," Medeiros assured her.

"Or maybe a piece of pizza," she teased, pointing to the last cold piece sitting on the tray.

Chapter Fourteen

It was the lobster's misfortune that he tasted so good. If evolution had exerted its pressure to selectively favor good looks or stringy tails, he would have been so much better off, thought Marguerite as she prepared her shopping list for Wednesday night's dinner. *Tant pis, too bad*, she consoled herself. *I have to feed my family.*

In a phenomenon inherent in a visit to Cape Cod, the urgent desire for lobster arose simultaneously with crossing the Cape Cod Canal. Postpone it though she might, Marguerite could not indefinitely delay this ritual. Her negotiation with Neil on the subject concluded with his agreeing to pop the creatures into the pot. Once they were red and dead, Marguerite had no hesitancy about cracking claws and tail, dipping them in butter, and downing this most succulent crustacean. That her behavior smacked of hypocrisy she acknowledged and did not defend. *Tant pis!*

Her shopping list had not progressed beyond the first item—three lobsters—when the telephone rang.

"Mother, it's Alex. I can't believe you've done it again." The voice was reproving. Marguerite rolled her eyes.

Her daughter, Alexandra, was a professor of English literature at a college in Washington, D.C. She lived in the Georgetown section with her husband, Preston Trowbridge, a former diplomat still with the State Department in a related but less motile capacity that permitted them to have a permanent residence.

135

Alex did not resemble her brother or her mother. Tall, slender, with reddish-brown hair one might be tempted to call auburn except that the red had more of a golden hue, and fair-skinned, she was more her father's child. Perhaps that was the reason Alex was the more unforgiving of the siblings toward her father's action in leaving Marguerite and, in effect, Alex herself. So bitter were her feelings that she refused to invite him to her college graduation although he had continued to pay the bills for her senior year as part of the divorce agreement.

"So good to hear from you, Alex," responded Marguerite, ignoring the reproach. "Did you know that Neil and his family are here?"

"Of course, I know. You wrote me that they were coming. I would have thought he could keep you out of trouble." Attempting to divert Alex was futile.

"I'm not in any trouble, dear. In fact, I was just going to order lobsters for tonight's dinner." Alex loved lobsters. Maybe this would distract her.

"That's great. I wish I could join you. We were thinking of visiting in late July and Preston would love one of your lobster dinners. However, that is not my reason for calling. I'm concerned about your being in danger. Whoever committed that horrible crime at the windmill had a reason for doing so and you appear to be right in the middle of it."

"No, Alex. Absolutely not. As soon as I found the man, I contacted the emergency service and the police, then left the scene. I have had nothing to do with it since then. By the way, how did you hear about it?"

"The newspaper. With crime such a topical issue here in D.C., the papers love to report crimes in other areas, particularly in a supposedly quiet place like Cape Cod. It was just one paragraph, but it was described as 'a fiendish, cultlike crime in a quaint New England village.' They included your name, too. 'Marguerite Smith, a grandmother accompanied by her toddler grandson, discovered the sacrificed man.' Why didn't you use another name?" Alex still used the name Smith professionally.

"And lie to the police? That would certainly get me in

trouble. When did you say you were coming to visit? Why don't I get my calendar and we'll make a definite date?''

"Mother, you are incorrigible. One last word. Don't get any further involved in this. It looks like there are some dangerous or crazy people behind it. Maybe both. I'll call you next week to set a date because Preston is in Atlanta on business until Saturday. Regards to Neil and Katie." And Alex was gone. She rarely wasted words on good-byes.

Relieved, Marguerite resumed her planning. "Three lobsters, butter—I'll need lots of that—and, oh yes, lettuce for a salad so Katie won't think it's a fatty meal."

Detective Glenda Watson drove slowly down the Hyannis street searching for a particular house number. Half the homes were bare of such identification and many of the others had numbers that were incomplete due to a missing numeral, or were difficult to read by dint of having been covered with paint. Extrapolating from the few readable addresses, she rang the bell of the likely house, waited a while, and rang again. A sleepy voice called out, "I'm coming. Hold your horses."

Wayne Mallory slowly shuffled to the door, his slippered feet never leaving the floor. Clad in a threadbare, loosely belted bathrobe and little else, as evidenced by his bare chest and by legs cloaked only in protuberant, gnarled veins, he searched in his pockets for a cigarette as he opened the door and growled, "I don't want any."

Flashing her ID, she smoothly replied, "I promise not to sell you anything. I just want to ask you a couple of questions. May I come in so that we can talk privately?"

She had shrewdly guessed that Wayne would prefer not to advertise any dealings with the police and was rewarded by his stepping grudgingly aside. She entered without formal invitation. After quickly assessing the collection of aging trays from frozen dinners, with the remains hardened and gray, discarded randomly on chair arms and tables and interspersed with empty beer cans, she elected to stand.

"Mr. Mallory, I apologize if I woke you up, but I didn't think you worked nights."

"That's a laugh! I hardly work at all anymore. Thirty years with the company and then they dumped me overboard with a measly pension and no health insurance. Downsizing, they called it. Greed is what I call it. Three months after they let us go they brought in new workers at a lower salary and no benefits. Can't get a job at my age either. All I was able to land was two days a week as a security guard. Guess I can thank the crooks for that. Security is a growth industry. Just like yours—cops. But what do you want with me? Is my jalopy over the yellow line?"

He had finally located a cigarette and started to search for a match. Wanting his attention, Watson retrieved a book of matches from her voluminous purse and offered it to him. Cigarette lighted, he inhaled deeply and slowly, very slowly, blew out the smoke, prolonging the pleasure of it.

"This has nothing to do with your car or with you personally. It's about Roberts Instruments. The records show that you were on duty for Acme Security last Saturday and Sunday and that you cover three buildings, including Roberts. Is that correct?"

"Yeah, that's right, but I didn't take anything."

"No, that's not the problem. We want to know if you saw anyone go into Roberts on either of those days."

"Is something missing?" he asked warily.

"No. It's an internal matter, not a burglary. It might have been someone who has the keys and could come and go without notice."

Wayne continued smoking and stalling, debating how to avoid trouble. This job was essential, at least until he could find something else. Was he better off keeping quiet, or would that land him in trouble with the cops?

Watson, sentient of the dichotomous relationship between the public and the law—fear of crime but reluctance to become involved—tried to allay his fears.

"I'm not referring to your employers at Acme. Was there anyone from Roberts who entered on Saturday or Sunday? Since it would be someone from management with the keys and the code to turn off the security system, there would be no reason for you to be suspicious of that person or to report it."

Somewhat reassured, Wayne remembered. "Come to think of it, someone did come in on Sunday. I didn't think nothing of it because he belongs there. Like you said, he has the keys. Usually he comes to me first though, but this time he didn't. I only knew someone was there because when I made my rounds I noticed the green light was on over the door. That meant the alarm was off. I was gonna go in but I noticed a movement through the first window to the left of the front door. When I looked in, I recognized the guy, so I just continued my rounds."

"What was he doing?"

"He had a couple of file drawers open and was going through them."

"What is his name?"

"I don't remember. But I know he works there," Wayne quickly added in a defensive manner.

"Was it one of these men?" asked Watson, extracting six photographs from her purse. Wayne studied the photographs of Ethan Quade, the two Roberts brothers, Henry Lawrence, Red Aumack, and a plant worker chosen at random. Ethan was dead on Sunday, the plant worker was not a suspect, and Red did not have the keys or the security code. Watson included them because a photo identification, like a lineup, had more validity if the witness had a choice of subjects from whom to select.

Wayne vacillated, hesitant to finger anyone. In his world, a stoolie had no standing. Finally, a nicotine-stained finger moved slowly over the pictures and stopped at one, as a husky voice said, "Yeah, it was him."

Gotcha, thought Watson gleefully.

Detective Sergeant Odoms had a knot in his stomach. Not the kind of knot precipitated by the wait before a dangerous mission that is obliterated by the welcome rush of adrenaline when the action starts. This was the sickening kind of knot that warned of an attack of nausea.

Odoms and State Trooper Fleming, armed with a search warrant, were ringing the bell to Anna Pochet's house. Odoms thought of a half-dozen reasons he could have given to be

excused from this assignment, ranging from a migraine headache to his daughter's softball game, for which he was an
assistant coach. This was supposed to be his day off.

He had attended Ethan's funeral in the morning, reques-
tioned Louis Perry at the hospital in the afternoon, and now,
at six-thirty in the evening, was at Anna's door, as nervous as
a rookie on his first day.

The nature of the search warrant was the principal reason for
Odoms's insistence on executing it personally. They were au-
thorized to search for hypodermic needles and illegal drugs.
The small size of the objects gave the holder of the warrant
wide latitude in searching. Every object in the house could be
examined, from cold cream jars to sugar canisters to shoe
boxes. It was the type of warrant that could be abused by an in-
sensitive or jaded officer, particularly in the home of a woman.
Rather than subject Anna to this potential humiliation, he chose
to do it himself and risk her hatred while preserving her privacy.

They knew she was home; they had been watching for her to
return from work. She finally answered the door, clad in cutoff
jeans and a pink T-shirt bearing the logo of the insurance company that employed her as an agent. Without the sheltering sunglasses her injured eye was in full view, a yellowish blue now
as the purple faded. Her delay in answering had been caused by
her change of clothes as she shed the flowered skirt, apricot silk
blouse, and business pumps of the workday.

"Lloyd, what do you want? I took Ethan's jacket to headquarters on Sunday. There's nothing more here."

Odoms nudged Fleming, the holder of the warrant. "Are
you Anna Pochet?" he inquired formally.

"Of course I am. Lloyd knows who I am."

"We have a warrant to search these premises, including all
outbuildings and vehicles, for the purpose of locating any hypodermic needles and/or illicit drugs that may be found on
said premises," Fleming recited in one breath.

Stunned, Anna ignored the young trooper and directed her
remarks to Odoms.

"Is this what we've come to? You actually think I killed

Ethan. How dare you suspect me and come to my house with re-
inforcements. Am I considered dangerous? Am I under arrest?''

''Anna, please try to understand. We have an unsolved
death linked to a needle and drugs. Louis Perry is a possible
suspect. He lived here and might have left behind some things
that could have been used to kill Ethan.''

Odoms was valiantly trying to convince Anna that it was
Louis alone on whom suspicion fell, despite his own foreboding
that it was Anna herself whom Medeiros mistrusted. He was
also aware of the flaw in his own excuse. According to Anna's
own statement, Louis had remained in the house on Friday
night only long enough to strike her. She made no mention of
his retrieving any articles that he might have left there.

Anna was breathing deeply, an irate breathing that caused
her nostrils to flare. The presence of the young trooper restrained her and she let her unspoken thoughts remain so.
Flopping down on the sofa, bare legs and bare feet spread
across the cushions in an attitude of resignation, she declared,
''Go ahead. Start ripping mattresses apart and emptying drawers in the middle of the floor. That's how you do it, isn't it?
I'll just wait right here.'' Her sullen guardedness betrayed the
attempted nonchalance.

The anguish in Odoms's mind was mirroring itself on his
face. Trooper Fleming was puzzled. He felt like an actor in a
play who had not been given the script. Breaking the electric
silence, he asked, ''Where do you want to start?''

''Anna, did Louis leave any of his things here when he left?
Things he may have forgotten or expected to take later?''

Studying him with wary eyes, Anna slowly replied, ''Yes.
There are a few boxes in the basement.''

''Would you show them to us?''

''No.''

''Where in the basement are they?''

''On the same side as the furnace.''

''Let's go,'' said Odoms, motioning to Fleming.

The boxes were easy to locate, taped closed and neatly labeled ''Louis'' as if Anna disclaimed any connection to them.
Using a penknife to slit the tape, they opened three cartons

and began sifting through personal items indicative of a past when Louis Perry was young and not yet soaked in alcohol and despair.

High school yearbooks, a letter sweater earned as a member of the baseball team, report cards revealing that Louis was a fair-to-middling student, a scuba mask and fins, several books, one of which had been borrowed from the Mashpee library twenty-five years ago—the flotsam and jetsam of a wrecked life began to accumulate on the cellar floor.

Testimony to change also appeared on the time line of his life: a passbook from a canceled bank account; a letter from the unemployment insurance agency notifying him of discontinuance of benefits because of his failure to seek work; odds and ends of clothes, unwearable but undiscarded; and a box for medical syringes, with four sterilely packaged syringes remaining.

Odoms was disconsolate. That Perry was diabetic and had needles was known. But finding some in Anna's house put her in a position of accessibility to them, implicating her.

Disguising his fear for her, he continued the search with the focus now on drugs, particularly fentanyl or any form of heroin. The two officers methodically examined the basement and its contents, admittedly an imperfect effort. The object of their search was so small and so easily concealed, the house would have to be taken apart board by board to ensure a total search.

Reluctant to subject the living area to their scrutiny, Odoms suggested the car be searched next. Trunk, engine, seats, floor mats, and glove compartment were all devoid of drugs except for a small container of aspirin.

Delaying tactics exhausted, Odoms announced they would search the house. Anna sat on the sofa as they had left her and did not look at them as they entered from the driveway. Despite Odoms's desire to spare Anna the indignity of having her personal possessions pawed by a stranger, he delegated the bedroom to Fleming and remained standing haplessly in the doorway, instructing Fleming to leave everything as he found it. With Odoms monitoring every move, Fleming made short work of it.

Moving from the bedroom through the remaining rooms,

they concluded the house was free of illicit drugs and any syringes other than the ones discovered in the basement.

Holding the now empty packing carton and the box of hypodermic needles, Odoms walked over to Anna who stared impassively at him. "Finished?" she asked.

"Almost," he answered.

"There's no place left. Unless you're going to search me, too."

"No, but we need to check the sofa. Would you kindly move?"

With a retort hot on her tongue, she swallowed it, refusing to engage in emotional dialogue which she was convinced would please her persecutors. Swinging her legs around, she stood and left the room.

A quick search of the sofa turned up only a used facial tissue and some crumbs. Sitting down and leaning on a coffee table cluttered with magazines, Odoms listed the box of needles and the brown carton on the search warrant as items they were removing, and tore off a copy to give to Anna.

"Anna, we're leaving," he called. "I want to give you a copy of what we're taking."

Perusing the search warrant, she commented, "I can understand why you're taking the needles, but what do you want with that old box?"

"Technically, it's the container in which the needles were hidden." Anna raised her eyebrows at the word hidden. "However, my real reason is for your benefit." Her questioning look encouraged him to continue. "The box was taped and the tape looks old and dusty. Maybe the lab crew can prove this box hasn't been opened in a long time, even years, except for where we just slit it."

"And if they can't prove that?"

"Well, they probably won't be able to prove that it has been opened either," he muttered.

"Thank you, Sir Galahad," uttered Anna, executing a mock curtsy while pointing to the door.

*   *   *

Frank Nadeau pondered the mixed news from the hospital. The good news was that Horton's brain swelling was receding. The bad news was that he was still unconscious and there was no certainty as to whether he would recover without brain damage.

For the present, the case was at a standstill. The motel in which Horton stayed had been almost fully occupied over the weekend, but by the period of Sunday night to Monday morning on which the assault and subsequent search had occurred, only one-fourth of the rooms were occupied, and even worse, the rooms on either side of his room were vacant.

By the time he was identified on Tuesday, two additional rooms had been vacated. Only four rooms remained in the possession of vacationers who had been there at the time of Horton's assault. Questioning the occupants had not been enlightening, except as to the activities of visitors.

No one noticed a car pull up or leave the area near Horton's room. Not surprising, since a stay in a motel implied that cars were a component of that stay—a convenience if it was your car, a nuisance if it was another's car door slamming, but definitely not something that one particularly noted. A careful criminal would not even have risked driving his car into the motel complex, and the man they were seeking appeared to be very careful.

There was no witness who saw anyone enter or leave room 112 Sunday night, or who heard any untoward noise. Horton himself was not even remembered.

Telephone calls to the two couples who had checked out Monday evening were fruitless. They managed to convey the impression that they had not seen or heard anyone or anything during the entire weekend at a nearly full motel.

Frank toyed with the idea of bringing Wilkinson in again but dismissed it. Wilkinson would come armed with a lawyer this time and would, no doubt, refuse to answer anything except name, rank, and serial number.

The chief frowned at his lapse into army terms. A veteran of Vietnam, he longed to put that morass behind him, but the army had shaped him more than he knew. He had enlisted young in a period of incipient rebellion against parents, society, and the confinement of that narrow spit of land that was Cape Cod.

Returning home disillusioned and disheartened from a war that lacked definition, he relished the ordered and orderly life he had capriciously abandoned. Though still distrusting absolute authority, such as that wielded by an army over its troops, Frank had become a policeman and prided himself that he treated people, whether law-abiding or otherwise, as individuals, not as dog tags.

Dismissing his fleeting thoughts of the past, Frank concentrated on the present. He decided to let Wilkinson cool his heels for a day or two. Make him nervous. A man of action detested uncertainty.

Meanwhile, maybe Horton would recover enough to talk. Without any other evidence, his testimony was vital.

Then again, Horton might never recover or might not remember anything about that night. Or he would not talk because he was involved in unsavory business himself.

Too many maybes, thought Frank, but he added another. Maybe only the windmill knew the truth, and would add this arcane deed to its three hundred years of secrets never to be revealed.

Chapter Fifteen

"Uh-oh, the fat's in the fire now," exclaimed Marguerite to no one in particular.

"As long as it's not our fat or our fire, Maman," remarked Neil distractedly, as he juggled utensils in an attempt to eat breakfast and encourage Thomas to retain at least half of the cereal the toddler placed in his mouth. Thomas thought it great fun to blow bubbles of the mushy cereal, and chuckled as they broke and oozed down his chin to be hastily scooped up by Neil in an endeavor to return the cereal to its source.

"Of course, it isn't. But listen to this. 'Drugstore czar, father-in-law of Wampanoag Indian found dead in mysterious circumstances, was seen leaving Eastham police headquarters.' He'll need some of his own medicine when he reads this."

Marguerite was silent as she read the complete article, then lamented, "Poor Rosebud! This article repeats the entire story of her mother's death and the custody battle. I don't think her classmates even knew about this. Now they will all be talking about it."

"They will for a while," agreed Neil, "but by the time school rolls around in September, they'll be thinking of other things. Besides, it will probably increase her prestige when her friends find out she has a millionaire grandfather."

Thomas reached over and dumped a spoonful of cereal on Neil's English muffin. Was it a gift or waste disposal?

"Katie, I think Thomas is finished," Neil bellowed.

Katie, fresh from the shower, came into the dining room in answer to that clarion call. Dressed in white shorts, a nautical black-and-white striped shirt, and white deck sneakers over the sides of which peeked the pink edging of her short socks, Katie had incompletely dried her hair so that one side hung wet and clung to her head, while the other side puffed out in a smooth, lustrous, dark coif.

"I'm almost ready. I'll dress Thomas next. What time are we leaving?"

"A quarter to eight would be good," answered Marguerite. "That will give us time to park and catch the eight-forty-five boat."

The Hy-Line boat trip to Nantucket was a popular one-day excursion for Cape Codders and their visitors. With a collapsible stroller along, the Smiths could enjoy a bus tour of the picturesque island, lunch at an historic inn, and shop or browse in the eclectic shops clustered within walking distance of the harbor, a former whaling port.

Marguerite carried the newspaper into the living room and placed it on the coffee table. Moments later she reconsidered, retrieved it, separated the front section, and thrust that into her pocketbook. Having read it glancingly, she wanted to reread it more thoroughly.

After all, how did one occupy oneself during a nearly two-hour boat trip on a gorgeous summer day, accompanied by family including an only grandchild? Read about murder, of course.

Esther gazed from the window in Ethan's room and absent-mindedly watched the bees plundering the patient flowers. Grandma Sunny's garden provided nectar and pollen from March through November. Delphinia, lilies, and foxgloves provisioned the early-summer insect larder.

Her fledgling confidence was inconstant and absented itself this morning. Pressing decisions weighed upon her psyche, which was normally accustomed to an unruffled routine.

Housing was the most immediate problem. Her job in Marstons Mills was further from Eastham than she would like to commute, particularly since she worked nights and would travel after midnight on roads made treacherous by winter's ice. The condominium in Mashpee was perfect for one, crowded for two, impossible for three.

Should she sell both places and start afresh? That would uproot Rosebud from what little continuity remained in her young life. Esther knew she could not make any mistakes in her decisions regarding her niece. Hovering in the wings was the dragon grandfather ready to whisk Rosebud to his castle in New Hampshire.

Her morning's task had uncovered another problem, one requiring finesse and tact, in both of which she considered herself lacking. Sorting through Ethan's papers, as instructed by Ethan's lawyer, Esther had discovered a bankbook in the name of Ethan Quade, in trust for Lily Sims, Grandma Sunny.

The first deposit was made four years ago, shortly after the deaths of Israel and Amelia Quade, parents of Esther and Ethan. This was also the time Grandma Sunny came to live with Ethan.

The deposits were small, the initial one two hundred fifty dollars with like amounts deposited three additional times that year, and varying amounts deposited quarterly, the last one in April of this year.

Puzzling at first, the quarterly regularity of the deposits struck a chord in her memory. Of course! Those were Sunny's tribal payments issued by the Passamaquoddy tribe.

Along with the Penobscots, another Maine tribe, they had brought suit against the United States Department of Interior, arguing that the 1790 Intercourse Act applied to them and entitled them to a federal trust relationship. Unlike the Mashpees, they were successful in their suit and, in 1980, the court ruled in their favor, affirming that they might have a valid claim to about two-thirds of Maine. They were also granted federal recognition as Indian tribes.

Out-of-court negotiations led to a settlement in which each tribe dropped its claim in exchange for monetary awards, one-third of which was designated to purchase large areas of trust land.

Another one-third of the fund went into capital investments at which the Passamaquoddy had great success, including a cement plant, blueberry farms, high stakes bingo, and ownership of a lucrative patent on a scrubber designed to control coal emissions that caused acid rain.

The remaining one-third of the settlement went into conservative investments, the proceeds of which were distributed to tribal members. When Sunny moved in with Ethan, she must have tendered her tribal payments to him. He had no need of the money, but this proud woman had always paid her way. Out of respect for her independence, he evidently had accepted her donations to his household and secretly placed them in a bank account for her.

This account was Esther's new problem. Returning the money to Grandma Sunny would humiliate her, but it was in trust and, with Ethan dead, the account must be settled.

Esther longed for someone with whom to discuss these problems. Anna! Funny that she should still associate Anna with Ethan. Anna was probably in need of consolation herself, for Ethan's death had been her loss as well. She had been the one blind spot in his otherwise perspicacious and sentient personality. He had never realized how much she cared or that their relationship was other than a high school crush. In later years, he considered her a good friend, nothing more.

A quick glance showed the time to be ten o'clock. If she called Anna, there would be plenty of time to meet her for lunch.

"Drat it!" she said aloud, startling into flight a black-capped chickadee who had perched on the windowsill, shopping among the insects for a mid-morning snack for the two chicks in the nest. "I just remembered Cat is supposed to come by for some of Grandma's work. I guess I can leave him a note on the door telling him to wait until Grandma and Rosebud return from clamming. They'll be home soon; the tide is coming in. Besides—" She giggled, covering her mouth in an uncanny duplication of Rosebud's similar reaction. "—the back door is open."

* * *

The boat broke smoothly through the waves, the seas no more than one to two feet high, creating a negligible spray even on the lower deck.

Neil was in a funk since having discovered they would be unable to ride in the bow of the boat, which was reserved as a lounge for first-class passengers.

"Maman, why didn't you reserve first-class tickets? That's the best part of the boat. I wanted Katie to see everything. Now we can only see what's on our right unless we keep moving from side to side."

"She can see the other side coming back. It's ridiculous to pay twice the price for a little boat ride like this. I have something important on my mind right now, Neil."

"I'm afraid to ask."

"I'll tell you anyway." Marguerite lowered her voice. "This article about Wilkinson. It claims he was photographed leaving Eastham police headquarters and then it goes on to repeat the story about Joy's death, Ethan's death, and so on. The reporter never mentioned that the windmill man was a private investigator from New Hampshire. If the reporter got this story from a police source, then Frank evidently is not pursuing the connection between my windmill man and Wilkinson."

"*Your* windmill man?" Neil's eyebrows arched almost to his hairline.

"I do feel some obligation to him. Remember the old saying that if you save someone's life you have a responsibility toward him?"

"When is he moving in?"

"Don't joke, Neil. I'm very concerned that Wilkinson's powerful connections will enable him to quash his involvement and let him get custody of Rosebud. Too bad the reporter didn't get the whole picture."

"Silly man," said Neil, hugging her shoulders affectionately. "He should have interviewed you."

There was a paucity of affection at Roberts Instruments on Thursday morning.

Red was in a ferociously bad humor, infecting the whole production unit with his distemper. Harboring the instinctive distrust of a blue-collar worker toward management, he was convinced he had been singled out as culpable in this crime. If they could not prove he stole the money, they would claim his procedures were faulty and blame him for the fraud having gone undetected for four years.

Either way, he was a loser with no options. He had limited educational background and no experience other than at Roberts. If they fired him, he would not even have a reference. Action being his chief form of expression, he banged boxes about and tongue-lashed anyone who dared approach him.

Leon Roberts was on the telephone with his travel agent. The trip to Europe must be postponed.

"What do you mean, some of it is nonrefundable? This is an emergency, a police matter!" he exploded in an uncharacteristic manner, indicative of the strain upon him. He paused to listen, then resumed shouting.

"The hotel can rent the room to someone else, some other fool who is willing to pay those exorbitant rates. Or they can cut the rate and offer it as a bargain, by shaving their markup to only two hundred percent. I wish I had that kind of a margin in my business."

The agent would do his best and call back later. Was Mr. Roberts certain he would not like to reconsider and go on the trip?

"Want to has nothing to do with this. I can't, I can't, I can't! My business is being stolen from under me and the police keep changing their minds about what happened. With all the taxes I pay I should get better service. And with all the business I give you, I should be able to get my money back. Just take care of it!"

Leon slammed down the phone and almost immediately broke into a grin. "I'm beginning to sound like James."

Trooper Stephen Fleming had begun his trek to Boston at seven-thirty in the morning and was at the first bank by nine o'clock in his now familiar quest to obtain an identification

of the elusive depositor. Same places, same questions, but he
had different pictures this time. Different shoes, too. He would
break in those new ones at another time—after the blisters
healed.

He had elected to reverse his route today, starting in Boston
and working his way back to the Cape. It was the wrong
decision, for it was in Braintree, the last stop of his revised
journey, that he got a positive identification.

Jeannie Browne, an employee at a mail drop, carefully studied the pictures he spread before her. She had previously failed
to recognize Ethan Quade, so she moved his picture aside and
concentrated on the others.

The pictures were duplicates of the set in the possession of
Detective Watson, with one addition, that of Doris Grimes.
Although she could not have entered the plant on a weekend,
she could have used Mrs. Lopes's typewriter during a lunch
hour with some excuse about hers being tied up or out of
order. As the individual who processed the new purchase orders, she was a suspect who could have been in collusion with
someone else.

After an endless time, actually only two minutes, she selected one and handed it to the trooper with conviction.

"That's the one. That's who I saw at the mailbox."

Fleming was excited and relieved. The lieutenant would
have to compliment him now. Medeiros had seemed dis-
pleased when the last trip had borne no results. This might get
Fleming a good report in his personnel file. He would investigate a little further.

"Can you remember when you saw him and what he was
doing?"

She could. About two weeks ago on a Saturday morning,
she had come out from the small office and walked into the
lobby where the boxes were situated in order to assist a new
subscriber who claimed his lock was jammed. It was. That
necessitated the selection of another box and the testing of
that lock.

As Jeannie had approached the client in need of assistance,
a man working the combination at an adjoining box, and wear-

ing a baseball cap with a long visor, visibly shrank at the sight of her. He turned away quickly and walked to a counter designed for customer use, where he stood with his back to her.

It was an exceptionally warm, humid day for June and the air conditioner in that room was pumping noise, but not cool air. The problems with the mailboxes took some time and the room was airless and suffocating. Carelessly, the otherwise stealthy man at the counter removed his cap to wipe the perspiration streaming from his head. Turning her head to speak with the frustrated new customer, Jeannie observed this action and the now uncovered head with the male pattern baldness tonsure at the back.

She saw more than that, too. The writing counter stood in front of a window on the outside of which had been placed a sign advertising new low rates. The dark back of the sign had turned the window into a mirror and Jeannie had a clear view of the man's full face, no longer shadowed by the baseball cap, clear enough for her to recognize him now.

"Would you show me the box this man was about to open?"

"Sure. It's right over here."

Fleming peeked through the small window and observed two letters in the box. When he asked if she would show him the letters, she balked. This was U.S. mail and she had no authority to give it to anyone but the addressee.

Fleming did not press her. He knew she was right. He would call Medeiros immediately and let him deal with the postal inspector and the warrants. Meanwhile, he would have lunch while the decisions were made and, from the restaurant across the street, watch the mail drop to be sure the suspect did not remove the mail which had become evidence.

Before leaving, he could not resist one final peek. Bending down, he was able to look up at the corner of one of the letters and, squinting into the dim light inside the box, could read the first three letters of the return address, a company letterhead.

They were ROB.

Chapter Sixteen

Nurse Patricia Nadeau monitored every blip and wave on the screens in the intensive care unit. With the patients wired like astronauts and the nurses' station resembling the flight deck of a spaceship, she felt more engineer than caregiver.

All the machines were beeping in concert. No dissonant sounds. It looked as if she might actually be able to go to lunch today.

A change in the pattern of lines emanating from the trauma patient alerted her, and she hurried to his bedside. His face was swaddled in bandages, but, for the first time since he entered on Monday, he was awake. The green eyes of Ralph Horton stared at her, confused, frightened, helpless.

Unable to talk because of a breathing tube and a wired jaw, he grimaced and moved his one free arm to his mouth and throat in an exploratory gesture. Patricia moved quickly to his right side to prevent him from displacing any of the wires or tubes and, as she held his arm, began to speak softly, informing him of where he was and attempting to allay his fear. Before she finished her explanation, his rudimentary recovery had exhausted itself, his eyes closed, and he lapsed again into unconsciousness.

Instructions on Horton's chart specified the measures to be taken if he regained consciousness: notify the doctor, notify the police. The doctor was in the building and easily located. The call to the police was easy, too. She dialed her own number.

Frank Nadeau was home today. As chief of police, he had the option of preparing his own work schedule and initially elected to be off weekends. That lasted about two months. In a resort area, most emergencies were clustered from Friday night to Sunday evening, with their frequency rising in direct correlation to the temperature. Frank switched his schedule to work weekends, and found it an advantage in the summer months when his Tuesdays and Wednesdays off allowed him to fish and golf on less crowded days.

The discovery of the windmill man on Monday had kept him at headquarters Tuesday and Wednesday. With the case now holding its breath awaiting the recovery of Horton, Frank took the day off. Nerves operating at high voltage, he rejected his usual leisure pursuits and roamed dispiritedly around the house.

A wasted morning behind him, he prepared lunch—a cold flounder sandwich on rye dabbed with tartar sauce. Reaching for a bottle of Sam Adams, he reconsidered and picked up a Diet Coke, a concession to his belt whose buckle had recently been forced to seek a new notch. Tall and trim, he refused to succumb to middle-age spread.

Munching his fish sandwich in rhythm to a violin concerto on the radio, he jumped when the phone rang and reflexively turned the radio knob, cutting off the violinist in mid stroke.

"Frank, it's Pat."

"How is Florence Nightingale today?"

"Looking for my lantern. It seems to have gotten lost among these computers."

"Touché. What's up?"

"Horton's up."

"When? Is he talking?" Frank lost all pretense of the casual air he had been feigning since Pat had warned him he was uptight.

"A few minutes ago. But only for a short while and he lapsed back. He didn't say anything but wouldn't have been able to because he has a breathing tube and his jaw is wired."

"He can write, can't he? His arms aren't broken."

"No, they're not, but he isn't able to do anything yet. I

don't know when he'll revive fully. The doctor is on his way to check him out. I just wanted to let you know he's improving."

Frank was considering the implications. "Pat, I'd like to keep this quiet. The man could be in danger. Does anyone else know about this?"

"The doctor does."

"Will this be on his chart?"

"Of course. But not many people see that. Only the people in this unit."

"Keep it as quiet as you can for now. Don't upgrade his condition at the front desk so if anyone calls the information will be the same. Is he still listed as critical?"

"Yes."

"Leave it that way. If the doctor has any questions about this situation, refer him to me. I'll talk to Medeiros. Maybe I can swing a guard for Horton. The hospital is out of my jurisdiction and the Barnstable police have no book on him. If I can convince Medeiros this is linked to the Quade case, I might get a man there."

"Frank, we don't want a policeman in here. Our patients are sick enough without being further upset by an armed guard."

"We can place him outside the door to the unit. I don't think we have to worry about anyone on staff being the culprit."

"Thanks for the vote of confidence. But you'll need to speak with the hospital director."

"Medeiros will, not me. One more thing, Pat. If anyone calls directly to the nurses' station making an inquiry about Horton, his improvement is not to be revealed. That goes for everyone except me or Medeiros. And be sure it's him you're talking to."

"Does that go for your friend, Marguerite, too?"

"Marguerite! What does she have to do with this?"

"She calls every day to inquire about him. She told me she has a responsibility toward him. Even sent him flowers so that if he wakes up he'll have something pleasant to look at. I didn't have the heart to tell her we don't allow anything in the room. She's so sweet.''

"Yeah, sweet, and sly too. She's dying to be involved. Don't tell her anything. This is too dangerous for a civilian, even a would-be sleuth. Another thing. Keep out any visitors until I talk to Medeiros and find out what he's going to do. I'll get back to you.''

"Yes, Chief,'' she answered in mock military fashion.

"One last thing, Pat. Don't go to lunch. Watch Horton until you hear from me.''

"Lunch? What's lunch?''

In another room of the same hospital, two floors and light-years away, reclined Louis Perry, reading the second section of the paper, the section which Marguerite had relegated to her coffee table. It would have interested her.

It certainly interested Louis. Sober and dried out on this, his fourth day in the hospital, with his blood sugar adjusted to a marginally acceptable level by frequent monitoring, he looked good. Until one noticed the tubes running from a shunt in his arm to a dialysis machine. Damage to the small blood vessels of the kidney, a degenerative complication of diabetes, had progressed to a point of near kidney failure. His drug arrest had saved his life—at least for the moment.

The prognosis was mixed. He would require dialysis treatment for the rest of his life unless he had a kidney transplant. A diabetic alcoholic with liver damage and a destructive lifestyle had little to no chance of receiving a donated kidney for which thousands of patients were competing. It was also unclear if he could summon the discipline required for a life dependent on regular dialysis and the accompanying restrictions as to diet, drinking, and smoking.

Confined to his chair by the umbilical tubes, he read the paper, front to back, to relieve the nervousness due to forced withdrawal from alcohol and nicotine. A small item in the second section, evidently received too late to make the first section, reported that there was a new development in the Ethan Quade case. An unnamed source revealed that a police

search of the house of Anna Pochet, the last person known to
have seen the victim alive, had uncovered a supply of hypodermic needles. No information was available as to whether
they were the same brand as the one which delivered the fatal
dose of fentanyl. The police would officially neither confirm
nor deny the report.

"Henry Lawrence, you have the right to remain silent," began
the uniformed officer, reading from a card which he extracted
from his pocket.

Henry's normally pale complexion was beyond pale now
and blanched of even a trace of life-giving hemoglobin.
Speechless, he buried his head in his hands as the officer
droned the rest of the warning familiarly called Miranda.
Henry had seen enough cop shows to know what happened
next. He was about to be arrested.

Warning completed, Henry raised his head and, summoning
his frail courage, managed a wan smile and ventured, "There
must be some mistake. It can't be me you're after. It was
Ethan. He was the one who robbed the company and he became frightened when I spoke to him about the fact that sales
were up but profits weren't keeping pace. He must have
known I would go to the Robertses. He knew how conscientious I was. That's why he committed suicide. Couldn't face
exposure. He was such a coward."

Refusing to engage in debate, and not wanting to jeopardize
the admissibility of any statements he might make at this time,
Detective Watson coolly informed him, "Mr. Lawrence, you
are under arrest. Please come with us." She signaled to the
uniformed officer.

As the handcuffs came out, the tears began. Unaccompanied
by sounds or sobs, they rolled down Henry's face, seeking the
low ground, overflowing the valleys between nose and cheeks,
the excess competing for space down the lateral sides of the
cheeks. Narrow shoulders drooped, spine crouched lower in
the chair, his body closed in on itself as if trying to become
invisible. In a tremulous voice, he finally spoke.

"I don't need the handcuffs. I'll come with you."

"It's procedure, Mr. Lawrence. No exceptions. Please stand."

Watson's authoritative voice caused Henry to respond as directed. The officer came around the desk, slapped on the handcuffs, and routinely patted him down for weapons.

As the little procession passed the offices of Leon and James Roberts, doors open as usual, the brothers, more alike than their temperaments indicated, reacted similarly. They sat agape as the handcuffed, tearful Henry passed their doors. Simultaneously, each reached over and knocked on the wall of his brother's office.

It seemed to take almost as long to exit the parking lot as it had taken the Hy-Line boat to return from Nantucket. Sun-weary, they longed to be out of this gridlock and into a cool, dark restaurant ordering an iced drink for their parched throats.

Everyone but Thomas, that is. Having slept during the nearly two-hour boat ride, he was full of vinegar, as Marguerite's father used to say in describing his own son.

Ever so slowly they crept forward and finally passed the traffic light on South Street that was creating the jam. At the intersection of Yarmouth Road and Route 28, as they waited for this final traffic signal to turn green, Marguerite noticed a familiar car which came from the opposite direction on Yarmouth Road and turned right, entering Route 28 in the direction of the rotary.

"Neil, quickly, turn left," Marguerite ordered excitedly.

"I thought we were having dinner in Orleans," objected Neil.

"We are, but first do this. Hurry, Neil! The light changed."

Neil shot out and turned left quickly without having signaled to the oncoming traffic, much to the consternation of the first driver in line, who made his displeasure known in a manner lacking elegance or subtlety. Neil assumed that his mother had suddenly remembered an errand in Hyannis, but that notion was soon dispelled as Marguerite leaned forward, pointing.

"See that silver Mercedes, three cars up? Follow it!"

Neil gulped. "Follow it? Are you crazy? Who's in that car?"

"Matthias Wilkinson, Rosebud's grandfather. I'm sure he is somehow involved in all these nefarious events. We have to get to the bottom of it."

"We don't have to do anything! That's why you pay taxes to have a police force."

"That's right, Neil, but the police aren't here now and we are. Don't let him get away! He's moving ahead."

Katie was smothering a laugh, not wanting to disconcert her already lathered husband. It escaped her best efforts at concealment and, amidst its gentle peals, she addressed Marguerite.

"Maman," she began, having adopted Neil's form of address as easier than saying Mother but warmer than saying Mrs. Smith, "Neil told me the Cape was the most peaceful, restful place in the world and we would get away from the stress of the city." She was laughing too hard to continue. Thomas, not understanding the reason for his mother's laugh, joined in anyway and added his joyful sounds to her half-suppressed ones.

Thus it was that two laughers, one seether, and one adventuress barreled down the road chasing a silver Mercedes.

"Neil, he's signaling to turn into that restaurant. Follow him but park at the opposite end of the lot. I'll duck down because he might remember me."

Stimulated by the chase, but averse to admitting it, Neil cruised by the Mercedes, pulled into a spot at the end of the lot, and positioned his car so that they could observe the pursued one. Then they waited.

Nothing happened. Matthias sat in his car and made no move to enter the restaurant. The Smiths felt exposed as four of them sat outside a restaurant, making no move to approach it. Thomas knew it was time to eat and was pushing the bar of his car seat, attempting release. Neil sat fuming at himself for having been so easily suckered into this; Katie continued chuckling; and Marguerite surreptitiously peeked through the car window from her position on the floor.

After ten minutes of this standoff, a woman drove her car into the driveway, stopped to survey the parking lot, then pulled into a spot two spaces away from Wilkinson. Marguerite, cramped from crouching down, stretched up a little further to watch. She sensed an ensuing climax to their chase.

The woman, smartly dressed in a short-sleeved, green linen two-piece dress, stepped out of her car and walked to the Mercedes. Her back was to Marguerite. After a brief exchange, Matthias got out of his car, carefully locked it, and walked with the woman toward the restaurant entrance.

"I can't believe it! I just can't believe it!" muttered Marguerite angrily.

Even with the large sunglasses, enough of the woman's flawless features were visible for Marguerite to recognize her.

"It's Esther's friend, Anna Pochet!"

Chapter Seventeen

An overnight stay in jail was not conducive to sartorial splendor. Particularly in the instance of Henry Lawrence, whose ensemble was notably lacking in splendor before incarceration. The synthetic fabrics he favored were laudable for their resistance to wrinkles, but notorious for their failure to breathe and their tendency to induce perspiration. In short, he stank.

Brought into the visitors' room at the jail early in the morning, he found a grim-faced Felicia waiting for him.

"Felicia, what are you doing here? I have to go to court this morning."

"I know you do. And were you planning to wear those disgusting clothes? And go without a lawyer?"

"I don't need a lawyer. Everything has been taken care of."

"What does that mean?"

"They told me if I confessed and agreed to make restitution, I would probably get off easy, maybe just probation. It wasn't much money and it's a first offense."

"And you confessed?" she asked incredulously.

"There was nothing else to do. They had the evidence. Some girl identified me at the mail drop. She saw the box I was opening. Even though I never went back, even for those letters, the cops managed to get permission to see who the letters were addressed to. They were two of the vendors I invented.

"Those stupid cleaning people messed me up, too, when

162

they switched the calendars. The police wouldn't have suspected me if they hadn't seen Ethan's notes to call H and notify police about H. I would have removed those pages if the calendar had remained on Ethan's desk where it belonged.''

''Henry, s-stop! S-stop saying these things!'' demanded an agitated Felicia.

''There's no use. The nosy watchman saw me in Ethan's office on Sunday when I was going through his files. I had told them I didn't have the keys for that file. It just happened that my keys fit his files. That's what started this whole mess. Ethan's keys worked on my files, too. When I was at the funeral last Friday, he needed some information on an order and when Doris couldn't find it he went into a special file of mine, one that Doris doesn't even have a key for, and found two new purchase orders for fake vendors with his forged signatures. I had typed those out on Thursday evening and would normally have given them to Doris to process next day, but I had to go to the funeral, so I couldn't leave them for her without my being there to control the distribution of the copies. She would have sent the pink slips to Red and the whole system would have fallen apart.''

Henry had lost the hangdog look with which he had entered. He was eagerly telling his story, bragging, trying to impress Felicia, anxious for her to acknowledge how clever he was. She was astonished at his frankness, but calm, in control of herself, speaking again in measured phrases.

''But, Henry, that's not much evidence. The identification at the mail drop could have been erroneous. Ethan's notes might have been referring to any one of a number of people whose names begin with H. You could have had a legitimate reason to check Ethan's files, perhaps the suspicion that Ethan was the one defrauding the company. The two orders in your file could have been planted by Ethan, whose key worked on that file. Come to think of it, how did you know he found those orders?''

''He called me on Friday, several times. Left messages that he had to speak to me about orders to certain vendors. I went

into the office Sunday because I knew he was dead and I could
take care of things. Those two orders from my file were on
his desk. I took them with me and destroyed them. I also
brought from home all the green and blue slips that would
have been in Ethan's possession if he had sent in the orders
and put them in his file. Luckily, I saved them in case something like this happened. The pink slips for all the completed
orders were already in the business office files as well as the
blue slips for the incomplete orders. I always made sure none
of those blue slips ever went back to Ethan after they were
stamped "Received" by handling that end of the operation
myself. I kept the phony pink slips at home until I was ready
to give them to Doris with Red's forged signature. Then she
would send the checks to the vendors at my mail drops. On
Sunday, I slipped three pink slips for outstanding fake orders
in Red's file and put the green slips for those orders in Ethan's
file. It was perfect." His pale eyes gleamed. His face was more
animated than Felicia had ever seen him.

"Perfect? Henry, you're in jail!"

"That's not my fault," he answered sharply. "If Ethan had
kept his nose out of my affairs this wouldn't have happened.
He had no right to go sneaking around behind my back. Those
files were private." Henry's voice was rising. "He was always
a thorn in my side. Got the job I should have had. I deserved
it. I had been with the company for years before he came
along with his Ivy League diploma and his Wall Street experience. We all know why he was hired and it wasn't because
he was smarter than me. I fixed him! I put his name on all
those orders. He would be the one in jail now if he hadn't
interfered. I was about ready to expose him."

For the first time in their three-year courtship, Felicia understood Henry. The mild-mannered, gentle underachiever
was a seething cauldron of hate and bitterness. She had un-
derestimated him. He was too bright not to have realized his
own shortcomings. Instead of addressing or correcting them,
he took the easy road and blamed his problems on others—
his mother, his classmates, his coworkers, and finally, cata-
strophically, on Ethan.

Felicia wanted to flee the room, but it would have been like abandoning a wounded fawn. She plunged on.

"Henry, they can't prove you put those papers in the file. Ethan could have put them there himself. As to his signature, he could have deliberately written it differently so it would appear forged if he was caught. You shouldn't have confessed."

"But they took my fingerprints. They are going to compare them with the ones on the papers. Only Doris's and mine will be there, not Ethan's."

"If he or someone else had done this, they could have worn gloves. Why didn't you request a lawyer? You had the right to one."

"I know. They told me that. But I thought it would just make things worse. All I want to do is give back the money and go home. I still have it all, you know. In a safe-deposit box. I didn't spend one cent. I really didn't need it," he finished proudly.

"Look, Henry, we have no more time to talk now. You have to get ready to appear in court. I stopped at your house and brought fresh clothes for you. I also brought a lawyer. He's waiting outside and will represent you this morning. He'll get you out on bail. Just listen to him and don't say anything more to the police."

"Which shyster did you get?" His contempt for lawyers stemmed from one experience at performing accounting work for an estate when he thought the lawyer had acted patronizingly toward him.

"No shyster. Arthur Bennington from Boston."

Henry gasped. "How do you think I can pay someone like that? His fees run into hundreds of thousands of dollars. I'd have to give him the stolen money." It was a rare and feeble attempt at a joke.

"He won't charge more than you can afford. He's been retained by my father."

"Your father! Who's your father?"

In his totally self-centered style, Henry had never inquired about Felicia's family or her job. He knew that she had a back office job at a hotel but had assumed she was a low-level staff member who entered charges in a computer. Wary of fortune hunters, Felicia had done nothing to disabuse him of this notion.

Standing up, gaining the advantage of towering over the seated figure, Felicia announced, "My father is Otis Murray. Haven't you ever heard of him? He's the biggest hotel and resort owner in the state. And that's only one of his businesses. You should have taken more interest in me, Henry. You could have married an heiress."

Joanne Parkinson, Eastham police dispatcher, put the call right through to the chief without asking questions. The caller had said the magic words Joanne knew the chief would like to hear.

"I have information about Matthias Wilkinson."

Frank had been sorting through the detested paperwork on his desk, giving each sheet a cursory glance before performing bureaucratic triage and assigning it to one of three piles— immediate attention, when he got to it, ignore. The news from the dispatcher energized him. He roughly pushed aside the papers, mingling the immediate with the ignore, to make room for a pad on which to take notes.

"Chief Nadeau speaking."

"I have some information for you on this Wilkinson guy."

"What is your name?"

"I can't tell you that. It's worth my job if I do. But I don't like to see people get away with things just because they're rich."

Frank hoped this was not a disgruntled employee of Wilkinson's trying to set up his boss, but plunged on anxiously.

"What is it you want to tell me?"

"I read in the paper that he was questioned by you so I thought you must suspect him of something. The story said he's been on the Cape since Sunday at the Sand Palace Motel."

"Do you know something different?"

"Yeah. I work at the Pleasant View Motel in Chatham. I

thought you would like to know that he stayed there on Friday and Saturday nights. Checked out Sunday about noon. You don't have to trace the call now. I just told you where I was calling from.''

The dial tone hummed. A red-faced Frank, who had been frantically reaching through his doorway and signaling to the officer in the outer room, placed the phone back in its cradle and rubbed his hands together gleefully.

''I knew we would get him if we waited.''

''Did you want me, Chief?'' blandly inquired David Morgan, the young officer who had been the recipient of Frank's incomprehensible signals to tape the call.

''I did, but I don't now. Yes, I do,'' he suddenly blurted as David started to walk away, wondering if the chief needed a vacation. ''Go over to the Pleasant View Motel in Chatham. I'll call police headquarters there to clear it for you. Take Wilkinson's picture from the newspaper and see if you can get a positive ID on him for Friday and Saturday nights. He supposedly left at noon Sunday. Check everyone—front desk, chambermaids, maintenance, pool attendant. Find out if any guests are still there who were there at the same time as he was. Question them. Ask to see his registration card and make a copy of it.''

David was feverishly writing in one of those little notebooks Frank detested. Using a variety of arty symbols to keep up with the rapid-fire commands, he hoped he would be able to decipher them.

An erstwhile artist, David had grudgingly applied for a job opening as a policeman after his floundering painting career presaged a hungry winter. To his surprise he was selected for the position and reluctantly accepted it, promising himself it was temporary. One year segued into the next and now, in his third year, David discovered he had a career, not just a paycheck. His love for painting had not cooled; it merely slipped one notch back in priority and sneaked to the fore in little ways like his eclectic notetaking or sketches of accident scenes suitable for framing.

''What are you waiting for?'' barked Frank. ''Get started.''

"Uh, Chief, where is the Pleasant View Motel located in Chatham?"

"You're a cop, Morgan. Find it!"

On this Friday morning, the gods must have decided to smile on police chiefs.

In Mashpee, Pedersen also received a telephone call, not an anonymous one, but an astonishing one. A hospital aide called at the behest of Louis Perry, who wanted to talk with a policeman. He had just remembered something. But he would not talk to Lloyd Odoms. They would have to send someone else.

Pedersen sent himself. It was a quiet morning in Mashpee. Store owners were hanging up the last of the bunting for Fourth of July; restaurant owners were checking the menus and the red, white, and blue iced cakes; and the children at breakfast were inquiring if this was the day for the fireworks. Mayhem awaited Friday evening: early evening for the onrush of weekend traffic and its resultant accidents; late evening for alcohol-induced fights, abuse, and the most serious road accidents.

Pedersen hated hospitals. Hated them even worse than jails. The criminals in jail put themselves there; the patients in hospitals were victims—victims of mortality. In vigorous health himself, the sights, sounds, and smells of a hospital floor made his flesh crawl. Maybe he should have sent someone else.

Too late. Here was Perry's room. Louis was seated in a chair next to the bed. Cleanly shaven, clad in a fresh hospital bathrobe, not hooked to or on anything at the moment, he looked good, certainly much better than the man Pedersen had seen cuffed and booked by Odoms last Sunday night. Only a nervous tapping of his foot and the restless movements of his hands betrayed his agitation at the multiple withdrawals forced upon his frail body.

"I must be more important than I thought. The big cheese himself came to see me," Louis wisecracked.

"What is it you have to say, Perry?" Pedersen remained standing, forcing Louis to look upward at him. It was not a position likely to inspire a cozy conference, but Louis's greeting had set the tone.

"I just remembered something about Friday night, you know, the night Quade OD'd. That's how come I'm in here, isn't it? Because I couldn't remember Friday night? That pet gorilla of yours, Odoms, he put me on ice."

"It looks to me like he did you a favor. Now what's on your mind that you suddenly remembered?" Pedersen asked impatiently.

"I remember going to Anna's house. Quade was leaving. I was upset and went into the house to see Anna. I was only there a couple of minutes."

"Just long enough to punch her."

"What do you expect me to do? That guy ruined my marriage."

"Get to the point, Perry."

"Well, as I said, I didn't stay long. When I came out, Quade pulled away. I don't think he saw me go into my wife's house."

"Ex-wife," Pedersen corrected. "Did you follow him?"

"Me? That's why you got here so quick, wasn't it? You're ready for a deathbed confession. Sorry to disappoint you, but I ain't dying and I ain't confessing."

"So you're just confirming Anna's story that Ethan left her house."

"No, I got more. I didn't follow him but someone else did. There was a car parked in front of the house next to Anna's. It was there when I came but it looked like no one was in it. I pulled in front of it. When I was leaving the house and Quade pulled away, the motor in that car started and I noticed a man in it. He must've been crouched down before. He pulled out right after Quade but stayed a little way back."

Pedersen's interest was piqued. He pulled up a chair, placed it directly in front of Louis, and leaned forward to look him right in the eyes.

"Could you see the man?"

Louis smiled. He had hooked this big fish, despite his hard nose. "No, I couldn't."

Pedersen frowned. This sounded like a convenient memory, one designed to get Louis out of jail and Anna into his debt.

"But I sussed the car." Louis dangled his new bait.

"What kind was it?"

"A white Grand Am, new looking. And I got the first three numbers on the plate."

"What are they? Don't hold back information!" sputtered Pedersen.

"Six one six. That's all I could see because he didn't put his lights on right away. Not till he was on the road. A car came behind him with lights but all I could read was the first three numbers."

"You're sure it was a man?"

"Yeah, I'm pretty sure of that. He had a man's short hair-cut. I couldn't see his face though."

"I'm going to have someone type this up and bring it back for you to sign."

"What's the matter? You afraid I'm gonna die?"

"No, I'm afraid you're going to have memory failure again."

As Pedersen lifted his long frame from the short chair, Louis had a question for him. "This gets Anna off the hook, doesn't it?"

"What makes you think she's a suspect?"

"I can read, that's what! You searched her house."

"Yes, but maybe she wasn't the one we were looking for."

Pedersen smiled enigmatically and left, hoping he hadn't said too much to scare Perry away from signing that statement.

He wondered if it was inevitable that big men had big mouths.

Joanne was not sure whether to put this call through to the chief. She diplomatically said she would see if he was avail-able and put the caller on hold. Buzzing through to his office, she announced the call.

"Chief, Marguerite Smith is on the line. She says she has important information. Should I tell her you're busy?"

"No, it's no use. She would just be down here at my door with a ham or something. Wouldn't have much trouble getting by you, either."

The embarrassed dispatcher protested, "Chief, I never—" but didn't finish her excuse because he ordered, "Put her through."

"*Ça va,* Marguerite?"

"*Bien,* François, *très bien.* And I have some news for you," she continued.

"Pray tell."

"I was with my family in Hyannis yesterday in late afternoon. We had just come back from Nantucket."

"Why were you in Nantucket?"

"*On prend les vacances.* One takes a vacation. Anyway, as we were driving, I spotted Matthias Wilkinson's Mercedes and saw it pull into a restaurant parking lot." Marguerite shaved the few minutes of the chase from her story. "We went into the same parking lot and, after pulling over, saw someone else come into the lot, park near him, and join him." She now shaved the ten-minute waiting period in the parking lot from her narrative. "Guess who it was?"

"I give up. Tell me."

"Anna Pochet."

"Are you sure?" Frank's attention was engaged. He had been kept advised of the Quade case and knew her connection to it. "How do you know her?"

"I was at the funeral—both of them—the one when Ethan was found and the one when he was buried. I couldn't help but notice her. She's so striking looking even with the sunglasses. And she was so sad. At Ethan's funeral, she was the only one of those four women to wear black. I know it was her with Wilkinson. She was even wearing the same shape sunglasses."

"Have you told anyone about this?"

"No one except my family. They were with me."

"Don't breathe a word of this to anyone. Tell your family

the same thing. This is a murder investigation. And, Marguerite, keep out of it. Don't go asking questions on your own. It could be dangerous.''

"Moi?" she asked innocently. "Would I ever do anything like that? *Bonne chance,* François!''

Chapter Eighteen

Henry was jubilant. He had been released on ten thousand dollars' bail, thanks to his ingenuity in confessing and agreeing to make restitution. He was a first offender, not violent or dangerous, and had roots in the community. The details of the final deal would be worked out between the district attorney and that fancy lawyer of Felicia's. Turning from the judge's bench with a self-congratulatory expression, he searched the benches for Felicia. Unable to locate her, he turned to his lawyer and crowed, "I told you I worked it all out."

Arthur Bennington was less sanguine about the outcome. He had pleaded with Henry to let him fight the fraud case and attack the confession as having been coerced and Henry's right to an attorney abrogated. Henry's naïveté about the mechanics of the law, and his refusal to look beyond the embezzlement to the myriad ramifications of his confession, placed him in jeopardy.

Bennington suspected that the fraud case was only the beginning of Henry's troubles. With a signed confession, attested to in court, the police now had a suspect with a motive for murder. That they had made no move in this direction was camouflage. They would want to put this nail firmly in place before swinging the hammer again.

During the hearing, Bennington furtively searched the small courtroom for uniformed officers. None in sight except the usual contingent of guards and the officer with Detective Watson. Clever!

As Henry cockily strode through the courtroom doors, his customary stooped posture a degree more vertical, and with Bennington behind him, Medeiros stepped forward, a state trooper at his side, and confronted Henry.

"Henry Lawrence, we are taking you in for questioning in the murder of Ethan Quade." Turning to the trooper, he ordered, "Read him his rights."

Bennington sighed.

Henry protested feebly, "I'm not a murderer. I'm a law-abiding citizen."

Frank Nadeau reviewed his strategy as he contemplated the interrogation soon to begin. David Morgan had received several positive identifications of Matthias Wilkinson, who had indeed been on the Cape since Friday night.

The ease with which he had been identified puzzled Frank. Would a man contemplating a near deadly assault, perhaps even a murder, leave himself so open to identification? Or had he not expected to commit any crimes when he first arrived on the Cape? Or perhaps he had calculated that his best defense was his undisguised person and truthful motel registrations. His mere presence on Cape Cod was not indicative of criminal activity. Though he had been less than candid with Frank about when he had arrived on the Cape, he had not lied but had cleverly finessed that question by confirming when he had checked into the Sand Palace Motel. Frank had missed this nuance and harshly criticized himself for his mistake. He was glad no one had been listening.

Wilkinson had been scheduled to appear at headquarters at two o'clock. Frank had granted a delay at Wilkinson's request because he wanted to contact a lawyer. There was nothing to be gained in denying this request. Without a lawyer, Wilkinson would refuse to talk at all.

The two-o'clock deadline had been Frank's bottom line. However, he had assumed that Wilkinson would be late, not due to unforeseen circumstances, but deliberately late. It was a tactic employed by powerful men to impress and subordinate.

Frank knew the game; he played it himself. Consequently, he had instructed Joanne that if Wilkinson and his lawyer came in later than five minutes after two o'clock, they were to be informed that the chief was in conference and they were to wait. The pair leisurely arrived at two-thirty and, despite protests, were instructed to wait.

At two-forty-five, Frank opened his door and waved them into his office. Sergeant Patterson was already seated and a tape recorder was visible on the desk.

Michael Leone, the attorney recommended to Simon Wagner by a New Hampshire colleague, and dressed for a postponed afternoon of sailing, walked in confidently and shook hands with the two policemen, much to the chagrin of Wilkinson.

Michael was in a good mood. Although his afternoon had been free of appointments at the start of this holiday weekend, he had played hard-to-get when Simon called. Detecting anxiety in Simon's voice and recognizing the name of the client, he decided to cash in on this emergency. The price of canceling his fictitious appointments in order to accompany Wilkinson was a thousand-dollar bonus on top of his usual hourly fee. Simon was the wily victor; he was prepared to offer two or three times that amount.

There was no handshaking with Wilkinson. He sat down without invitation and waited sullenly for this unwelcome intrusion into his personal life. Frank wasted no time and, after advising him of his rights, confronted Wilkinson aggressively.

"Mr. Wilkinson, you have been on Cape Cod since last Friday night, June twenty-fifth, and stayed at the Pleasant View Motel on Friday and Saturday nights. Is that correct?"

Without even looking at his lawyer, Wilkinson answered, "That's correct."

Frank suppressed the natural follow-up question as to why he had not admitted that when first questioned, knowing Wilkinson would answer that he had not been asked. Saving face, he jumped ahead.

"That means you were on the Cape the night your son-in-law was murdered."

"It is my understanding that he took an overdose of drugs, either accidentally or to commit suicide because he was a swindler about to be uncovered." Wilkinson sidestepped the question.

"It is not your understanding that counts—it's ours. Please answer the question."

Wilkinson glanced at Michael, who nodded. The police already knew he was on the Cape.

"I was in Chatham on Friday night."

"What was the purpose of your being in Chatham?"

"I was vacationing like all the other tourists in Chatham. I might even buy a place there for the summer."

"But you left Chatham on Sunday morning and checked into a motel in Eastham. Why?"

Michael was still pondering his advice on this question, when Wilkinson answered, "As you well know, my granddaughter lives in Eastham. I wanted to see her."

"And forcibly take her with you?"

"My client denies any use of force," declared Michael pompously.

"I assumed I had custody after her father died. My lawyer later informed me that I was mistaken and had to apply for legal custody. He has been instructed to prepare the papers. I have not been near her since then."

Frank could understand why this man had been so successful. He admitted what it was fruitless to deny but put his own spin on it. Frank resumed.

"How did you know her father was dead?"

"It wasn't a secret. It was in the papers."

"Had you been informed of this death earlier, perhaps as early as Saturday, by Ralph Horton?"

Wilkinson was quiet, indicating by the set of his jaw that he declined to answer.

"We know that Horton telephoned you twice at your home in New Hampshire."

"When do you claim he called?"

"On Saturday."

Wilkinson threw up his hands in disgust.

"You know I was not home on Saturday. I was here. This business has nothing to do with me." He began to stand.

"Sit down!" barked Frank. "I'll tell you when to leave," he announced in a harsher tone than was usual for him. He had to gain control of this interview. "We made some other checks. You placed a few phone calls to New Hampshire yourself on Saturday. Foolish of you to use the motel phone. It seems you have an answering system to which you gain access by telephone. That's why Horton's calls were so brief. He never spoke to you. He just left messages which you later picked up by telephone."

"You can suppose whatever you want. The fact that I collected my messages proves nothing. I'm an important businessman. I keep in touch with my office."

"You called your personal line, not the business line you have in your house. Where were you on Sunday night when Ralph Horton was attacked?"

"In my motel room," he answered, despite Michael's signals to him.

"Where were you on Friday night when Ethan Quade was murdered?"

"In my motel room." Michael was furiously signaling.

"For a rich man on vacation, you spend a lot of time in your motel room. Can you prove any of this?"

Michael Leone was nervous, very nervous. This was much heavier than he had expected and he had a client who was ignoring him. He had to stop this interrogation.

"Chief, my client refuses to answer any more questions." That should give him time to figure out how to handle them—the case and the client. And to demand a bigger retainer.

Wilkinson reconsidered also. He knew these small-town cops. They would love to collar a prize like him on a murder charge. It would guarantee them a lot more publicity than drug dealers or wife beaters. He decided to take the initiative, having assessed shrewdly that this lawyer was over his head and would not get a cent from him. He would feed this cop a little information, enough to divert him.

In a belligerent tone, with his icy unblinking eyes fixed on the chief to exercise control, Matthias began his statement.

"I'm going to say this only once, so be sure that toy is turned on," he commanded, indicating the tape recorder. "I employed Ralph Horton as a private investigator to assure myself whether or not my granddaughter was in a suitable environment. As you are aware, her father had a sleazy history and he induced my daughter to take drugs resulting in her untimely death. I did not intend to let my granddaughter meet the same tragic fate."

Wilkinson paused with a catch in his voice. He shook it off and continued.

"Horton was observing Ethan Quade's life-style."

"You mean he was tailing him," interrupted Frank. He wanted no misinterpretations on the transcript of this statement.

"If you are more comfortable with police jargon, have it your way. In any event, he observed Quade going into a bar on Friday evening and noted that he was drinking heavily. Knowing that I was interested in such character flaws, he phoned me at home."

With a mirthless laugh, he said in an aside to Frank, "There's a call you missed, Chief." Frank ignored the jibe.

"Since it was only about seven o'clock when he called, I decided to go to the Cape myself and contacted a motel in Chatham for a reservation. It only takes a few hours in my Merc."

"At the legal speed limit, I assume?" asked Frank.

Seizing the opportunity to speak, Michael warned Wilkinson, "You should not be talking. You don't have to say anything."

"Shut up, you fool! You're fired!"

That made Frank uneasy. "Mr. Wilkinson, you have the right to an attorney. Are you voluntarily giving up that right?"

"You just heard me, didn't you? Stop interrupting and let me finish. When I arrived at the motel, I dialed Horton's motel but he wasn't there. I called my answering service and there was a message from him that Quade and a woman were about to leave the bar and he would follow them. He said he would call me Saturday to report. I decided to leave it at that and not let him know I was on the Cape because I didn't want him hanging around me. He's not the type of person I associate with.

"Saturday afternoon I picked up two messages from him. On the first one he said he had to talk with me; on the second he told me Quade was dead under strange circumstances. I located him Saturday evening at his motel and he said he had stopped watching the woman's house about eleven o'clock Friday night but went back Saturday afternoon and heard from someone in Mashpee that Quade was found dead in an open grave and drugs were suspected. That was my last contact with Horton."

"Did he say who told him?" queried Frank.

"No, he didn't, and I never asked. This was exactly the type of ending I expected for that bum. I knew I had to take Rose away from here, but I decided to wait until the death was announced in the papers."

"I guess you didn't want to admit to your undercover activities," suggested Frank. Wilkinson shrugged and continued.

"Sunday morning I checked out of the motel and went to one in Eastham. I read about Quade's death. I considered my options and decided that I had the strongest claim to custody and that the best thing for Rose was for me to take her right out of that hovel."

Frank was not amused at this slur on the Quade house, as his was of much the same design, but he refrained from commenting.

"I went to the house and you know the rest. That crazy woman kept screaming at me, then some busybody demanded to know who I was, then I was attacked by an old hippie with a ponytail. My lawyer, my *real* lawyer," he stressed with a sidelong glance at Michael, "is arranging for me to have legal custody of Rose."

Wilkinson sat back, relaxed now that he had clarified and justified his role, convinced he had put an end to this police

harassment. He was mistaken. The chief was not the simpleton
he had thought him to be.

"Very interesting story, Mr. Wilkinson, and I appreciate
your cooperation."

Wilkinson smiled at Frank in his best noblesse oblige manner. Frank resumed his interrogation in a folksy manner.

"We could straighten this whole thing out and let you go
on your way if you would just answer a couple of more questions. What time did you say it was when you checked into
that motel on Friday night?"

"About eleven o'clock," Wilkinson answered civilly.

"And where were you between eleven o'clock that night
and three o'clock Saturday morning?"

Wilkinson exploded, chopping the air with his hands as he
spoke. "You dumb cluck! Do you still think I'm involved
with Quade's death? This is slander! This is libel! I'll have
that badge taken away from you. I had nothing to do with
Quade's death, or even his life. The less I saw him or any of
his family or any of his friends, the better I liked it."

Michael Leone threw up his hands in despair and wished
he were anywhere but here. He hoped he would not be reported to the bar association for failing to properly advise his
client. It would be the second complaint.

"You are certainly entitled to associate with anyone you
want to," remarked Frank patiently. "It's a free country.
However, one thing puzzles me. Since you have such a strong
aversion to the Quades and their friends, why did you have
dinner on Thursday night with Anna Pochet?" Checkmate.

There was no predictability to police work. One day an investigation seemed dead in the water; the next day something
broke loose and the case was resuscitated.

The Quade case was coming to life. One of its weak-
nesses had been lack of a compelling motive for murder.
Now they had a bona fide suspect with a strong motive.
Henry Lawrence had confessed to stealing company money,
and Ethan Quade had uncovered the fraud and was about to
reveal it on Monday, according to his calendar. He was

murdered before he could implicate Henry, who then used the weekend to plant papers incriminating Ethan, and promptly uncovered the fraud on Monday.

Henry had motive and opportunity. By his own admission, confirmed by Felicia, he had left her house about midnight, leaving plenty of time to commit a murder which could have occurred as late as two-fifteen, even two-thirty in the morning if Anna's story was true.

But Medeiros hesitated to charge him with the murder. Too many questions were unanswered. Where did Henry obtain the syringe and the fentanyl at such short notice? He had only become aware of Ethan's suspicions at about seven o'clock Friday night when he listened to his phone messages and had spent the remaining hours until midnight with Felicia. His story of attending a funeral in Connecticut checked out.

If Henry had killed Ethan early Saturday morning, why retain the incriminating purchase orders in his home and two newly typed ones in his file at the office until Sunday?

How did he know where to find Ethan when Ethan himself did not know he would meet Anna and leave the bar with her? She claimed he made no phone calls while with her. If Ethan had called Henry after leaving Anna at twelve-thirty, that left very little time to arrange such a complicated murder.

Unless Felicia was involved herself and they were providing alibis for each other. The complications inherent in bringing Otis Murray's daughter into this case gave Medeiros a headache.

Henry himself was of no assistance, either to his defense or prosecution. Mostly he just cried. Too late he understood what Arthur Bennington had predicted. He was less cavalier now about wanting Bennington's counsel.

But Bennington was not to be found. Otis Murray objected to his personal lawyer defending a suspected murderer who might be linked in the press with Otis's daughter. Fraud, Otis understood; murder, no. Bennington withdrew from the case with the explanation that he had no experience in murder cases.

To Medeiros, this case did not seem right. Something was

still missing. When he returned to his office from the jail, a message awaited him to call Chief Pedersen immediately.

"Walter, Al Medeiros here."

"Where have you been? I called you this morning."

"In court and questioning Henry Lawrence. Mostly wasting time, I think."

"Well, some of us have been productive. Louis Perry regained his memory. Chivalry isn't dead. When he read the piece in the paper about us searching Anna's house, he wanted to talk to someone."

"What did he say? Did he do it?"

"Not according to him. But he saw Ethan pull away from Anna's house and a car that had been parked outside pulled after him with lights out. It was driven by a man and was a white Grand Am with a Massachusetts plate beginning six one six. Familiar?"

"It sure is. This is beginning to make sense. That nerd Lawrence is larcenous but not murderous. He just doesn't fit. Did you get a signed statement?"

"Absolutely. The officer just returned with it. Got it on tape, too."

"Good work. Thanks, Walt."

Medeiros had barely begun to mull this development when he realized that he still had a loose end. If Horton had murdered Ethan, who had attacked Horton? Perhaps he would never recover enough to tell them. Another phone call interrupted his musings.

"Al, Frank Nadeau."

"This is my lucky day. Two chiefs in a row."

"It may be luckier than you think. Wilkinson just left and he told us plenty. He finally admitted to hiring Horton. Claims he wanted Horton to discover something to use against Ethan Quade in order to get custody of the granddaughter. Horton left a message that he followed Ethan to a bar on Friday night and that Ethan was leaving with a woman. Said he was going to follow them to see where they were going."

"Don't stop now! You've got me salivating," cried Medeiros.

"Horton told Wilkinson they went to the woman's house and he waited outside for a couple of hours but the lights went out and he assumed they were there for the night so he left about eleven o'clock. When he came back to Mashpee on Saturday to check out the woman, he heard about Ethan's death and called Wilkinson."

"Then Wilkinson came to the Cape to grab his granddaughter," Medeiros surmised.

"Wrong," corrected Frank, pleased to have one more surprise for Al. "Wilkinson was already on the Cape. He checked into the Pleasant View Motel in Chatham at eleven o'clock Friday night."

Medeiros rearranged in his head the pieces of the puzzle before he responded.

"Frank, we have a big lie in here somewhere. Perry claims Horton was outside Anna's house at twelve-thirty and followed Ethan. Wilkinson claims Horton said he left Anna's house at eleven o'clock. The key to this, Horton, hasn't been able to tell us anything."

"No, but he soon will be, according to Pat. Maybe even by Saturday or Sunday."

Medeiros had the puzzle almost completed; just one piece remained to be added, one very fragile piece.

"Frank, remember that request you made for a policeman outside the intensive care unit? He's on his way."

Chapter Nineteen

Marguerite's blender whirred as she spoke to Katie over the noise.

"It's hard to blend in the beginning. You have to keep stopping the motor to loosen the fish until it's all broken up."

Katie was the attentive recipient of a lesson in the utilization of Atlantic salmon, a favorite of local smokehouses. On Friday nights, Marguerite played bridge and tonight the rotating game was at her house. Smoked salmon pâté was to be the only homemade refreshment. Finger sandwiches and a cake had been ordered from the bakery. Marguerite deferred to the experts.

"Now that the mixture is fairly smooth, I'll add a little more cream cheese to get it to the consistency I want, and some softened butter, too."

Katie winced. She hoped Neil was not going to eat this pâté. The spareribs he had on the grill for dinner had more than enough fat for today. Unperturbed, Marguerite continued.

"Now some sherry and seasonings. In summer, I use whatever herbs are growing in the garden. I snipped some chive and some dill for this batch. That should do it." Marguerite tasted it with satisfaction.

"Try it, Katie."

Politely, Katie complied and was amazed at the delightful, heady taste of this spread. Perhaps Neil could have a little of it. Maybe she could, too.

As Marguerite scooped the pâté into a serving bowl, the phone rang and Katie answered it.

"Maman, it's for you. It's Rosebud. She seems very excited."

Marguerite picked up the phone. "Rosebud, is something wrong?"

"Yes, it's Grandma Sunny. She fell down and can't move."

"Is your Aunt Esther there?"

"No, she left to go to her apartment in Mashpee to pick up some clothes. She's not there yet. I called."

"Listen carefully, Rosebud. Stay by your grandmother. Don't try to move her. I'm going to call the emergency squad, then I'll come right over. Try to be calm."

After giving the ambulance dispatcher specific locator directions, Marguerite ran headlong out of the house and down the road to the Quade place. An ambulance arrived as she reached the path to the back door.

It appeared to be a stroke. Sunny was conscious but could not raise herself and was having difficulty speaking. The crew made a quick check of her respiration and pulse, then placed her on a stretcher for the trip to the hospital in Hyannis.

Marguerite asked Rosebud for Esther's number in Mashpee and dialed it. Breathlessly, Esther answered. Quickly assessing the situation, she told Marguerite she would drive immediately to the hospital and to pass this information to the ambulance crew so they could inform the admissions office of such if the ambulance arrived first. She implored Marguerite to prevent Rosebud from going in the ambulance and to take care of her. Marguerite sympathetically agreed.

Rosebud watched the procedures of the EMTs with mournful sobs. She was sure her grandmother was dying. Sunny noted Rosebud's grief and, as she was carried out of the house with Rosebud trailing, attempted a smile for her. Only one side of her mouth moved, resulting in a crooked expression more tortured than tender. Rosebud hid her face in her hands.

A small cluster of neighbors had gathered, attracted by the flashing lights. Thanking them for their offers of assistance, Marguerite put her arm around Rosebud's shoulders and they walked back into the house. Marguerite let her cry until her tears were exhausted, a catharsis of mind and body. As she became quieter, Marguerite reviewed with her the plans she had been mentally organizing.

"Rosebud, I think I should stay here with you tonight instead of us both staying at my house because your aunt is supposed to call here to let us know how your grandmother is."

Marguerite remembered her bridge game but hid from Rosebud the inconvenience of rearranging it. Besides, she had an idea about how to resolve that.

"Let's walk over to my house so I can pick up my night clothes and tell everyone where I'll be staying."

Rosebud valiantly produced a weak smile and said, "Thank you, Mrs. Smith."

As they left the house through the back door, Marguerite asked, "Rosebud, is there a key for this door?"

"Yes, in the kitchen drawer next to the sink."

"Let's lock it. There are all women living here and it would be safer for you to keep it locked."

The key located, they locked the door and left, holding hands as they walked.

The smell and smoke of barbecued spareribs greeted them as well as the outthrust arms of Thomas, who ran down the driveway happily squealing, "Gramma, Gramma."

The playful toddler distracted Rosebud from her sadness long enough to tempt her to eat some of the food placed in front of her at the outdoor table. Marguerite ate and issued directions without missing a beat.

"I'm going to stay at Rosebud's tonight. Neil, you're a wonderful bridge player; you can take my place. It would be too complicated to change houses now. Katie, when we're finished, you can pick up the sandwiches and cake I ordered so Neil can wait here in case anyone comes early. You know how old folks are, always early. I'll take Rusty with me so she won't bark at everyone. And, Neil, watch Laura Eldredge. She cheats." Marguerite paused to select another rib.

"How do you know she cheats?"

"She must. Laura wins too often for someone who has no card sense, no feel for the table."

Neil suspected that Laura and his mother vied for the role of best player, but wisely kept his thoughts to himself.

A low muttering of thunder sounded in the background. Rusty, indifferent as a clam to most weather, stood up, perked her ears, dropped her tail, and headed for the door into the house. She was terrified of thunderstorms.

Marguerite greeted the thunder with relief. The days had been uniformly bright, blue, and sunny—chamber of commerce weather. Ardent sunbeams daily caressed the flowers in her garden but the lack of rain had bowed their beautiful crowns.

A race to clear the table began. Rosebud joined in the effort. Thomas grabbed his teddy bear and carried it to safety. Laughing and with total disorder, they managed to escape without a drenching.

Lightning flashed in the evening sky from zenith to horizon. The thunder was steady, like cannonading. Rain poured down so heavily the gutters could not handle it and water poured over their sides, obscuring the view from the windows.

It was just as well. The wind had picked up fiercely and the trees were swaying, some perilously close to the house. They were spared the sight.

Rusty hid under a table. Thomas clapped his hands over his ears and tried to induce Rosebud to follow suit. The adults gritted their teeth and steeled themselves against showing fear in front of the children.

Suddenly it was over. Like an eraser cleaning a slate, the fast-moving storm was cleared from the sky, west to east, by the gusty winds that propelled it belligerently out to sea, firing parting shots as it retreated. The sky seemed bluer than ever, the air fresher. Flowers were bent almost to the ground as if in obeisance to Thor, god of thunder.

Marguerite gathered the few things she would need for the night and emitted further directions.

"It's so wet out, why don't you drive us to Rosebud's house, Katie, and pick up the food on the same trip?"

Leaving Neil to sort out the chaos in the kitchen, the three women, Thomas, and the dog piled into the car and pulled out of the driveway. A small tree had fallen on the side road, blocking their access to the main road. Katie looked at Marguerite questioningly and was advised to turn around and drive the opposite way down the dirt road and to circle the block.

Marguerite and Rosebud entered the empty house and began mopping up windowsills and floors drenched from the storm. In Grandma Sunny's room, Marguerite saw, hanging on the closet door, a small buckskin dress with fringed bottom and sleeves, and beautiful beaded designs. A matching pair of moccasins sat nearby on the floor. As Marguerite fingered the soft material of the dress, Rosebud appeared at the door.

"That's my dress for the powwow. Grandma Sunny beaded it for me. I was supposed to dance in the girls' fancy dance. Aunt Esther has been taking me for lessons. I guess I won't be able to go now." She lowered her eyelids.

"Maybe you will," Marguerite consoled her. "Your grandmother was conscious so she may not be seriously ill. You might be dancing yet."

"It's all right if I don't. Daddy always told me not to let my *wuttah*"—Rosebud placed her hand on her heart—"rule my *wuttip*"—then on her head, translating with gestures. "Those are Wampanoag words."

"Did your father speak Wampanoag?"

"Not really; hardly anyone does anymore. But when he was at Dartmouth he became interested in the language and culture and learned a lot of the words."

Marguerite continued mopping and reached for the windowsill behind Sunny's worktable. The table was covered with an array of glass beads, each size and color with its own compartment in one of several clear plastic trays; with beads shaped from clamshells, only roughly finished and with no holes as yet, most of them purple, a few white; and with the simple hand tools Sunny had been given as a young girl and still used. The center front of the table contained papers on which Sunny had been working. The wind from the open window had scattered them and some sheets were on the floor.

Marguerite was attracted to the design of the paper, as it resembled graph paper and reminded her of her past struggles to instill in science students the techniques and principles of graphing. But this was not traditional graph paper, which had a grid of perfect squares. This paper was scored in small rectangles with blocks comprising ten spaces across and six down. One sheet had a partially completed design which Sunny had been creating by filling in the rectangles with colored pencils.

So this is how she creates a design, thought Marguerite.

Bending down to pick up the fallen papers, she discovered among the blank pages some photographs of a magnificent beaded belt. There were two pictures showing the entire belt, front and back, and many enlarged pictures of specific areas that revealed the intricate beadwork.

Comparing the belt with the work on the unusual graph paper, Marguerite noted that Sunny had been transferring this design to paper, bead by bead. She was not creating a design, she was copying one. Surprised but not unduly so, Marguerite assumed that designs were traditional and frequently reused.

The telephone ring drew her attention and she heard Rosebud talking to her aunt, looking cheerful as she returned to the bedroom.

"It's good news, Mrs. Smith. Grandma had a stroke but not a serious one and is expected to recover. Aunt Esther would like to stay there tonight if it's okay with you."

Nodding her agreement, Marguerite went back to sopping up the water on the floor and placed the photographs on the desk.

Work completed, she and Rosebud sat in the beautiful living room and Rosebud, relieved about her grandmother, began to talk. She spoke of her grandmother and her aunt but, mostly, of her father. Marguerite remained quiet and let Rosebud reminisce in a stream of consciousness. She had restrained herself all through this terrible week and now unleashed her thoughts and memories.

Finally she was through; the exorcism had tired her. She leaned against Marguerite and soon fell peacefully asleep. Marguerite waited until she was sure Rosebud was soundly asleep, then, with arms strengthened by gardening, lifted and carried her to bed. She removed the chunky shoes and put a summer blanket over her.

Tiptoeing from Rosebud's room, Marguerite went into Sunny's room and picked up the photographs. Something in the pictures had belatedly struck a memory chord, a disturbing one. She selected the two photographs of the entire belt to study more closely. Just as she had remembered, there was a white rectangle visible in the lower right-hand corner of the pictures. Not wearing her glasses, Marguerite picked up Sunny's magnifier to examine the pictures more clearly. There were numbers at the top of the rectangle and what appeared to be writing beneath them that she was unable to decipher.

It was getting dark and Marguerite had not turned on any lights. Desiring to study the photographs in greater detail, she returned to the living room, retrieved her eyeglasses from her purse, and sat down on the welcoming, though firm, sofa, enjoying the restful darkness that made no demands on her senses. Lulled by the companionable quietness, she rested in the dark pondering the events of the day, loath to turn on the lights and risk uncovering a secret she did not wish to know.

Suddenly Rusty stood up, growled softly low in her throat, and twitched her ears. A frisson ran through Marguerite. She usually ignored Rusty, who growled at a myriad of sounds—animals, falling twigs, motorcycles—but Marguerite's nerves were on edge and the dog's behavior frightened her and alerted her drowsing senses. She was glad she had insisted on locking the back door, but most of the windows were open with the screens affording flimsy protection.

Rusty growled again. Then Marguerite smelled it. Gas! Seeping through the house! Maybe Sunny had left a gas jet on before she was stricken. Marguerite ran toward the kitchen but was knocked off her feet by an explosion. Dazed, but unhurt, she struggled to her knees and, accompanied by a furiously barking Rusty, crawled the short distance to the kitchen.

A fire blazed on one side of the room. The wall behind the stove had a gaping hole and the stove itself was blackened and ruptured, with the oven door hanging open and askew, attached by only one hinge. The kitchen was replete with flammables—curtains, dried-out wallpaper, old wooden cabinets, table, and chairs—and the fire was sending out great licks of flame testing for areas of vulnerability.

Rusty whimpered and cringed on the floor. Marguerite grabbed her collar and backed out, still crawling, pulling the dog who was unhurt but immobilized by fear.

Although the fire was limited as yet in scope, smoke was filling the air and escaping the kitchen to spread its breath-robbing haze throughout the house. Marguerite's first thought was of Rosebud. That blast must surely have awakened her, yet she made no sound nor had she come from her room to see what had happened.

Luckily, Rosebud's bedroom was the room furthest from the kitchen. Moving quickly but carefully, Marguerite stayed low to the ground as she had practiced with thousands of students, instructing them how to behave in a fire. Away from the threatening flames, Rusty ran instinctively toward the nearest fresh air and was in Rosebud's room with its opened windows before Marguerite reached there in her awkward crouch. The light switch was right inside the door and easily located by touch, but it did not respond. The wiring must have been knocked out by the explosion or the fire.

"Rosebud, where are you?" she called in the dark room, which was beginning to fill with smoke.

There was no answer. Frantically, Marguerite groped around the room until she heard Rusty whine, and followed that sound. Rusty was standing over Rosebud who was on the floor with something on top of her—a bookcase. Exerting all her ebbing strength against its weight, Marguerite managed to lift it sufficiently to prop it on some fallen books, leaving enough clearance to drag Rosebud's trapped leg from under it.

"Come on, girl," she instinctively urged Rusty. "Let's get out of here."

Not wanting to risk traversing the smoke-filled rooms, she raised the screen on the window and clumsily attempted to climb through it while carrying the unconscious Rosebud. Her strength was fading. She got no further than to lift one leg over the sill and to protrude her own and Rosebud's head out into the life-giving air.

A neighbor, who had heard the explosion and called the fire department, ran to the house and spied Marguerite. Running to the window, illuminated by the fire, he took Rosebud from Marguerite's arms, laid her gently on the ground away from the burning house, and rushed back to assist Marguerite.

She was gone! Poking his head through the window into the smoky room, he saw her bending down trying to lift something.

"Leave that! Get out of there!" he yelled.

"I can't! She needs help."

Convinced that another child was in the room, the man climbed in and reached down to discover a hairy lump—a dog. A pet owner himself, he offered no recriminations but hastily lifted the dog through the window before helping Marguerite escape, then exited himself. After a few deep breaths, he hurried back to his house and called for an ambulance.

Marguerite said nothing. She just breathed.

The taxi pulled into a dark driveway. Marguerite, weary, her clothes covered with soot, instructed the driver to wait while she went into the house for the fare. Her pocketbook had been abandoned in the fire and she had no money for the trip back from the hospital.

Quiet though she was, Katie heard her with the sensitive ears of a mother attuned to the least stirring of child or home. Nudging her husband, she whispered, "Someone is in the house."

Grabbing a heavy flashlight as a weapon, Neil crept into the hallway and toward the stairs as a figure quietly ascended. With flashlight poised to strike, Neil heard the burglar cough, a woman's cough.

"Maman?" he inquired.

"Of course, it is. What are you doing creeping around in the dark?"

Chapter Twenty

Nurse Costa nearly jumped out of her skin as a harsh, guttural sound exploded directly behind her. Turning to meet the challenge, she encountered only the sheeted and sheathed figure of Ralph Horton, immobile amidst a tangle of tubes and wires, but with eyes glaring fiercely at her. It was the first time she had seen him awake.

Breathing on his own since Friday afternoon when the mechanical assistance had been removed, he had been checked every hour since she came on duty late Friday night but he had slept through her ministrations. He was trying to talk now but the wired jaw did not permit movement and the sounds were nearly incomprehensible. They sounded like "Autta, autta."

Repeating the sounds to herself, she decided he wanted water, which he affirmed with a nod of his head. Quickly checking his chart, she found no prohibition against fluids and was soon holding a glass with a flexible straw for him to drink. It was his first awkward attempt and water was soon running down the side of his mouth. Nevertheless, he smiled at her in gratitude, the smile emanating more from his sea-green eyes than his frozen mouth.

She allowed him only a few sips, resettled him with encouraging patter, and left to comply with the nonmedical orders on this patient. She was to immediately notify the doctor covering the intensive care unit of any change in Horton's condition. The doctor would assess the patient and relay the appropriate information to the trooper sitting patiently outside the door of the unit.

The rookie trooper was relieved to have some excuse to move as he asked to use the telephone to contact headquarters. It was only six in the morning. Lieutenant Medeiros would be notified and could be expected by eight. "Don't let anyone except staff near the patient," were the strict orders.

Ralph Horton had two hours to enjoy his recovery.

Despite her exhaustion, Marguerite had slept very little. The events had overstimulated her. Though she attempted to calm herself by drinking a cup of tension-tamer herbal tea while reciting her story to Neil and Katie last night, every time she closed her eyes she smelled smoke and leaped out of bed to check the house, distrustful of the fire alarms on each floor.

At six o'clock in the morning she gave up the pretense of resting and slipped quietly down the stairs wearing a bathrobe. Might as well have some caffeine and be fully awake, she decided.

The water took forever to boil; it took even longer to drip through the filter. Her agitation manifested itself in her hands which restlessly leafed through an assortment of yesterday's newspapers on the table and uncovered Katie's sketchbook. Marguerite flipped through the pages, hardly cognizant of the subjects, until she came to the last one and bolted upright in her chair, studying the familiar face.

Neil and Katie were still sleeping. Their toddler alarm had not sounded yet. Marguerite added more water to the pot, more coffee to the filter, and pounded at their door. "Katie, I must talk to you. Right away."

Heavy-eyed, but valiantly attempting to be good-natured, Katie emerged wearing a cotton robe with a beautiful abstract pattern of her own design which had been silk-screened onto the fabric by a friend of hers. They had recently sold the design to a fabric manufacturer.

Marguerite, a connoisseur of fine fabrics, gave it nary a glance. She was pointing to the sketch that had shocked her. "Katie, when did you do this one?"

"Last evening. After I returned from the bakery and helped Neil set up for the bridge game, I took Thomas to the playground across the road. He was too excited to sleep so I thought that would tire him and get him out of the way of the card players. This man was there when we got there and I thought he was with one of the children. He seemed to be waiting for someone because he stood so that he could see the road. His face was so interesting, I took a small pad I always carry in my pocket and sketched him roughly. That larger drawing was done later when Thomas went to bed. It probably isn't very accurate because I only had a small sketch to use," she explained defensively, then continued.

"It's funny though. He wasn't with one of the children and no one came to meet him. Thomas and I were the last ones to leave the playground when it started to get dark and this man was still there. I wonder what he was doing?"

"I think I know what he was doing!" exclaimed Marguerite as she ran for the phone book. "I hope Frank doesn't have an unlisted number at home."

"Maman, it's only six-thirty in the morning," protested a yawning Neil, just emerging reluctantly from his room, wearing a humdrum bathrobe of no noticeable design. "Can't this wait?"

"No, Neil, it can't wait. I think this man tried to murder me last night."

Lieutenant Medeiros arrived in the hospital accompanied by Trooper Fleming, who carried what to the uninitiated might appear to be a briefcase but was actually a laptop computer. Horton might not be able to talk clearly but he still had one free arm. Medeiros had never known a single-operator PI who could not type. They were ready for him.

Medeiros started gently. "Mr. Horton, I'm glad to see you're looking so much better."

" 'Ank you," came from behind the clamped mouth.

"We have a few questions to ask you but don't want you to exert yourself trying to talk. Can you type?"

Unwittingly he nodded his head, affirming his ability to be

questioned. He was not up to his usual standards of self-protection.

Fleming had already set up the laptop and put it on the movable stand reaching over the bed. He gave a few instructions and let Horton test it.

"First, Mr. Horton," began Medeiros, "we're anxious to find out who did this to you. Do you know the person who beat you up like this?"

"No," he typed.

"You must have seen him. What did he look like?"

"It was dark. Two men. Young."

"Had you ever seen them before?"

"No."

"How did they happen to pick you out to beat up?"

"Do not know. Sitting on bench. Drove up."

"They just walked up to you and started to beat you, a total stranger."

"Yes."

It was slow going. Horton had only his left hand and the computer was at an awkward angle. He was also weak and they had to be careful not to push him too hard. He revealed nothing. They knew he was lying.

He persisted in his claim that he had just happened to be sitting on a bench on the windmill green late at night when two young men in a pickup truck stopped, approached him, and beat him up, then apparently strung him up on the windmill, all for no reason of which he was aware.

When faced with the information that he had been drugged with triazolam, he remembered that they had a bottle of vodka and offered him some. He took a couple of drinks, then they beat him.

"Okay, Mr. Horton, let's talk about Friday night. Mr. Wilkinson informs us that you were working for him and followed Ethan to Anna Pochet's house. Correct?"

"Do not know whose house," appeared slowly and protectively on the screen.

"And you left there about eleven o'clock at night to go back to your motel?"

A nod of the head.

"Let's go back over that a little."

"Sorry, Lieutenant, you'll have to leave now. I need to examine my patient and he'll need to rest after that. He's barely regained consciousness and you're overtiring him," scolded the doctor, identified by a name tag as Irene Kozlowski, and identified by her stern face as tolerating no objections.

The phone would not stop ringing. She tried to ignore it and pulled the sheet over her head but it kept ringing. "It's probably for you, Frank," Pat Nadeau complained before opening her eyes and realizing she was alone in the bedroom.

"Yes?" she finally mouthed into the intrusive instrument.

"I'm sorry to call so early but it is very important that I speak to the chief. This is Marguerite Smith and it's an emergency."

Isn't it always? thought Pat, but retained a modicum of politeness. "He isn't here. I'll check to see if he's downstairs."

On the kitchen table she found a note indicating that he could not sleep so had left early to go down to the site of that suspicious fire last night. He wanted to be there when the fire marshals came to inspect it.

Conveying this message to the caller, Pat went back to bed smiling. She'd gotten even with Frank for leaving early and letting her be wakened on her day off. That Smith woman was probably hotfooting it down to the fire site right now.

Pat's timing was a little off. Marguerite breakfasted, showered, and dressed first. When she finally arrived at the burned-out house site, Frank had already left. He was not at headquarters either when she arrived there. The dispatcher said he had stopped for a belated breakfast.

Comfortably fed herself, Marguerite chafed at Frank's perceived inattention to duty and walked up and down the reception room as she waited, a spectre at the feast, ruining the morning camaraderie of officers changing shifts and gathering around the coffeepot. When he finally appeared, she bom-

barded him with a barrage of facts, circumstances, and con-
jecture, pointing agitatedly at the sketchbook as she did so.
He was impressed enough to make some exploratory phone
calls, making sure that she waited outside his office while he
did so, much to the consternation of the coffee crowd.

Medeiros and Fleming were still in the hospital. Though temporarily exiled from the intensive care unit, they kept in touch
with it through the trooper stationed outside. After what they
considered a suitable rest period for the patient, they returned
to the area on the all-clear signal of the officer on guard who
had been monitoring the movements of Dr. Kozlowski,
dubbed by them as the iron maiden without any information
as to the accuracy of this designation.

But they knew better than to just barge into the room. Medeiros did not want any statement thrown out on the grounds
that the patient was ill and incompetent at the time. Knowing
the hospital routine, they waited until the next doctor came
on duty. After he examined Horton, they asked for and received permission to question him, then strode in and set up
the computer again.

Informed for the first time that there was a witness to the
fact that Horton had remained outside Anna Pochet's house
until twelve-thirty and then followed Ethan when he left, Horton admitted this sequence of events but claimed he had
started to follow Ethan but lost him at a red light which he
could not run because cars were coming through the intersection from the side road. He had been too afraid to admit this
when he learned Ethan had been murdered. But now he was
telling the truth.

Asked the same question in various ways, he stuck to his
new story, pointing to the same answers on the screen. Medeiros wearily ran his fingers through his untidy hair, disar-
ranging it further, while searching for the next question.
Horton sank back on the pillow and closed his eyes. Physically
drained, emotionally terrified, he wanted to halt the questions
without having to say so.

Pulling the sheet up to his neck, he tucked his free arm

under it as if cold and, while Medeiros had his head down and Fleming was checking the latest blister on his foot, Horton jiggled the wires attached to the cathodes on his chest and loosened one cathode entirely. Eyes closed, he suppressed his breathing to a minimum and waited.

He gave the duty nurse good grades. Seconds after the green line on his monitor began to jump crazily, she was at his side with only one word for the police—an emphatic "Out!" Medeiros complied wordlessly. He was out of questions anyway.

They took their time leaving, stopping to talk with the officer outside, the lieutenant renewing his instructions about no visitors. The nurse's aide found them. There was a message for Medeiros to call the Eastham police chief. It was important.

Medeiros reacted immediately and, through the Barnstable police force, had officers dispatched to two locations to locate a suspect and bring him in for questioning.

The police were too late. When they arrived at his house, Herbert Catlaw was swinging from the end of a rope attached to the high-beamed ceiling.

Chapter Twenty-one

Two envelopes were propped on the mantel over Cat's fireplace. The police officer in charge opened the one addressed to "Police" and read it aloud.

I never meant to hurt Rosebud. She was very dear to me, the daughter I never had. I thought the Quade house was empty. It was quiet and dark. Earlier I saw Rosebud walking with that Smith woman to her house after Sunny went in the ambulance. I watched from the schoolyard to see if they came down the road again back to Rosebud's house but they never did.

I would have broken in and taken those pictures of the Indian belt but couldn't because I was seen at the house earlier after everybody had left and I tried to enter the back door which is usually open, but it was locked. A neighbor saw me trying the door and came over to tell me no one was home, which I already knew. He had a good look at me and my van and would have been able to identify me if the house was broken into.

So I decided to burn down the house and make it look like an accident. It was easy. I just loosened the nuts connecting one of the small tubes leading from a propane tank to the house and stuffed the end of a long strip of cloth in it. I ran out the cloth to a safe distance and lit it. The pipes were old and rusty. I could have gotten away with it.

Then I saw Rosebud being carried out. I never meant to hurt her. If she lives I have tried to make it up to her.

But I had to do it. I accidentally got mixed up with a couple of guys who were planning to switch fakes for valuable Indian antiques that were in a museum. They had an in with a couple of security guards who could be bribed. The stuff they were going to steal sat in glass cases and would not be examined unless something was suspected. The phonies were going to be faded and dirtied up a little so they would look old and would all be switched the same night. They knew they could sell the stuff. Some collectors don't mind hot merchandise even if they can never show it. They just want to own it.

They included me in because they knew I could get quality stuff made. They had seen the wampum beads I had Sunny making that I was passing off as antiques. She never knew. They gave me several pictures of a belt they wanted copied and I asked her to make the belt as a favor to me to give to a lady friend. She had no idea what belt that was. But Ethan saw the pictures and recognized it as a famous belt captured from a warrior in combat during the Revolutionary War. Who knew that he had seen it in New York? That was his bad luck.

He called me and told me he knew what I was doing. It all added up when he thought about those wampum beads Sunny was making look old. He told me to call off the whole operation or he would turn me in. Monday morning was my deadline. I called him a couple of times but he wouldn't budge.

I was caught in the middle. When I let my partners know what happened they told me to get rid of him. Big money was involved. I didn't want to do it but they said if it wasn't done by Sunday they would off him and take care of me too.

I had no choice. I followed Ethan all Friday night and talked to him when he left Anna's house. Claimed I was working it out and needed to talk to him but not where we could be heard. He was half drunk and agreed to

*follow me. I led him to the cemetery and took out a bottle
of whiskey. I took a little and got him to take a lot. He
wasn't used to drinking and this was hundred proof. He
passed out.*

*That's when I injected him with the drug that I still
had from years ago when I dealt for a few steady cus-
tomers. Luckily I found out this stuff was dangerous. I
meant to get rid of it but stalled and stashed it in a coffee
can full of nails. Insurance, you know. Then I wrapped
his fingers around the needle for fingerprints, planted the
packet of drugs in his pocket, and threw him into that
grave so no one would find him till I could work out an
alibi. Funny thing is I was never questioned.*

*Everything would have been great except for that pri-
vate eye. He was tailing Ethan, but I was so nervous I
didn't notice. He watched everything in the cemetery.
Never tried to stop me either. Tailed me home, got my
name from the mailbox, and called me Saturday morning
to blackmail me. Said he had taped everything Ethan and
me said with one of those enhanced listening devices.
Told me to get the money and he would call me in twenty-
four hours. When he called me Sunday I said I had the
money but would only hand it over in person and get the
tapes at the same time. He arranged to meet me at the
windmill at two in the morning. That was a lucky break
for me. I knew it wasn't lighted at night. He probably
didn't know that.*

*I bought a bottle of vodka and doctored it with knock-
out stuff. I pretended to drink it and his mouth was wa-
tering. He couldn't resist. Guess he never learned not to
drink on the job.*

*When he passed out I hit him. I thought he was dead.
Then I searched him. He had a small gun that he never
got to use. I threw it in the woods off Route 6. He had
no tapes and no ID but his motel key was stuck in his
waistband and the name of the motel was on it.*

*I got the idea to tie him to the windmill because I
thought it would look like some kooks done it and it*

wouldn't be connected to Ethan's death. I stood on a folding display table from my van. It was harder to do than I thought it would be. Then I searched his motel room. There were no tapes. He was bluffing.

Then I found out he was alive. I figured that if he talked it would be his word against mine if I got rid of the stuff at Sunny's house. Maybe I could even turn it around and make it look like he killed Ethan. But I was caught trying to enter the back door and had to burn down the house instead. I realized later that it was a stupid move because Horton couldn't be blamed for that and the nosy neighbor would probably remember me prowling around. This is the only way out for me. I'd rather be dead than behind bars for life.

I didn't mean to hurt Rosebud. Maybe I even killed her. If she is okay give her the envelope on the mantel.

Tell her Uncle Cat loved her.

Chapter Twenty-two

Chief Pedersen was elated. The murder case was off his books. Best of all, the murder had nothing to do with Mashpee. The victim was from Eastham, the murderer from Hyannis Port, and the blackmailer from New Hampshire. It had been an imported problem, soon resolved, sooner forgotten. While downing a Boston cream doughnut, he reviewed his schedule, hoping to squeeze enough time off on Sunday to take charge of the Fourth of July barbecue at home. Irene was a disaster at the grill.

Detective Watson was in a celebratory mood. She skipped her workout at the gym and went shopping. This had been her first big case and she had pulled it off—with a little help, of course. She was relieved that Henry was not the murderer. A murder trial would have overshadowed the embezzlement case. Now she was sure to be highlighted. Her only immediate problem was to decide whether the lime green or the pale blue silk shirt would be more flattering in a color news photo.

Chief Nadeau was pensive. Ralph Horton was not a murderer but he was a blackmailer and likely to be charged with obstruction of justice as well. Did they have a case? Would it stand up in court? They had only the written confession of a dead man, without any corroboration—no blackmail letters, no tapes, no pictures, only a suicide note from an admitted murderer. The DA would have to figure this one out. But there was no hurry. Horton wasn't going anywhere for a long time. Meanwhile, Frank had a busy day ahead of him. He hoped he wouldn't be too tired tonight to open those Wellfleet oysters Pat had on ice.

Lieutenant Medeiros was depressed. Ethan Quade had left the best, in fact the only, clue to his murderer and he, Al Medeiros, had misinterpreted it. The calendar notes—*see about H, call H, call police about H*—could have led them to Herbert Catlaw if they had looked beyond their noses and investigated other aspects of Ethan's life. The fraud had seduced them, enticed them, wooed them into implicating Henry Lawrence in the murder. They should have listened to Henry. He told them there were lots of people whose names begin with H.

Marguerite slept through it all. Upon returning from police headquarters, she launched into an animated description of her encounter with the noncommittal Frank Nadeau, then ran out of steam. Taking a book to her room just to relax for a few minutes, she jumped when she heard the doorbell ring. The digital display on her radio-alarm shamelessly advertised that it was two o'clock in the afternoon. Preposterous! She never napped.

The soft murmur of voices downstairs, just out of range of her hearing, tantalized her to move frenetically while straightening her slept-in clothes and barely running a comb through her hair.

Esther Quade sat in the living room, dark circles under her eyes, looking exhausted but not despondent, more at peace than at any time during this horrible week.

"Is Rosebud all right?" Marguerite asked, intuitively knowing the answer.

"Yes, she's fine. She has no injuries except a huge bruise on her leg where something fell on her. She must've panicked when she was pinned down and fainted. The hospital released her. I took her home before coming here."

"Home? Her home is gone. I guess you mean your place."

"No. My place is too small. We're staying at Anna Pochet's

house and she's moving temporarily to my condo. Both places are going to be sold. I'll look for another house for Rosebud and me, and for Grandma Sunny if she wants to live with us. But I have a feeling she'll want to go back to Maine finally, to her people.''

"Is she going to be able to live on her own and take care of herself?''

"She won't have to. When I told the social worker at the hospital that Grandma Sunny is Passamaquoddy, she checked her information on the Indian Health Service. They're a federally recognized tribe, which means they have health care. There are good facilities on the reservation, even a housing complex for the elderly, right on the water, and a place for meals.''

"Will she be able to get around?''

"It's too soon to tell, but the doctor said her stroke was only on one side and wasn't severe. She should be able to use a walker, maybe even a cane. They can take better care of her in Maine than I could here.'' A shadow crossed Esther's face. "It would get her away from the gossip, too.''

"About the beading?''

"Yeah. That belt was a famous one. She was being used by Cat. I don't want her to know that right now. Maybe never. She would feel responsible for Ethan's murder.''

"Ethan's murder! What did Sunny have to do with that? I thought the police arrested that accountant for the murder. To tell you the truth, I was surprised to hear it because I suspected that Wilkinson was behind it. I thought Cat was just copying Indian antiques and tried to get rid of the evidence because Sunny was taken to the hospital and one of you might find the pictures, the ones that I found. He did succeed in destroying them, after all. I left them on the table in the living room when all the excitement started.''

"Himself as well. I guess you haven't heard.''

Esther summarized the unfolding saga. The police had sought her out because of the note Cat left for Rosebud. They wanted it opened and followed her to Rosebud's hospital room where Esther gave the note to Rosebud after firmly closing the door behind her, shutting out the police.

It was Cat's handwritten will, leaving his house and business to Rosebud. Evidently anticipating a legal challenge from his two ex-wives, he had gone to the house of nearby friends and had the will witnessed. They later recounted that he had left hurriedly, saying he had an appointment. He never mentioned that it was to death he was racing.

Marguerite had tears in her eyes. Cat was a murderer but he, too, had loved and walked the earth encumbered by the human frailties that burden us all. Wiping her eyes, she resumed her questions.

"Esther, can you tell me the name of the man who lives in the house nearest to Ethan's? I want to call him. They refused to let Rusty in the ambulance," she explained indignantly, "so that man offered to keep her. I'm worried about her."

"That's Mr. Anderson. I was just over there to look at what's left and he told me he took her to the vet because she inhaled a lot of smoke. You can pick her up anytime you want. He's the one who carried her out of the house."

Marguerite was folding and refolding the front of her skirt, trying to find a tactful way to approach her next topic.

"Esther, you said you are staying at Anna's house. I know you're good friends but there's something you should be told. I think she might be conspiring with Matthias Wilkinson to help him gain custody of Rosebud."

Esther laughed and her rich, deep peals brought Neil and Katie into the room. They took the laughter to indicate the end of the private conversation.

"I guess you found out that Anna met Mr. Wilkinson."

Marguerite guiltily mumbled, "We, er, accidentally saw them," hoping that Neil and Katie would keep her secret. They did. Esther continued.

"I met Anna for lunch one day and laid all my troubles on her, about Ethan's death and Wilkinson wanting Rosebud. Anna is so smart. She saw right away that neither of us was thinking of Rosebud's welfare. We were selfishly fighting because of past hatreds. She persuaded him to meet her for dinner and offered to help mend fences between us. She told me the same thing. It worked. In fact, Mr. Wil . . . I mean, Matthias—he asked us to call him that—is enchanted with her. I think he has a crush.'' She giggled, covering her mouth with her hand in the familiar gesture.

''Friday night, when Rosebud was in the hospital and so was Grandma Sunny, it was too much for me so I decided to give Anna's plan a try and called Matthias. He rushed to the hospital and made all kinds of demands—a private room, private nurses. He had everyone buzzing. I realized then that Rosebud is all the family he has, the same as me, except that I have Grandma Sunny, too. We're going to try to get along better. It will be nice for Rosebud to have a grandfather.''

''Will you be staying at Anna's house long?''

''No, just temporarily until I find a house. Anna's insurance company is starting a new office in Boston and asked her to be assistant manager with the possibility of being manager in three years. She's selling the house and moving to Boston.''

''You certainly had a lot to think about in one week,'' commiserated Marguerite.

''Lucky for you and Rosebud that I did,'' Esther answered enigmatically.

''What do you mean?''

''I was so busy and upset that I didn't pay attention to the propane tanks. Ethan always took care of that but he had so many things on his mind between his office and Grandma Sunny that he must have forgotten. They were nearly empty. The police told me that if the tanks were full, you both could have been blown to bits. Aren't you lucky?''

''Yes, aren't I,'' groaned Marguerite, sinking back in her chair, unable to decide if her sick stomach was due to an escape from death or a desire to escape Neil's embryonic recriminations.

Epilogue

Blue Feather called for the drummers to come forward and take their places at the large drum under a shaded pavilion fashioned from tree trunks and branches. As master of ceremonies for the powwow, he was cajoling participants to get ready for the Grand Entry which had been scheduled to start at noon.

Apologizing to the assembled audience, he explained, "We're a little late getting started. It's about twelve minutes after noontime. Actually we're right on schedule, Indian time."

Using the time before the procession began, Blue Feather explained that the dances were to express thankfulness and to honor Mother Earth. He then lighted the smudge pot and, with a long black feather, walked around the roped-off circle and wafted the ceremonial smoke toward the assembled crowd.

The procession was finally ready to begin and the waiting crowd was requested to stand and remove their hats. Carrying a huge staff, the lead dancer entered the ring, his garb including a feathered headdress and a circle of tail feathers worn behind the hips.

Behind him followed, one by one, the men in traditional dress, a diverse category, unique to the individual as well as his tribe. They sported moccasins; breechcloths; headdresses of fur, feathers, bonework, or beadwork; breastplates; armbands; legbands; and facepaint. Some of the more flamboyant costumes sported tail feathers and shoulder feathers tipped with streamers dyed in brilliant colors. One costume included a wolfskin cape with the wolf's head extending over the wearer's forehead, and his face painted with wide vertical white stripes. He danced in a crouching, staccato step. All the men carried short staffs or ceremonial rattles.

After the men came the women, some dressed in elaborately beaded and fringed buckskin dresses and moccasins, others in long cotton dresses. Children, too, joined the procession, many dressed for the dance contests in which they would compete. The tiniest tots often had headdresses slipping down over their eyes, and armbands and sashes changing positions rapidly as they were pulled at and tugged on by their rebellious wearers.

The drummers continued the familiar cadence throughout the Grand Entry, with the participants dancing the traditional two-beat steps.

Katie nudged Marguerite and whispered, "Isn't that Rosebud? I'm surprised to see her here."

"Yes, it is. I'm not surprised she's here because she wasn't badly hurt, just stunned and very frightened. She was awake and speaking to me in the ambulance. I wonder where she got the costume? Hers was burned in the fire. Someone must have lent her one. The outfit Sunny made for her was much more beautiful than the one she is wearing."

"Mama, Mama, look!" urged Thomas, pulling on the leg of Katie's shorts.

The scene to which they turned was spectacular. The Aztec Dancers from Mexico City had been introduced. Barefoot, wearing black and gold breechcloths with wide belts and gold-lined capes, they entered the ring and began an athletic dance, each dancer shaking a rattle in his right hand and carrying an ornamental shield in his left hand. The three-feet-long feathered headdresses, some of yellow-tipped rooster feathers, others of purple-tipped pheasant feathers, waved and swayed in rhythm to the dancers. The effect was mesmerizing.

When this exotic dance ended, the Smiths look a lunch break and wandered among the food stands, assembling their choices on a picnic bench. Unable to speak with a mouthful of fry bread and beans, Marguerite nodded her head in the direction to which Katie and Neil had their backs. They turned in unison and saw an amazing sight. Matthias Wilkinson was strolling toward them flanked on either side by Anna Pochet and Esther Quade.

Beaming, he tipped his straw hat in a courtly manner and said to Marguerite, "Did you see my Rose out there dancing? Just like Joy and my wife, Rose. They were terrific dancers. I used to cut quite a rug myself. Yup, that kid is a Wilkinson all right, through and through."

Finis origine pendet.
The end depends upon the beginning.

This book only hints at the rich culture established by the Native Americans on this continent. For more information about customs or events mentioned in this book, I recommend the following resources:

Erdoes, Richard and Ortiz, Alfonso, *American Indian Myths and Legends*. New York: Pantheon Books, 1984.

Stribling, Mary Lou, *Crafts from North American Indian Arts*. New York: Crown Publishers, Inc., 1975.

Thomas, David Hurst, et al., *The Native Americans*. Atlanta, Georgia: Turner Publishing, Inc., 1993.

Vuilleumier, Marion, *Indians on Olde Cape Cod*. Taunton, Massachusetts: William S. Sullwold Publishing, 1970.

For the details and history of the Mashpee Indian land suit, I recommend the following comprehensive account:

Campisi, Jack, *The Mashpee Indians*. Syracuse, New York: Syracuse University Press, 1991.

—Marie Lee